# TOE *the* LINE

Editing: Jessica Royer Ocken
Proofreading and Formatting: Elaine York, Allusion Publishing
www.allusionpublishing.com
Proofreading: Julia Griffis
Cover Model: Christian Ganon, @christianganon46
Cover Photographer: Martin Traynor
Cover Design: Letitia Hasser, RBA Designs

# TOE *the* LINE

*NEW YORK TIMES* BESTSELLING AUTHOR
PENELOPE WARD

# CHAPTER 1

## Noelle
### *Present*

**IT'S FUNNY HOW** you always remember where you were and what you were doing when something pivotal happens in your life.

I'd certainly never forget being in the art room in kindergarten when I heard my teacher had died in a car accident on the way to school that morning. And I'd always recall getting my period for the first time while bowling with my dad.

Today I had something else to add to that list. I would always remember where I was when I received Archie Remington's wedding invitation: in the pedicure seat at Wonder Nails, choking back tears after opening the envelope while simultaneously fighting unwanted laughter from the tickle of the loofa being rubbed on the bottom of my feet.

*Giggle.*
*Sniffle.*
*Giggle.*
*Sniffle.*

I'd taken a pile of my mail with me to sort through while I was in the chair in an effort to maximize my time. In the middle of the stack was an envelope containing a thick piece of crème stationery that read:

*Please honor us with your presence*
*as we join our lives in love.*
*Mariah and Archie*
*Saturday, October 12th at 5 PM*
*St. Catherine's Church*
*Sonoma, California*
*Cocktail Hour and Reception to follow at Lindall Estates*

For the past seven years, Archie had been my best friend. I'd known he was dating Mariah; I'd even met her once when I flew out to California on business and used it as an opportunity to visit Archie. But surely he could've had the decency to tell me he was engaged before sending me this invite? We'd exchanged many candid emails over the years. He'd never hesitated to relay anything going on in his life. So why keep this major piece of news from me and have me find out as if I were a virtual stranger? It made no sense.

I continued to stew over this and fidget as the woman finished my pedicure.

Toes completed and bursting with a sense of betrayal, the second I exited the nail salon, I dialed Archie. Flustered, I hadn't even bothered to remove the paper flip-flops they'd given me to wear out while I stood on the busy New York City sidewalk.

Archie picked up on the second ring, his deep voice a grating sound against my already-sensitized nerves.

"Noelle?" He paused. "Is everything okay?"

He was likely asking because, while we'd been close over the years, you could probably count on one hand the number of times we'd actually spoken on the phone. Our preferred method of communication had always been email.

"How could you not have told me you're getting married?" My voice cracked.

"What? How the hell do you know that?"

"You didn't mean for me to know? What are you talking about? You sent me an invitation!"

The line went silent for a moment. "Shit. All I did was hand over a list of names and addresses. I had no idea they were going to send anything out so soon. I was planning on telling you next weekend."

Archie and I planned to meet at Whaite's Island, Maine, where our families co-owned a summer home. Since their half was now half in Archie's name, he and I were meeting with a realtor to discuss listing the property. I would be going in place of my parents, who'd moved down to Florida. It was a seller's market right now, so it seemed the right time to unload it. We'd been renting the house to seasonal tenants for several years.

"I'm so sorry, Noelle. Mariah's mother must have gotten ahead of herself. I swear I would never have wanted you to find out like this. Please know that."

Swarms of people rushed past me while I stood there in a daze. I concluded that Archie was telling the truth, but despite his explanation, I still felt a pang of sadness.

When the silence on the line grew awkward, Archie said, "I'll cook you your favorite pasta with vodka sauce next week to make up for it."

"Yeah…" I muttered. "Okay." My chest hurt.

Not because of the damn pasta. My best friend was getting married, and that was complicated.

The thing about Archie? He was my best friend now, but at one time…we'd almost been more. That summer I learned the biggest lesson of my life: A good way to have your heart broken by your best friend is to forget how to toe the line.

# CHAPTER 2

## Noelle
*Past*

**THERE WAS NOTHING** like that first hint of salty air. I'd come to Whaite's Island, Maine, for a couple of summers before this one, but the excitement of arriving was just like the first time. It never got old. When you breathed the noxious fumes of the city most of the year, it was easy to appreciate the literal breath of fresh air here.

I stepped out of my parents' car and looked up at our new summer house. Although I'd seen photos, this was my first time viewing it in person. It was your typical oceanside, shingle-style home, with a wide, spacious porch and tons of large windows. The lawn was beautifully manicured, and bushes bursting with flowers surrounded the property.

"It's even more stunning than I imagined," my mother said.

If only this house was solely ours. My dad had gone in fifty-fifty with his friend and mentor, Archer Remington. They were both criminal defense attorneys, and my dad had worked under Archer for a while in New York.

When Mr. Remington left to head the West Coast division of their firm, Dad and he had stayed friendly. Archer and his wife, Nora, had one son, Archie, who was a few years older than me and going into his senior year of college as a pre-law student. Previous times we'd met them here over the years, we'd rented our own place. This was the first time my family, the Benedicts, would be staying under the same roof as the Remingtons.

"I can't believe this is half our house," I muttered, my eyes wandering across the road to the ocean in the distance.

My grandmother had been ill, so we hadn't traveled for the past few years, and it'd been a while since I'd seen the Remingtons. They, however, had been coming here consistently during the summers since their son was young. Archie had a ton of friends on the island, whereas I'd kept to myself or hung out with my family during the couple of times we'd been here previously. I wanted this summer to be different and planned to force myself to socialize, even if it killed me. It would be good practice for starting college at Boston University in the fall. Considering we now half-owned this property, it would be in my best interest to make some permanent friends, especially since there were a fair number of people who lived here year-round.

My heart pounded as we approached the front door. I was apprehensive about seeing Archie. I'd always had an unwanted crush on him, even though he and I had never really interacted. In fact, I didn't *like* him much at all, and he'd never made an effort to get to know me. But now, under the same roof, we'd have no choice but to acknowledge one another.

The Remingtons' SUV was parked outside, so they'd definitely already arrived. My dad used the key Archer had sent him to open the door, and I heard footsteps before I spotted a smiling Nora Remington.

"You made it!" She beamed. "Noelle! Oh my goodness—look at you. You're so grown up."

The last time Nora saw me, I was about fifteen. I was eighteen and a half now, so I'd certainly changed a lot since then.

"I'm ready for my tour," my mother Amy said before I could formulate a response.

Archer Remington descended the stairs and patted my father on the shoulder. "How was the ride, Mark?"

"Uneventful," Dad answered as he looked around the space.

"Where's Archie?" Mom asked.

"He had some things to wrap up at the university, so he's coming straight from school," Nora answered. "He'll be arriving tomorrow."

Relief washed over me. I had the rest of the day to acclimate to my new surroundings in peace.

Mr. Remington looked over at me. "When did Noelle grow up?"

I shrugged and smiled shyly, looking down at my feet.

My dad smacked him on the arm. "You'd better have a cold beer waiting for me, old man."

"Already have a cooler set up by the tennis court."

"Ah...we're wasting no time, are we?" My dad chuckled. As he followed Archer out back, I heard him say, "I trust you're ready for me to kick your ass?"

Archer and Nora Remington were about a decade older than my parents. Nora was nearly forty when she had Archie, so she had to be over sixty now. My dad had been fresh out of law school when Archer became his mentor. Now my dad was a successful trial attorney in his own right. Both Dad and Archer would work remotely from the island this summer, with occasional trips if they needed to meet clients.

"Let me show you to your room, Noelle." Nora smiled.

"I'd love that."

As my mother ventured toward the kitchen, I followed Nora up the large staircase.

She opened the door to my room. "I think you have the best view in the house."

The second-floor window did indeed provide a lovely view of the ocean across the road. I could hear the waves crashing in the distance and could even spot a lighthouse. Something told me I was going to sleep like a baby here.

"I'll give you a chance to unpack," Nora said. "Then you should come down for something to eat. You must be hungry."

I nodded. "Thank you."

My bedroom had a connected bathroom and a large closet. The white linens looked freshly laundered, and the room was decorated in a nautical motif. A weathered wooden anchor hung on the wall, and there was an accent chair with thick navy and white stripes in the corner.

Once I got most of my things unpacked, I joined my parents and the Remingtons downstairs. Nora had prepared a charcuterie board with smoked salmon, olives, and an assortment of crackers and cheeses.

While the parents lingered at the table after we noshed, I decided to take a walk and scope out the area.

I'd planned on jogging while I was here, so I wanted to decide on a route before tomorrow morning.

I walked for a bit but ended up stopping at a cute boutique clothing store down the road. A bell dinged as I entered.

I was perusing the selection of beachy wear when a girl around my age came up to me.

"Can I help you find something?" she asked.

"Oh no." I shook my head. "I was just browsing."

"Are you a tourist?" she asked.

"My family just bought a house here, so I guess I'm not exactly a tourist anymore, although I'll only be here in the summertime."

"Where's your house?"

"On Shady Oak Drive."

"Nice." She paused a moment then asked, "Is it you and your parents or...husband?"

"No husband." I laughed. "I'm only eighteen."

"I figured you were close to my age. I'm nineteen."

I nodded. "It's just my parents and me. We bought the house together with some family friends. Do you know the Remingtons?"

Her eyes widened. "I do, actually. My sister dated Archie one summer."

"Oh wow. Okay."

"Yeah. He broke her heart, ended things before he left for college. She sort of hates him now." She shrugged.

"I'm sorry." I frowned. "I mean, I don't know Archie very well. But that really sucks."

She tilted her head. "You don't know him, but you're living with him?"

"He's not even here yet. Our parents are friends, but the past summers I spent here, he acted like I didn't exist. So I've barely spoken to him."

"Ah, I see." She nodded. "Anyway, I'm sorry. I should've properly introduced myself. I'm Cici. I live here year-round, and this is my mother's shop."

I looked over at a mannequin in a terry-cloth swim-suit coverup. "I'm Noelle. This shop is really nice. I'm just kind of wandering around today."

"If you're bored and want to chill, a few of my friends and I get together by the clam shack at the beach most nights. There's usually live music and a bonfire. It's pretty much where everyone goes to hang out."

"That would be awesome. I don't know anyone here."

"Well, you do now." She winked. "Give me your phone. I'll enter my contact information."

"Cool." I handed it to her.

"I'll check in with you tomorrow," she said as she gave the phone back to me.

"Sounds good."

I walked out of there with a new pep in my step. I'd vowed to meet people while I was here, and I'd done it within the first couple of hours. All I needed was one person who knew their way around this place, and it seemed I'd found her.

• • •

The following morning, I started my day with a run at sun-rise. I left the house right around 5 AM before anyone else got up. It was as if I had the entire island to myself, and jogging with the beautiful Atlantic Ocean as the backdrop was like a dream.

When I returned to the house, my parents were at the kitchen table with the Remingtons. I joined them for breakfast and listened as they discussed plans to charter a boat later that day. That sounded like a recipe for barfing, with my tendency toward seasickness, so I opted out of that.

Once they'd departed, an anxious feeling loomed over me, as I knew Archie would be here sometime today. I had no idea what time he was arriving and hadn't wanted to seem interested by asking.

Rather than hang around the house with my nervous energy, I texted my new friend, Cici, to find out what she was up to. She told me she had to work at the shop until two but would be free after that.

At 3 PM, I rode my bike to Cici's house. The property was just as beautiful as the one we now co-owned. Gorgeous hydrangea bushes surrounded the home, which had a wide staircase leading up to the front porch.

I texted her that I'd arrived, and she met me out front.

"Hey! You found it." Cici's long, blond hair blew in the sea breeze as she came out to greet me.

"Yeah." I stepped off my bike and parked it. "It's beautiful."

"I was just making some lemonade to bring out to the pool." She waved me in. "Come meet my friends."

Cici led me through the house to the pool out back. Her parents didn't seem to be home.

She introduced me to two girls who were sunbathing on lounge chairs.

"This is Lara. And that's Crystal."

I lifted my hand. "Hey."

While Crystal offered a simple wave, Lara held her hand up to her forehead to block the sun. "Nice to meet you, Noelle."

Just then another girl burst through the French doors at the back of the house.

"Hey, have you seen my Michael Kors wedges?" she asked Cici.

"They're in my room."

The tall blond gritted her teeth. "Stop taking my shit." She stormed away.

Cici turned to me. "And that rude bitch is my sister, Amanda."

"I see."

I assumed Amanda was the sister who'd dated Archie Remington. It was no surprise that she was beautiful and bitchy. I would expect no less from him.

"Where are you headed in the fall?" Cici asked.

"Boston University."

"Oh, cool. What's your major?"

"Journalism. Not sure what I want to do with it after graduation, but I'm gonna give it a go."

She nodded. "At least you have some idea what you want. I can't decide. I'm in general studies at U of Maine."

"Nothing wrong with that."

The conversation continued to be pretty light the rest of the afternoon. We swam in the pool and drank lemonade—which Cici had spiked with vodka. I limited myself to two since I had to bike home.

When I returned to the house that evening, the parents weren't home—still out boating, I supposed. The house seemed quiet, so I assumed I was alone and Archie hadn't arrived yet.

Mr. Remington had mentioned a clam bake tonight for dinner to celebrate his son's arrival, so rather than eat anything now, I figured I'd just clean up.

Upstairs in my room, I untied the top of my bathing suit and let it fall to the ground before slipping out of my bikini bottoms, readying to hop in the shower.

Then I opened the door to my bathroom and froze at the sight of him.

"What the fuck?" he growled, running a hand through his thick, golden-brown hair.

My heart pounded in my chest. Archie stood before me, his sizeable dick hanging freely in the air.

Mortified, I stepped back out of the bathroom and closed the door behind me, my heart still hammering. *Okay.* What a difference a few years made. Not the Archie I remembered. That was a *grown-ass* man in there. A total Adonis. Rippled muscles. Tattoo on his arm—*when did he get that?* And a huge cock from what I'd gathered in the millisecond I saw it.

"Have you ever heard of knocking?" he finally called from behind the door.

*Seriously?* His attitude pissed me off. "Knock? It's my bathroom!"

"*Your* bathroom? Then why does it connect to my room, too?"

*Ahhh...* I hadn't bothered to actually open that other door. I'd only hung my robe on the back of it. "I thought that other door was a linen closet," I answered after a moment.

Throwing a T-shirt over myself, I sat on the edge of my bed and bounced my knees. As the shock started to wear off, it hit me that Archie had also seen *me* naked. Seems he'd put that together, too.

"You look *different* than I remembered," he said from behind the door. "Can't put my finger on it." He paused. "Oh, that's right. The last time I saw you, you were wearing clothes."

"Jerk." I laughed. "And your..." *Dick wasn't on display.* "...hair wasn't that long."

"You're pretty funny-looking when you're shocked." After a few-second pause, his voice softened. "I'll be right out so you can come in and do your thing."

"Okay," I breathed.

I suspected my "thing" would consist of replaying the past couple of minutes repeatedly under the shower—half mortified, half turned on by what had just happened.

# CHAPTER 3

## Noelle
### *Past*

**ARCHIE WAS THE** last to stroll into the dining room that night for dinner. A piece of his longish hair fell over his eyes as he plopped down into his seat. I was seated between my parents on the other side of the table.

Nora turned to me. "Did you and Archie have a chance to say hello to each other yet?"

Archie looked up at me with a mischievous grin. "We sure did," he said. "We were hanging out." He lowered his voice. "*Everything* was hanging out."

I cleared my throat, wishing the floor would somehow magically open under me so I could disappear.

My mom placed her hand on my arm. "Are you okay, honey?"

"Yeah, of course," I lied. I was probably red as a beet.

Once we dug into the pot of steamed shellfish and corn on the cob, I was able to focus my attention on the food and avoid making eye contact with Archie.

At one point, Nora turned to her husband and whispered, "Are you gonna tell him?"

"Tell me what?" Archie mumbled, sounding annoyed.

Archer straightened in his seat. "The alumni association is granting me its distinguished alumni award. As is tradition with alumni who have children attending the college, they've asked that you be the one to present it to me."

Rumor had it Archer had pulled some strings to get Archie into his alma mater, Ford University, which was located on the outskirts of San Francisco.

"What does that entail?" Archie poked at his food.

"It entails you writing something poignant and articulate."

Archie dropped his fork. "I'm supposed to write a speech about you?"

"That's what I said, yes. Just a few kind words about your dear old dad." Archer smiled tauntingly. "Surely, you can handle that, can't you? It'll be good practice for you—writing instead of those foolish doodles you do in your free time."

"Yeah," Archie muttered. "Sure."

He did *not* look happy. He actually seemed very on edge.

After another tense moment, Nora interrupted his silence. "How was your flight, Archie?"

"It was fine."

"Do you have plans tonight?" she asked.

"Not sure yet," he murmured. Then he looked up from his plate, making eye contact with her for the first time in a while. "How are you feeling, Mom?"

Nora seemed to force a smile. "Good, honey. I'm great."

"Good." He reached over and squeezed her hand, a surprisingly tender gesture.

The dynamic between Archie and his mother was certainly different than the one he seemed to have with his dad.

I kept waiting for Archie to say something—anything—to me during dinner, but he never did. After his initial joke about our encounter, I'd ceased to exist to him. Things were just as I'd always remembered them to be.

Just when the tension from earlier seemed to have dissipated, Mr. Remington reignited it.

"I was talking to Rodney Erickson the other day, Archie. He says he can get you in for a law internship at his practice here on the island this summer."

Archie sighed. "Can't I just enjoy my summer in peace?"

His father glared. "It's a great opportunity and will look good on your law school applications. Now is not the time to be burying your head in the sand. I've already discussed it with him. You can't embarrass me by not showing up."

"It doesn't take much to embarrass you, does it, Dad?" Archie shook his head. "Yeah, sure. Give me his number. I'll call him."

"Good."

Things once again went quiet. Archie's face reddened, the stress seeming to emanate from him despite the silence. His father definitely had some kind of hold on him. "Dinner was great. Thank you, everyone," he suddenly announced. His chair skidded against the floor as he got up from his seat.

Everyone watched as Archie swiftly left the dining room—even before the dessert I knew Nora had made. As expected, he'd graced us with the bare minimum of his presence. But given his father's antagonizing nature, I couldn't say I blamed him.

• • •

It wasn't long before I saw Archie again. That night, rather than ignoring me at home, he was ignoring me in front of a bunch of people at the beach. I sat on the sand across from him, yet no one would have known we lived under the same roof.

He'd also wasted no time hooking up with some girl. A blond clung to his side, laughing at his every word. *How does one step off a plane in the afternoon and have a girl at the ready that same night?*

Cici's breath smelled like alcohol as she leaned in and whispered in my ear, "Archie's back in town, I see."

"Yep."

After the introduction in the bathroom and the tense dinner, I was kind of hoping I could forget about him for the rest of the night. Instead, my eyes constantly wandered over. If Archie was upset about anything that had happened over dinner with his dad, you wouldn't know it now. He stood talking and laughing, soaking up attention from not only the blond but from everyone around him.

It was interesting how you could have a miserable personality but still attract so much attention based on looks alone.

My observation of Archie was interrupted when a couple of guys entered our space.

"What's up, Cici? Who's your friend?" one of them asked.

"Noelle, this is my cousin, Xavier." Cici pointed her cup toward him. "X, this is my new friend, Noelle, from New York."

Xavier had a full-sleeve tat, a lip piercing, and wore a knit hat despite the warm weather. "Well, hello, Noelle from New York," he said.

"Xavier actually goes to school in Boston, too," Cici told me as I nodded his way.

My eyes widened. "Really?"

"Yeah. I'm at Berklee College of Music."

"Oh cool."

"What about you?" he asked.

"Heading to BU in the fall."

"Nice. We should exchange numbers before the end of the summer and meet up in the city."

I shrugged. "Sure."

I ended up spending the next half hour chatting with Xavier. He was apparently a talented bass player. He seemed nice enough, although he got a tad touchy-feely with me, occasionally placing his hand at the small of my back as we talked. I didn't mind it too much, but it seemed a bit forward, especially considering how close his hand was to my ass. Before he left, we made informal plans to "hang out" more this summer, although I wasn't entirely sure what I thought about that.

I spent the remainder of the evening hanging with Cici and her friends while sneaking glances at Archie. After a couple of hours, I figured I should head back. Overall, I felt good about how my first night out had gone. I'd met new people and was already managing not to be a loner, unlike the other two summers I'd spent on Whaite's Island. And even though Archie had never bothered to acknowledge me, he *had* to have noticed I was there. At one point, he'd gone off somewhere with that girl, and I'd lost track of his whereabouts.

Despite my unhealthy preoccupation with him, I went home that night in a great mood. That is, until I got back to my bedroom, turned the knob on the bathroom door, and realized it was locked.

His voice was jarring. "I'm in here."

*He's home already?* "Well, nice to see you know how to use the lock," I said.

"And once again, you didn't knock," he responded. "Hey, that rhymes."

*Damn it.* He was right. If he hadn't locked it, I would've walked right in on him again. But I really hadn't thought he'd be home yet.

I sighed. "Just let me know when you're out."

Listening to the on-and-off sound of the water running, I paced in my room as I waited.

"That guy you were talking to is a douche, by the way," he called out.

*Hmmmm...* "I'm surprised you noticed me there tonight."

"What does that mean?"

The vodka lemonade Cici had poured into my cup now granted me a bit of liquid courage. "Seriously, Archie? You've never bothered to get to know me at all. Mostly you pretend I don't exist."

"Have you bothered to get to know *me*?" he spat back.

I guessed I really hadn't. I'd always assumed he thought he was better than me. But maybe that's because somehow *I* believed he was better than me.

The door opened.

I swallowed. Archie was so handsome. The sight of him entering my room took my breath away for a moment. He had changed into a fitted white T-shirt and gray sweatpants. He was tall, muscular, and had the angular features Disney prince faces were made of. And let's not even talk about that thick mane of hair or the way he smelled— freaking amazing. Very few people had this effect on me, but Archie Remington was certainly at the top of the list. *And that sucks.*

Clearing my throat, I chided, "Who's the one not knocking now?"

"That was pretty crazy earlier, huh? The way we first ran into each other?"

*Uh, why is he bringing that up?* "Not my finest moment," I mumbled.

"You should've seen your face." He laughed.

I rolled my eyes. "I can only imagine."

He grinned. "Actually, you *want* to see your face?"

"What are you talking about?"

He then presented a piece of paper I hadn't realized he was holding behind his back. "I drew you."

He handed me a sketch. It was a female...who looked remarkably like me. She was totally naked. And upon closer inspection, her body looked like mine, too—from the shape of her breasts to the amount of pubic hair. Okay, so this was a full-on portrait of me. I'd assumed he barely had time to notice my *features*, but apparently not.

"My, don't you have a photographic memory," I said, continuing to stare at the drawing. Then I noticed a caption underneath: *Naked and Afraid, AR*

A and R were his initials.

"Consider it a peace offering." He smirked.

"You could've given me, oh, I don't know...flowers, instead of a frighteningly accurate naked portrait of myself."

He chuckled. "Where's the fun in that?"

"Anyway..." I looked down at it again, noticing even more details, like the freckles on my chest. "You're really good."

"Well, my dad would disagree. He calls my artwork *doodling*, so..."

"Don't listen to him," I snapped. "You're talented."

His eyes darted to mine and stayed there a few seconds before he looked away. "Anyway, who the fuck puts a bathroom between two bedrooms like this, anyway? It's like...pick one or the other."

"I think it was designed for siblings to share or something."

"Dumb." His eyes lingered on mine again. "I know I joked about it earlier, but you do look a lot different than I remember."

My cheeks burned. "What you mean to say is you don't remember what I looked like before because I was invisible to you." I glanced down at the drawing. "Based on this, I sort of wish I was *still* invisible."

His eyes narrowed. "What are you talking about? Of course, I remember you. Even if you seem to think I was a dick and anti-social, I remember you. You used to wear two different-colored socks and pull them up to your knees."

*Wow.* That was my thing when I was fifteen. "That was in back then."

"You also used to have braces, and now you don't."

I shook my head. "I'm blown away that you remember those things."

"So, anyway, as I was saying earlier, Xavier is a douche. Stay away from him. Those girls you're hanging out with? Douchettes. They're trouble, too."

"Who in particular?"

"Cici Kravitz."

"You don't like her? Didn't you used to date her sister?"

"Ah, we're doing our research, are we?" He raised a brow. "I did, for a brief time the summer before my freshman year of college."

"Well, it seems you hurt her pretty badly."

"I guess you believe everything you're told."

"It's not true?"

"I never promised her anything. It was a summer thing. She's bitter, so she talks shit about me. Just remember what I said about them. They're no good. I've been coming here every summer since I was a kid. I know everyone. You want to know whether someone's legit, just ask me."

I lifted my brow. "And you're so respectable yourself?"

His eyes widened. "You really dislike me, huh?"

"No." I shook my head and chuckled. "I don't know you. I can't hate someone I don't know."

"You've just assumed certain things in the meantime."

"Yes, because of how distant you've seemed in the past."

"Maybe I was just shy. Did you ever think of that?"

"I doubt it."

"Let's clear some things up." He moved to sit on the edge of my bed, putting *me* on edge. "What's one impression you have of me?"

"That you're stuck up," I said immediately.

He crossed his arms. "I could've assumed the same about you—that you were a smart, know-it-all, overachiever who wanted nothing to do with the dumb jock son of your parents' friends. Because *you* also never made an effort to get to know *me*."

"I don't think you're dumb." My eyes narrowed. "And who said I was smart?"

"Your parents are always bragging about you."

"Yeah, well, your mom brags about you, too."

"Exactly." He huffed. "My *mom*, not my dad, right?"

*Crap.* I'd touched that sore spot. "Yeah...your mom always has amazing things to say about you."

"And yet you think I'm an asshole, for some godforsaken reason."

"You know what? You're right. I made assumptions about you. You've just always been elusive." I crossed my arms.

Archie stood up and inched closer, putting my body on high alert. "If you want to get to know me, then get to know me. But don't make assumptions without anything to back them up." He looked me in the eyes. "And I promise to do the same." He then stood and walked backward toward the bathroom door. "Anyway, the bathroom's free. But FYI, only the door on your side seems to lock from the inside. So while I can lock you out, you can't lock me out.

I'll be extra careful to knock first, though." He winked and turned away. "Unlike some people."

*Great.* "Thank you."

He turned around one final time. "Nice to *actually* meet you, Noelle Simone Benedict."

*He knows my middle name? Interesting.* "You, too," I murmured.

He headed through the bathroom and disappeared into his room. It felt a little like that bathroom was a gateway to heaven—or hell, depending on how you looked at it.

Imagining him listening to every move I made, I washed my face and brushed my teeth as quickly as possible. I almost opted to go to sleep without using the toilet for fear that I'd fart or something, but then I figured out that I could run the water to hide any potential sounds. He was just too close for comfort.

I had trouble getting to sleep after that, albeit with a reluctant smile on my face. Because Archie Remington? He was a bit different than I'd imagined. He was...alright.

• • •

The following morning, I dragged my butt out of bed at 5 AM for another morning run. I spent a few minutes watching the sun beginning to rise over the ocean as I stretched, the sound of seagulls the only sign of life.

But about a minute after I took off down the road, I heard footsteps on the gravel behind me. My heart raced. It sounded like I was being chased—until the footsteps caught up with me. My adrenaline waned after I turned to find Archie jogging beside me.

"You scared the shit out of me," I panted.

"You shouldn't be running this early by yourself."

"Why not? This is a nice area."

"It's not as nice as you think. There are plenty of low-lifes lurking around, ready to take advantage of people they think deserve it because they're rich and entitled. People travel here to prey on others. And you're the perfect victim, all alone out here with no one else around. It's practically the middle of the night. The sun isn't even fully up yet."

"How did you know I went running?"

"Well, your fucking alarm woke me up, for one. Then I looked and saw you stretching out front. Figured I'd catch up with you." He turned to look straight ahead. "Anyway, I run too and don't mind having a partner."

"Well, I don't exactly need one, so..."

He shook his head. "You were upset because I was anti-social, and now you don't want my company? Isn't that a bit of a contradiction? I get no points for effort here?"

Speeding up a bit, I said, "I like running alone to clear my head. And I can already see you talk too much."

"Now I talk *too much*?" He chuckled. "Damn, you're hard to please, Noelle. How about if I agree to shut up while we're running?"

*God, he looks fucking hot right now.* He wore a Dodgers cap backward, which was barely able to contain the golden-brown hair peeking out from under it. And his black athletic shirt hugged his muscles impeccably.

"Okay..." I sighed. "I can deal with running and no talking."

As requested, the remainder of the jog was surprisingly quiet, though his mere presence next to me was overwhelming and seemed to be all I could focus on. So much for clearing my head when all I could do was breathe his delicious scent and focus on his nearness.

We stopped for a break at the top of a hill.

Archie leaned his hands against his knees. "You're pretty fast, Benedict. Impressive."

"I was trying to lose you," I teased.

"You're a brat." He laughed.

I shook my index finger at him. "You don't have to force yourself to hang out with me just to prove you're not an asshole. I told you I wouldn't assume anything about you anymore."

"I do feel bad that you thought I was intentionally ignoring you in the past, but that's not why I'm here. I came because I didn't want you running alone this early."

If that was true, it kind of warmed my heart. I looked up and noticed the way the sun caught his eyes, making them appear even icier than they already were. I cleared my throat. "Well...thank you for your concern."

"Translation: fuck off." He grinned.

I smiled and shook my head. "No."

After a minute, we resumed our run, heading back toward the house.

When we stepped inside, our parents were at the kitchen table having coffee. My mother's jaw dropped at the sight of us together.

"Nice to see you two getting along," Nora said.

"I wouldn't go that far," Archie muttered, smirking over at me.

"He was nice enough to accompany me so I didn't have to run alone," I said.

"We appreciate that, Archie," my mom said. "I've always worried about her running alone so early. She does it at home, too."

Archie came up behind me as I popped a coffee pod into the machine, his closeness sending a shiver down my spine. "You wanna shower?"

My face flushed with heat. My thirsty brain interpreted that question entirely incorrectly. But then...*duh*...we shared a bathroom. I cleared my throat. "I'll just use my mom's bathroom. You go ahead."

He nodded. "Okay."

Nora smiled over at her son before he disappeared up the stairs. Then she sighed. "It's so good to have my baby back."

"I'm sure we'll feel the same next year once Noelle's away in Boston," my dad said.

"Archie needs to start getting serious," Archer interjected. "This time is precious. I'm afraid he's wasting it. He needs to call—"

"He just got here!" Nora said. "He'll call him. Don't worry."

*Has this guy never heard of summer vacation?* I brought my coffee to the table and joined them, reaching for an apple fritter.

To my surprise, Archer turned his attention toward me. "Noelle, your mother tells me you're majoring in journalism at BU?"

I nodded. "Yes."

"You don't think that's a bit of a waste?"

My chewing slowed. "How so?"

"Well, journalists don't make much money, from what I understand."

I straightened in my seat. "Someone has to document what's happening in the world. Whether journalists get paid a lot or not, it's an important job. You can't deny that."

"Just because someone has to do it doesn't mean you should. Are you going to become a garbage collector because someone needs to take out the trash?"

*God, he's so condescending.* "There's nothing wrong with that, either," I responded.

I was definitely starting to understand how Archie felt around his dad. I was a confident person, but he had a way of making you feel less-than. I wasn't entirely sure what my father saw in him. I wondered if Dad mainly associated with Archer because it helped him professionally.

I glanced around the table, but my parents and Nora stayed quiet. It would've been nice if someone had come to my defense. But I suspected no one in this room quite knew how to stand up to Archer. So it would have to be me.

I opened my mouth again, unable to help myself. "Even if I don't end up becoming a journalist, I think a major in journalism shows prospective employers that my writing and communication skills are strong. Those things can be applied to many different industries." I took another bite of my apple fritter and spoke with my mouth full. "Many people end up majoring in one thing and landing in another field. You don't have to commit to anything based on your major."

He shook his head. "If you're smart, you will. I would consider switching to business. BU has a great school of management."

Feeling disgusted, I stood up from the table. "If you'll excuse me, I think I'm going to take a shower."

Upstairs in my parents' bathroom, as the water rained down on me, I replayed the conversation in my head. That was only five minutes, but life must be like that for Archie all the time.

• • •

I didn't see Archie for the rest of that day until dinner. And we didn't say much to each other during the meal. I mostly just listened as his dad grilled him yet again while I stole glances at Archie's gorgeous face, broad shoulders, strong forearms. The way the overhead light brought out the gorgeous blond streaks in his hair. Yeah, I was pathetically hot for him.

At one point, Nora started posing questions that I remembered her asking the other night at dinner—how Archie's flight here had been, among other things. It perplexed me, and I wondered if she was just making shit up without thinking as a distraction in the hopes that his dad would pipe down.

Archie was once again the first to leave the dinner table. Could I blame him? Absolutely not.

# CHAPTER 4

## Noelle
### *Past*

**LATER THAT EVENING,** Cici's cousin, Xavier, asked me if I wanted to go for a walk on the beach. It seemed harmless enough, so we went for a stroll and talked—him mostly about his musical aspirations and me mostly asking him questions about life in Boston.

When we arrived back in the general area of the bonfire, we stood closer to the shore, away from people. Xavier reached out and caressed my hair.

"Your eyes are so striking, Noelle."

I stiffened. "Thank you."

"Seriously, they're like...translucent. I love your dimples, too."

I looked down at my flip-flops and repeated, "Thanks."

When I looked up again, he was still staring at me. Then suddenly he went in for the kill. My body tensed. I hadn't been expecting him to kiss me, and I *definitely* hadn't been expecting the rough way he shoved his tongue down my throat. Flailing my arms, I leaned back to try to get him to stop, but he only pushed forward, kissing me harder. It didn't help that he was a little drunk.

It was too much for me, all of it—the kiss, the weight of him. There were people not that far from us, but I still felt totally alone.

Then the weight lifted. When I looked up, Archie's hand was around Xavier's neck.

"What the fuck are you doing?" he demanded. "Could you not see she was trying to push you off?"

"Hey, man, calm down."

Archie shoved Xavier across the sand, causing him to land on his ass. "She clearly didn't want it, and you kept pushing," he spat.

Xavier looked over at me, his eyes groggy. "I didn't do that, did I? Tell him."

In total shock, I shook my head and stammered, "Umm...I think you should leave, Xavier."

Xavier stood up and stumbled away.

Archie was out of breath. "Are you okay?"

"Yeah," I exhaled. "He was drunk. I don't think he meant anything by it—"

"Don't make excuses for him! I saw it. You were trying to get him to stop. He didn't. End of story."

I took a deep breath. "You're right. I'm just a little rattled. Nothing like that has ever happened to me before." I smoothed out my shirt. "I guess you were right about him, huh?"

Archie gave me side-eye. "That doesn't make me feel good, by the way."

"How did you see us all the way over here?"

"I saw you walk away with him earlier, so I kept an eye out. When I noticed you down by the shore, I came to make sure you were okay."

I straightened the wrinkles in my shirt. "I'm sorry for not listening to you."

"Well, I guess I haven't given you a reason to trust me yet." He tilted his head toward where his friends were congregated in the distance. "Come on. Let's go over there."

The waves crashed behind us, and I looked over at him as we walked. "You must be right about Cici, too. What's the deal with her? You were never specific."

He raised a brow. "You really want to know?"

"Yeah."

"I was dating her sister, as you already found out. Like I told you, it was just a summer hookup with Amanda and nothing more, despite what Cici might have told you. That stuff about me breaking her heart is a total joke." He sighed. "Anyway, one night, we were all hanging out down in their parents' basement. Amanda was drunk. When she went upstairs to throw up, Cici tried to go down on me."

My mouth dropped.

"I bet she'd deny it if you asked her," he added. "But she did. You can't trust someone who would stab her own sister in the back like that."

That news really rubbed me the wrong way. "Yeah. No shit." I'd only hung out with Cici a couple of times, but that seemed like a betrayal.

"Anyway..." he said. "The people you see me with, they're all cool. Good people I've known for years. You should hang out with us instead."

*Well, alright then.* "You mean the girl you've been sucking face with this summer? She's the only person I've seen you with."

"I wasn't really referring to Bree. She's part of the crew, though."

"Is she your girlfriend?"

"No. I don't have a girlfriend. She's just someone I..." He hesitated.

"Someone you fuck?"

Archie squinted. "Why does that word sound wrong coming from Little Miss Goody-Goody?" He laughed. "We've hooked up, yeah. I've known her for years. She's just a friend."

"With benefits," I added as jealousy burned my cheeks.

"I suppose. But we have an understanding about it. So it's all good."

We arrived at the spot where his friends always hung out, and he waved me closer. Until now I'd only gazed over at this group.

"Come on," he said. "I'll introduce you."

Three guys, Bree, and another girl were talking and laughing.

"Guys, this is Noelle. She's the daughter of my parents' friends—the ones we share the house with now."

Archie's something-or-other held out her hand as her long hair blew in the breeze. "Hey. I'm Bree. Nice to meet you."

"You, too."

Bree was the opposite of me looks-wise: tall, skinny, and blond to my short, brunette, and curvy.

A guy smiled and waved. "I'm James."

I nodded. "Hey." Dark-haired James was cute, although only a little taller than me.

Archie then introduced me to Linus and Sean, along with Sean's girlfriend, Sarina.

It turned out Archie's friends were pretty cool. They were all around his age—a bit older than me—and everyone was home from college. I stayed quiet and mostly listened as they told stories from summers past on the island.

Bree was still hanging all over Archie, but he seemed unfazed as he chatted with the others. Out of everyone, James seemed the most interested in getting to know me. He stood next to me and kept asking me questions about myself.

"So how did you and Archie's family become friends?"

"Our dads work for the same law firm. Mr. Remington was my father's mentor for many years, and then they decided to invest in a property together. So we're all staying for the summer."

"Gotcha." He dug his feet in the sand. "Archie's a good dude. I've known him for years."

"You're from here?"

"Yes. Born and bred. It was a great place to grow up."

"I would imagine. It's so idyllic. But it's probably a little strange when everyone converges on you in the summer, huh? When you have to share it with us city dwellers?"

He looked out toward the water a moment. "Strange but awesome. Always the best time of year, if you ask me." He shrugged. "I appreciate being home even more now that I'm away at school. You can't beat coming back to this."

I learned a lot about James during the next half hour or so. He was pre-med, loved nineties alternative rock, and had an older sister who was already in med school. And unlike Archie's dad, James seemed impressed with my journalistic aspirations and the opportunities that could result from that major.

Our conversation was flowing nicely, but it was getting late. I felt like I needed a breather. Tonight had been *a lot*, particularly what happened with Xavier. So I excused myself from talking with James and went over to Archie.

"Hey, I think I'm gonna head back to the house," I told him.

He let go of Bree and placed the cup he was holding down in the sand. "I'll walk you." His breath smelled like beer.

"You don't have to."

"You shouldn't walk home alone this late."

Archie was nothing if not protective, so I chose not to argue with him.

After I said my goodbyes, the short walk from the beach to our house started off quiet. Then I decided to ask him something. "How did you know my middle name?"

His eyes filled with mirth.

"What?" I asked.

He stopped walking and placed his hands on his hips. "Let me demonstrate." He flipped his hair before putting on his best female voice. "Representing the great state of New York, I'm Noelle Simone Benedict."

*Uh...* A rush of adrenaline hit with the embarrassment. "Where did you see that?"

"I Googled you once when my mother told me you were in a beauty pageant. I had to see it for myself. They had the replay online."

"It *wasn't* a beauty pageant," I clarified. "It was for a scholarship."

"You were wearing a gown. Looked like a beauty pageant to me."

"Well, yeah, that was part of it, but this particular pageant is geared toward academics and declamation, not beauty."

"By the way, I'm not making fun of you. I hope you know that. I think it's fucking awesome."

"I only entered for the scholarship money."

"You got robbed. That Rhode Island chick who won had nothing on you."

"She took nothing from me because I didn't even place in the top ten." I laughed.

"Still, it took a lot of balls to put yourself out there like that. I couldn't have done that shit. I have mad respect for you."

My chest swelled with pride, though the pageant wasn't something I was usually boastful about.

"Thanks again for rescuing me from Xavier," I said when we approached the house.

"I'm still pissed and want to fuck him up. I never thought he'd be *that* big of a douche. If I'd known he would pull something like that, I would've pushed harder for you to stay away from him."

"Had he done something in the past to tip you off?"

"I just know how he treats girls in general—fucking them and then bragging about it. His parents are super rich. He's very entitled. I know that sounds funny coming from me, by the way." He chuckled. "It takes one to know one."

"Yeah." I laughed. "But you're not a douche like him."

"Not to that level, no." He grinned. "I'm like a douche level two maybe. He's a douche level ten."

I elbowed him. "I suspect you're not a douche at all, despite my earlier preconceived notions."

"Well, one thing's for certain. I would never push myself on a girl."

"You're too busy pushing them off." I winked.

He shrugged, unable to argue with that.

We stopped in front of the door at the house. "I assume you're not coming in. It's still a little early for you."

He shook his head and looked down at the ground. "Nah. My dad's probably still up, so..."

"I don't blame you for wanting to avoid him." I sighed. "He's tough on you."

"Yeah. It wasn't always as bad as it is now, but..."

"I got a little taste of it myself earlier."

He drew in his brows. "What did he do?"

"He quizzed me about my decision to major in journalism this morning. He didn't approve."

"Typical, yeah. Unless you're gonna be a doctor or lawyer—or something else that promises good money—it's not worth pursuing in his mind." He rolled his eyes.

I opened the door. "Well...have fun...with Bree, I presume."

He kicked some dirt. "Thanks."

I watched as he walked away, wondering why the hell I had butterflies in my stomach when the dude I was apparently crushing on was about to have sex with another girl.

• • •

The following morning, as I set out on my jog, there was something missing: Archie. I couldn't help but look back from time to time, hoping he'd show up. He'd made it sound like coming with me would be a regular thing, since it wasn't safe to be alone. But apparently, it was a *one-time* thing.

The fact that I was disappointed bugged the shit out of me. Why did I care so much about Archie all of a sudden? Why had I thought of little else but him since the moment he arrived? I pondered such things for three miles.

When I returned to the house, no one was up yet. I popped one of the coffee pods into the machine and made myself a quick cup before I went upstairs and jumped in the shower.

As I shampooed my hair, a deep voice startled me from behind the shower curtain.

"I overslept."

My hands froze mid-lather. "You just come in here without knocking?"

He sounded groggy. "I knew you were in the shower. Figured it was safe." He paused. "But it's nothing I haven't seen before anyway, right?"

I rolled my eyes. "You did *not* just say that."

"Anyway...I'm sorry I missed our run."

"It's not your responsibility to accompany me." I resumed rubbing the shampoo into my scalp.

"But I meant to."

"Not sure how you can stay out all night and expect to get up early to run. I heard you come in pretty late."

"Did I wake you when I came home?"

I rinsed the shampoo out of my hair. "Just for like five minutes when you went to brush your teeth."

"Sorry."

A few seconds passed.

"Are you going to stand there while I shower?"

"No. I just wanted to apologize."

"Apology accepted." I squirted conditioner into my hand. Then I heard the door close.

As I got dressed in my room, I was painfully aware of Archie's presence nearby. I was also aware of a weird tension within me. I was bummed he hadn't joined me this morning, but I was probably more bummed about the *reason* he was out so late.

A few minutes later, I heard his voice from behind the bathroom door.

"Are you decent?"

I looked down at myself to make sure I wasn't missing anything. "Yes."

"Can I come in?"

I swallowed. "Yeah."

He entered the room and plopped down on my bed. I couldn't help noticing the way his shirt rode up, displaying sculpted abs. My eyes explored the tattoo on his upper arm as he wrapped his hand around the back of his head. It looked like a wolf's face. Maybe a school mascot? Archie had played football in high school, but it hadn't carried over into college.

He let out a deep sigh. "Today's gonna suck."

"Why?"

"I have to meet that attorney my father wants me to intern with this summer."

"Might there be anything good to come of that?"

"Possibly. But...if I know Dad, he'll find a way to say I'm fucking the whole thing up and embarrassing him."

"Whatever happened to just enjoying the summer?"

"Right? This final year before law school is going to be hard enough." He stared up at the ceiling for a bit and then turned to me. "I need to ask you for a favor."

I blinked. "What is it?"

"I'd like you to change your running time in the morning."

Tying my hair up into a ponytail, I looked at him through the mirror. "Why would I do that?"

"So I can go with you. Five AM is too fucking early, Noelle. I can't have a social life at night and get up at five."

"Well, you snooze you lose," I teased.

"Seriously, can we just move it to six? I'd like to be able to join you. Six I can handle."

He seemed serious about this—not even a hint of a smile. *How could I say no?* I turned to face him. "Are you gonna set your alarm? Because I'm not waiting for you."

"Yeah." He nodded. "I'll do that."

Secretly thrilled, I pretended to think it over. "Okay, then."

"Cool." He hopped up. "I gotta go get dressed for this shit."

"Archie?"

"Yeah?"

"Good luck today."

"Thanks." He let out a long breath. "I'll need it."

About ten minutes after Archie left, my phone rang. It was my best friend, Ashley Carrera, from home.

"Hey, you!" I bounced on the mattress.

"How's it going over there?" she asked.

It was so good to hear her voice; it reminded me there was an entire world outside this little bubble and the intoxicating guy I now lived with.

"Good, actually."

"Have you run into Asshole Archie?"

I cringed. Before leaving to come here, I'd made it sound like he was the devil. I looked out the window and saw Archie getting into his parents' Jeep. He wore a collared shirt and dress pants and looked tense as he slammed the door. My chest tightened. I felt bad for ever calling him an asshole. "Actually...he's nothing like I had him pegged."

"Really? Do tell."

"I've just realized I never really knew him before." I sighed. "He and I are getting along. It's weird."

"Like...getting along or *getting along.*"

"No." I shook my head. "Nothing like *that.* He doesn't see me that way. And he has this girl here he hooks up with. But he and I...talk and stuff. He's gone running with me in the mornings. He's pretty nice."

"Wow. I wasn't expecting you to say that."

"I know. Me neither."

"Is he just as hot as you remembered?"

"No."

"No?"

"No." I sighed. "He's hotter, unfortunately."

I could've gone into detail about what I'd walked in on that first day—how his dick was, in fact, much bigger than his ego. But bringing up his body felt exploitative and unnecessary.

"The summer is long, Noelle. Anything can happen." She laughed. "Now I'm really looking forward to my week there in August. We're going to have a blast."

"I'm looking forward to that, too," I said. I'd been so stuck in my head lately that I'd practically forgotten I'd invited her to visit.

• • •

Archie strolled into the dining room fashionably late that night. It was nice to see him after he'd been out all day. While he was gone, I'd spent some of the afternoon lying out in the yard and reading.

Dinner, on the other hand, was spent listening to Archie's father grill him about his first day at Rodney Erickson's law practice. Apparently, after the interview, the attorney had invited Archie to stay and shadow him.

Tonight Archie had chosen the seat next to me. That didn't go unnoticed. He also stayed through dessert for the first time ever.

As we finished eating, he leaned in and whispered, "You comin' to the beach tonight?"

The heat of his breath against my neck gave me goose bumps. "I was thinking about it, yeah."

His eyes fell briefly to my lips. "You should."

"Okay. Maybe I will." I could feel my dumb self getting excited. Why? So I could watch Bree all over him? *What are you doing, Noelle?*

When he'd cleaned his plate, Archie got up and left the table, and Nora went out back with the two dads, leaving my mother and me alone in the kitchen.

Mom tackled the dishes, and I stayed to help.

She smiled over at me. "You and Archie seem to be getting along."

"Strange, right?" I took a pan from her to dry it.

Mom lowered her voice. "I know you were dreading interacting with him. It's nice to see you enjoying yourself."

"Yeah. I had him all wrong."

"He's awfully handsome, too, isn't he?"

I looked over my shoulder. "Mom..."

"I won't tell if you like him that way."

My skin tingled. "Just because we're getting along doesn't mean I like him *that way.*"

"I suppose you're right."

"Although..." I added. "He's obviously quite good-looking. And smart, regardless of what his father seems to think."

My mother sighed. "I want to smack Archer sometimes." She exhaled. "He's under a lot of stress lately, and that's making his behavior toward Archie worse."

I narrowed my eyes. "Stress? About what?"

My mother shut off the water and spoke in a low voice. "I'm not at liberty to divulge. But things have certainly been better for their family. That's all I can say right now."

My stomach sank. "Mom, you can't just hint at something serious and not elaborate."

"I shouldn't have said anything at all. Okay? Pretend I didn't, please." She turned on the water again and immersed herself in the rest of the dishes.

Dread settled in my stomach. *What is going on with the Remingtons?*

A few seconds later, Archer and Nora entered the kitchen, and Mom and I put on fake smiles, as if we hadn't just been talking about them.

# CHAPTER 5

## Noelle
*Present*

**STANDING BY THE** window in my old bedroom at the beach house on Whaite's Island, I gazed out at the ocean across the road. Seven years had passed since that first summer here, but it felt like yesterday.

The anxiousness running through my veins reminded me of the nerves I'd had back when I first arrived, waiting for Archie and expecting the worst. But facing him this time would be a whole lot harder.

Neither of us had known that first summer would also be our last at this house. It had turned out to be the most memorable season of my life, despite how it ended.

Archie called from downstairs. "Did someone say penne a la vodka?"

I took a deep breath and glanced at myself in the mirror. *Let's go.*

My heart pummeled against my chest as I rushed down the stairs. "All I heard was *vodka*. And I'm totally game."

Archie dropped the bag of groceries he was holding and held his arms out wide. "Fuck, Noelle... It's been too damn long."

I leapt into his arms. "You made it!" I took a deep breath of his scent as he held me tightly, and all of the unwanted memories flooded back. This trip would be short, but I would cherish every moment, while also trying to keep my heart from breaking.

He pulled away, his eyes wandering over me. "You look great."

"So do you."

It was hard to look at him, in fact. Archie was even more beautiful in his late twenties than he had been seven years ago, and that was saying a lot. With the same gorgeous, thick hair, he had even more definition to his jaw and slightly more facial hair.

"I figured I'd stop at the market on my way here instead of having to go back out. That way we could just enjoy the day."

"Makes sense."

Archie picked up the bag and took it to the kitchen as I followed. He placed it on the center island. "Can I ask a favor?"

"What?"

"I know we have a lot to discuss—namely the wedding invitation and my not telling you sooner. But can we put all of that off for one day?" He sighed as he took a package of pasta out of the bag. "I just want to enjoy your company without any heavy talk." He flashed a sad smile. "Just today."

I was in no rush at all to think about him marrying Mariah. I was perfectly happy to live in denial on this one. "Okay." I nodded. "We can do that."

"Cool." He wriggled his brows. "How about a cocktail before we have to meet the realtor?"

• • •

Later that afternoon, we met with Dawn Mahoney, the agent we'd tasked with putting this property on the market. She did a walkthrough of the house and stayed for a longer time than I'd anticipated. But she also felt we could list it for about a hundred grand more than we'd estimated, so that was good news.

By the time she left, it was almost dinnertime. Archie poured us glasses of white wine, and I sat at the kitchen island to watch as he prepared dinner.

I was so proud of Archie for following his dream and becoming a chef. He and his buddy co-owned a restaurant now out in Irvine. Archie was the head chef while his friend, Max, handled the business side of things. Archie had almost chosen a profession his heart wasn't into. This was so much better.

As he diced the garlic and mellow piano music played from his phone, my heart swelled. When he put the knife down and moved over to the stove, I decided to squelch the inappropriate feelings building inside me by bringing up his bride-to-be. That would cool things down.

"I'm surprised you didn't bring Mariah with you..." I took a sip of my wine.

He stopped stirring for a moment and tapped the long spoon against the edge of the pot. "She had a friend's bridal shower this weekend. She wasn't thrilled about me coming alone, but I'm glad it worked out this way, because I needed the space."

*Space? Interesting.*

I'd only met Mariah once when I was passing through California on an assignment. As a field producer for a national news magazine show, my job often took me to different parts of the country. Whenever I was on the West Coast, I tried to meet up with Archie. The last visit had been five months ago, and he'd introduced me to his girlfriend.

"Why do you need space?" I asked.

"There's just…a lot going on."

"The wedding?"

Archie took a long sip of his wine and set the glass down. "You promised we could have a day off from wedding talk."

"Okay." I ran my finger along the stem of my glass. "You're right."

Once we sat down to eat, we kept the conversation light. I told him about the latest piece I was working on—the story of a man who lived multiple secret lives and scammed several women out of thousands of dollars. Archie filled me in on the possibility of him opening a second restaurant.

The wine was flowing, and when what I'd consumed started to hit me, my ability to hold back left the building. I unleashed a question that didn't *technically* fall under the banned category of wedding talk.

"Does Mariah know about us?" I asked.

"Does she know we're here together? Of course."

"That's not what I meant."

Archie looked up from his empty dessert plate. "You mean did I tell her you and I hooked up that one summer?"

"Yeah. I'm just curious if she knows about that...blip, if you will." Sadness settled in my chest at the way I'd reduced what we'd had to a mere *blip*. It was so much more than that to me.

Archie fiddled with his napkin. "No. I don't see a good reason to tell her." He looked up at me. "Do you?"

"Probably not."

His eyes seared into mine. "Did you ever tell Shane?"

"No." I chuckled. "He didn't like you as it was."

"Well, there you go." Archie rolled up his napkin and tossed it aside. "For the record, I never liked him, either."

Archie had only met my ex-boyfriend once, when Shane had accompanied me on one of my work trips to California, pre-Mariah. The three of us had dinner together one night, and Shane kept telling me all Archie really wanted was to get in my pants. I'd neglected to tell my ex that was what *I'd* wanted for quite some time, too—until Archie rejected me.

Things went quiet for a bit, as Archie cleared the table and I felt more emotions bubbling to the surface. Archie and I had decided a long time ago that we were better off as friends. Well, it was more *his* decision, though I went along with it. Either distance or circumstances had made being anything more than friends pretty much impossible anyway. And for most of the time we'd been physically apart, I'd had a boyfriend.

Shane and I had been together for five-and-a-half years. We'd met at BU, dating exclusively up until about six months ago. We'd both gotten TV-industry jobs in New York after college and had stayed together until we finally grew apart. Shane decided he didn't want kids after previously saying he did, and that was a dealbreaker for me. But by the time he and I ended things, Archie was with Mariah. I'd missed the window to explore things with Archie again. The universe must've had other plans. Fate had to be telling us something.

"What room are you sleeping in tonight?" he asked.

"My old one."

He nodded. "I'll probably take the bedroom down here."

That shouldn't have come as a surprise. I'd wondered, though, if maybe he'd sleep in the room adjacent to mine for old times' sake. Hiding my slight disappointment, I folded my hands together. "There's plenty of space to choose from, right?"

Him sleeping downstairs was probably better anyway. I knew Archie would never cheat on his girlfriend— excuse me, *fiancée*—but knowing he was right next door would likely ignite old feelings in me that were better kept buried.

Eventually, I helped Archie finish cleaning up the mess we'd made. Then we sat out back and gazed up at the stars. It was a beautiful, clear evening on Whaite's Island, albeit a little cool. I had a knit blanket from the living room couch over myself as I sat on the Adirondack chair.

Archie looked up at the sky. "Do you think we're making the right decision about selling this place?"

"I do. My parents agree that it's the best time to sell."

"It just...feels like the last piece of that simpler time."

"I know," I whispered.

"That was the best summer of my life, you know."

Turning to him, I nodded in agreement.

"And maybe also the worst," he added.

We stared at each other in silence.

I wanted to say so much, but I was afraid of what opening up even a little would cause me to say next. Because there was *a lot* I wanted to tell Archie right now. I wanted to tell him I loved him—as more than a friend. That I'd always loved him, from that first summer we lived together. It had taken me a long time to figure out that my inability to love Shane the way he deserved was probably because I'd been harboring feelings for Archie.

Instead, I cowered. I said nothing but wondered if everything would come flooding out before the end of this weekend.

One thing was for certain: if there was ever a time to tell Archie Remington how I truly felt, it was now. I might not have another chance.

● ● ●

A loud knock woke me the next morning.

My groggy eyes fluttered open. *What the?*

His deep voice was grating as he spoke from behind the door. "Come on, Benedict. You're late for our run."

I looked at my phone. 6 AM. Our old running time. "Run?" I rubbed my eyes. "I don't do that anymore."

"Are you serious? You used to be so disciplined."

"I know. I lost my mojo a while back."

He clapped his hands. "Well, chop chop! Time to get your mojo back."

I straightened up and looked out toward the sunrise, then at the still-closed door. I could sense his presence there. "You're not going to let me get out of this, are you?"

"Not a chance."

I dragged my ass out of bed. "Okay, give me a minute to get dressed."

"I'll grab some coffee and wait downstairs for you."

My mouth curved into a smile. "Since when do you drink coffee, Remington?"

"I started about a year ago. I think of you every time I drink it. Now I'm hooked."

He pounded on the door one last time, and I heard his footsteps fade into the distance. Still half asleep, I took my time getting dressed.

When I joined him in the kitchen, Archie's eyes very obviously traced over the revealing athletic tank top and tight Spandex shorts I'd put on. *What can I say?* If Mariah was going to have him forever, I at least wanted to *borrow* his admiration this weekend. *It's just innocent fun,* I told myself. Nothing more.

"I thought you said you were getting...dressed." He swallowed. "I think you might have accidentally gotten *undressed.*"

I shrugged. "It's hot out."

Archie cleared his throat. "True."

In that moment, I realized for the first time in years that I did still have an effect on him. Physical chemistry was hard to gauge from across the continent. Then again, I'd never put it to the test the way I had just now.

Archie waited for me to gulp down some coffee.

After about five minutes, we left the house, hit the gravel, and took off down the road. The warm ocean breeze followed, the salty air like an old friend. How I'd missed this feeling—Archie running alongside me.

It was smooth and uneventful for about thirty minutes until Archie suddenly stopped. His face went white as he panted. "Can we take a break for a minute?"

"What's wrong?"

I wasn't even sure why I'd asked. Because as I watched him clutch his chest and gasp for air, I knew *exactly* what was happening. Let's just say, it wasn't Archie's first rodeo.

# CHAPTER 6

## Noelle
*Past*

**WHEN I ARRIVED** at the beach, Archie was already set up in his usual spot. Bree was once again glued to his side, with a beer in hand. I did my best to ignore Cici and the old crew on the other side of the bonfire. She probably wondered why I'd abandoned their ship, though it was possible Xavier had badmouthed me to her.

Archie waved when he spotted me approaching his group.

"We were talking about heading to the cliff walk tonight," James said.

I nodded. "That sounds like fun. I haven't been over there yet."

Soon after, we walked over to the scenic, rocky trail. Archie disappeared with Bree, and I was left with James, who was always interesting to talk to.

"Would you want to hang out this weekend?" he asked. "Maybe go to Abe's Seafood Shack for some fish and chips?"

"You mean like a date?" I stupidly said.

"Unless you'd rather it not be. We could just go as friends. But yeah, to be clear, I'm asking you out."

I wasn't sure how I wanted to respond. But ultimately, I decided I had nothing to lose. "Yeah. Alright. That sounds like fun."

"Cool." He beamed.

We then returned to normal conversation.

After a while, Archie emerged with Bree, after doing God knows what.

When I realized how late it was, I hugged James goodbye. He offered to walk me home, but before I could answer, Archie came running over.

"You headed back to the house?" he asked.

"Yeah."

"I am, too. I'll walk you."

"You're leaving?" I said, surprised.

"I have to go to my internship tomorrow."

"I didn't realize you were starting so soon."

"Yup. So I can't be doing an all-nighter. Plus..." He winked. "I have to run at 6 AM sharp."

James looked between us. I said goodnight to him again and made my way down the road with Archie.

I couldn't stop my mouth. "You disappeared for a while with Bree. I didn't think you were coming back."

"Did my absence bother you?"

A rush of heat tore through me. Shit. *Am I giving that impression?* "Of course not," I answered, laughing it off.

"I'm only hanging out with her because it's...easy," he admitted. "She knows me. I know her. There's nothing to prove. It's just a summer thing, and I know I won't have to feel guilty at the end of the season when we don't talk again until next year."

I swallowed the bitter taste in my mouth. "Easy for the summer. I get it." After some silence, I asked, "James is a good guy, right?"

"He is. A real good guy." He knocked into my shoulder. "Why? You like him or something?"

"I'm not sure. But he asked me to go out with him this weekend, and I said yes."

It was hard to see Archie's expression in the dark, but his pace slowed. "Oh." After a moment, he added, "Yeah... Like I said, he's cool."

"Okay. Just making sure."

We didn't say much else for the rest of the walk home.

After Archie and I went to our rooms, I tossed and turned for most of that night—thinking about James and me, Bree and Archie, Archie and me, and the various ways I knew my heart could end up broken this summer.

• • •

The following morning, Archie was already waiting outside when I emerged from the house at 6:05.

"Someone set his alarm," I teased.

"Well, you gave me the extra hour. I told you I would. I don't play games. By the way, who's the late one now?"

After a minute of stretching, I turned to him. "Ready?"

"Lead the way."

The extra hour of sleep had also done me good; I seemed to have more energy this morning. It didn't hurt that I had one of the most gorgeous guys I'd ever laid eyes on as a personal chaperone, either.

We were two miles into our run, and everything was going smoothly until Archie suddenly slowed down and clutched his chest.

My pulse picked up. "Are you okay?"

He panted, pointing to the side of the road. "I don't know. Can we sit over there for a minute?"

"Yeah. Of course."

We planted ourselves on a large rock.

"What are you experiencing right now?" I asked. "Talk to me."

His hand was still at his chest. "It just...feels like I can't catch my breath." He looked at me. "I think it's a panic attack."

"You've been through this before?"

He nodded.

I put my hand on his shoulder. "We should go back home."

"No. I can't let him see me like this."

*His dad.* "Okay. We'll stay here. It's okay. Just breathe." I rubbed his arm. "You get these a lot?"

"Only randomly when I'm under stress, but always at inopportune times." He forced a smile. "Like running with you. I have a reputation as an asshole to uphold. I can't have you thinking I'm some weak dude who gets panic attacks." He flashed a crooked smile.

I was probably meant to laugh at that, but I couldn't. "Did something specific cause you to panic?"

"I think this attack's been brewing for a while now. But, in general, they come out of nowhere."

With each minute we sat, he seemed to calm down a little more.

I remembered what my mom had alluded to briefly last night. "Is everything okay with you and your parents? Is something going on?"

Several seconds passed before he turned to me.

"Things aren't okay." He shook his head. "They're not okay at all."

My hand landed on his arm. "You can tell me."

He kept shaking his head. "I don't even know where to start."

"The beginning?" I offered a sympathetic smile. "Or not. I just want you to know you can vent. I won't tell anyone."

He closed his eyes for a long while. "This may be the last summer that anything looks remotely the same, Noelle."

A sinking feeling came over me. "What's happening?"

"My mother is losing her mind."

"What do you mean?"

"She was diagnosed with early-onset dementia."

*Oh no.* "When?"

"The signs had been there for a while, but the diagnosis came about six months ago."

That explained why she was asking him the same questions again that one night at dinner.

"I'm so sorry, Archie."

"That's not even all of it." He blew out a shaky breath. "Sorry. I need a minute. I haven't spoken about this with anyone."

"Take your time."

"I think my dad is having an affair," he finally said. "Actually, I *know* he is."

My mouth fell open. "Oh my God."

"So while my poor mother is suffering, that bastard is taking full advantage of her not being in her right mind."

I held my stomach. "That sickens me."

Archie looked up at the sky. "I just feel...so much pressure—to be there for my mother, to please my father, because he expects me to follow in his footsteps and work for his firm someday. The thing is, I want to do that, if just to prove myself to him. There's nothing I want more. But there's something you don't know about me—why it's gonna be so goddamn difficult."

My heartbeat accelerated. "What?"

"I might seem outgoing from the outside. But I...don't speak in front of people. Public speaking is not my thing. I get terrified. How the fuck do you become a trial attorney when you freeze up?"

Relief washed over me. I'd expected something worse. "I would never have known that about you."

"I come across as cool and confident, I know. I have everyone fucking fooled."

"It's actually quite common, a fear of public speaking."

"That's why my father volunteered me to present him with that award in the fall. I made the mistake of opening up to him about my issue once. So now he wants to throw me into the fire."

No wonder he'd had a panic attack today.

He raked a hand through his hair. "So between the stress of that dumb speech I have to write by the fall, applying to law schools, my father's affair, and most of all, worrying about my mom...I think I've been falling apart for a long time. Today I just finally lost it altogether. Unfortunately, you got a front row seat to the show."

"Well, I want my money back."

He looked over at me and smiled.

"Kidding." I squeezed his knee. "There are some things you can't change. But other things you can."

"Meaning..."

"Why don't we work on it this summer? The whole public speaking thing."

"*We*? You're gonna help me what—learn how to not be a blubbering idiot?"

"Yeah. You can practice on me. It won't matter how many times you flub up. We'll keep working on it until you get more comfortable. This kind of thing is my forte."

"I almost forgot, Miss America."

"Miss America *Scholastic*," I clarified. "Anyway, it's not just about learning to communicate in front of an audience; it's about how to not give a shit what other people think in that scenario." Excitement grew within me at the prospect of working with him. "Seriously, let me help you."

"You don't need me as a summer project."

"Actually, I do. You have your internship. What am I good for if I can't accomplish something useful here?"

He paused. "When are we supposed to do this?"

"Anytime you want."

"You know I'm desperate if I'm agreeing to let you coach me."

"How about a couple nights a week, like after dinner but before we go to the beach? It can be whenever, really.

It's the middle of June, so we have two months to work on it."

He laughed. "I hope you're not sorely disappointed when you can't help me. But I guess we can give it a shot."

"Cool." I smiled.

"*You're* pretty cool, Noelle. Nothing like the goody-two-shoes know-it-all I might've assumed you were." He winked.

"And you're nothing like the snobby jackass I thought you were," I replied. "I mean, you're a jackass, but not a snob."

"Fair enough."

"Kidding again." I elbowed him.

He took another deep breath, looked around, and finally got up from the rock.

"Ready to roll?" he asked.

I brushed off my butt. "If you are..."

We ran together back to the house in silence. The Archie alongside me now was nothing like the Archie I thought I'd known this morning.

# CHAPTER 7

## Archie
*Past*

**NOELLE LOOKED SO** damn cute when she was being all serious. A couple of nights after my panic attack, we were in her room for my first how-not-to-be-a-fucking-blubbering-idiot lesson. She paced as I sat up against the headboard on her bed. She didn't realize it, but I was sketching her while she spoke.

"I was Googling today," she said. "And I found many articles that talked about the seven Ps of public speaking." She tried to recall what they were as she counted on her fingers. "Purpose...people...preparation...planning...personality..." She paused.

"Penis," I deadpanned. *Already, I'm not taking this seriously enough.*

"Good guess, but no."

"Penetration?"

She laughed. "It's...performance."

"Sexual performance. See? I was right."

"Very funny."

"All right. I'm sorry." I sighed. "I'll try to be good."

She waved her hand dismissively. "Okay, never mind the seven Ps. The first rule of public speaking is knowing what the hell you're talking about. If you're not confident in what you're relaying, that's gonna be an issue."

I sat up straight. "Well, that's problem number one. I have to make a speech about how wonderful my father is when he's been nothing but an asshole to me almost my entire life."

She scratched her chin. "Hmm... Well, even if he hasn't been the best father, you can agree that he's had a remarkable career. There's probably a lot we can compile that will have you convinced he's worthy of accolades, even if Father of the Year isn't one of them."

"Yeah...of course. I just have to put it all together."

"Can you interview him?"

I immediately shook my head. "No. He wants me to do this on my own, and he'll only end up pissing me off if I ask him for any help."

"Okay." She nodded. "That's why you're going to have homework."

Shading in some of my drawing, I said, "I didn't realize I'd enrolled in school."

Noelle winked. "No actual grades though, which is pretty nice for you." She took a seat and kicked her feet up on the edge of her bed. "In my research on public-speaking fear, it seems one of the biggest challenges is the false impression people have of their importance as the speaker. People are listening to what you have to *say*. They don't care as much about *you* as you perceive. Somehow the person who's nervous assumes they're being judged on a personal level. So we have to get you to somehow... lose yourself."

64

I pointed my thumb behind me. "I've got a bottle of tequila in my room. That usually does the trick. Will that work?"

"As tempting as that might be... No."

I snapped my fingers. "Damn."

Noelle stood up and started pacing again. She waved her hand as she spoke as if she were conducting an orchestra instead of my blubbering-idiot class.

"You have to *become* someone else when you're up there. Like an alter ego." She stopped and turned to me. "Let's pick who you're gonna be up on that stage."

I squinted. "You're losing me a little..."

"He needs a name. Your alter ego. Something very opposite of the egotistical person who worries about what everyone thinks."

"Fred," I said. That's the first name that came to mind.

"Fred?" She laughed.

"Yeah. Generic. Boring. He doesn't give a shit what anyone thinks."

"Okay...Fred." She wrote it down.

"Why are *you* taking notes on this shit?" I asked.

"This isn't *shit*..." She threw her notebook on the bed. "This is your future, Archie. And you should be taking notes, too, instead of drawing. Don't think I don't notice. At least *pretend* to take it seriously."

I sighed. "You're right. I'm sorry."

She picked her notebook back up and tapped her pen against it. "Okay...so a few things we have to work on. First, you've got to get to know your dad better."

"Hard no."

"I don't mean spending more time with him. But Google him. Memorize his bio on the firm's website—that kind of thing. Second, you have to lose yourself and *become* Fred. The challenging part is going to be not avoiding eye contact while you do that. It's easy to want to look down when you're not comfortable."

"Kind of like *you* the first night I arrived," I pointed out.

"What do you mean?" she asked.

"You avoided eye contact with me at the dinner table that first night."

"I did?"

"Yeah."

"That's probably because I was intimidated. So that would make sense. My ego cared too much about what you thought of me."

"And now? You know I'm really a blubbering idiot who panics, so I don't intimidate you anymore?"

She smacked me with her notebook. "Stop calling yourself that."

"Okay..." I sighed.

She cleared her throat. "As I was saying, we're conditioned to think if we avoid eye contact, we're somehow protecting ourselves, when in fact, we're making it worse. That active avoidance alone is enough to make you anxious. So, as Fred, you're not going to avoid eye contact."

"How am I supposed to read off my paper and look at people at the same time? Because you know I'm not memorizing that shit."

"You'll just look up between sentences from time to time."

"What if I lose my place? Then I'll repeat the same line." I laughed, even though I didn't find that funny. "Can you imagine? I'm totally gonna do that." I started to sweat just thinking about it.

"You're catastrophizing now. Don't do that, or we'll have to develop another curriculum."

"No more curriculums, teacher."

She placed her hands on my shoulders, shaking me. "It's gonna be fine. You'll get to practice on me all summer. By the time you get to that event, it will be old hat."

"Old hat." I chuckled. "You talk like an old lady sometimes."

"I do have an old soul." She raised her chin proudly. "Thank you for noticing."

I flashed a mischievous smile. "You know what else they say about public speaking?"

"What?"

"That you should picture your audience naked."

She nodded. "Sure, that's another strategy you could use."

She hadn't figured out what I was getting at. "So, if I'm going to be practicing on *you* all summer, that means…"

Noelle squinted when it hit her. "Ew."

"Nothing I haven't seen before, Miss America."

She threw her pen at me and laughed. "Shut up."

"I have to warn you, *Fred* is a bit of a perv."

Her face turned red. "He'd better not be."

"Even better, can I picture you with welts all over your skin?"

"No."

Still chuckling, I got up from the bed. "Are we done for today?"

"Yeah." She sighed. "We can be." She tucked her notebook away in a drawer. "Lesson adjourned."

She turned back around to face me, and I caught myself staring at her mouth. *Wow. Let's not do that again.* I was attracted to Noelle, which was a little unnerving, since I knew I couldn't *go there.* Not with this one. She was the only good thing in my life right now, and fucking that up was not an option. Plus, not only was she a family friend, we lived on different coasts. Also, I got the impression she was inexperienced. Aside from thinking she was adorable, though, for the first time in a long time, I felt a strong connection to someone.

"You were cute playing teacher," I said.

She blushed. She did that a lot around me. I wondered if she had a little crush. Maybe that was wishful thinking. But it would be kind of fun to mess with her if she did. Make her blush even more.

I handed her the drawing I'd sketched while she was lecturing.

"What the heck?" She covered her mouth as she looked down at the image of herself. I'd dressed her in an evening gown featuring a sash that read *Miss Whaite's Island.* Instead of a normal bouquet, in the drawing, Noelle held a giant penis bursting with flowers at the tip. In the bubble above her head, it said, *The Seven Ps of Public Speaking.*

• • •

The following night, Noelle wasn't at dinner with our parents. I knew she was getting ready for her date with James, but I asked her mother where she was to seem nonchalant about it. When Amy told me her daughter had a date tonight, I acted like I was surprised.

I decided to go bug Noelle upstairs after I left the dining room. The door to her bedroom was open, and I looked in as she stood in front of the mirror.

Once again I decided to play dumb. "Where are you off to? You weren't at dinner."

She turned, looking surprised that I was so clueless. "I have that date with James, remember?"

When I got a full look at her, it took my breath away for a moment. Noelle wore a form-fitting shirt that displayed a little cleavage, along with a black leather miniskirt. There was no denying how freaking hot she looked.

But I pretended not to notice. "Oh, that's right. Where's he taking you again?"

She resumed brushing her long, brown hair. "Some fish and chips place."

"Ah. Nothing sexier on a first date than greasy food seeping out your pores."

"I suppose you take Bree to the fancy places?"

I lay back on her bed. "Bree and I don't really go anywhere. We're not dating."

"That's right. You're just hooking up."

I sat up. "You say that like there's something wrong with it."

"There's not."

"I don't believe you. I feel judged. Do I need to transform into Fred right now?"

She laughed. "I swear I'm not judging you."

"I don't believe in leading people on," I said. "I can't have a girlfriend over the summer and break up with her before I go back to school. There's no way in hell I'm doing a long-distance relationship, either. So, it's either be alone for the summer or have an agreement with someone that we're just hooking up."

She stopped brushing for a moment and turned around to face me. "Have you ever had a serious girlfriend?"

Again, I tried not to admire how beautiful Noelle looked tonight. "Once. In high school."

"What happened?"

I swallowed the bitter taste in my mouth. "She cheated on me with my friend, actually."

"Wow. Okay. I can see why you're turned off by relationships, then."

"I'm long over that. But I don't have time for a girlfriend. I've got too much to worry about. Bree's not the type of girl who cares."

"Well, lucky you."

"She says with sarcasm."

"No, truly. I'm happy for you."

I mocked her. "'I'm happy for you and that little floozie, Archie.' Is that what you mean to say?"

"I didn't say that."

"I can read your face." I took her in again. She'd put on makeup, which made her look older than her eighteen years. "You clean up nice, by the way."

"Too bad I'll have grease coming out of my pores later."

"You should have him take you to the beach after. Jump in the water and get clean."

"Maybe I will." She rolled her eyes. "You'll be there tonight, I take it?"

I placed my hands behind my head. "Is there anything else to do on this island?"

"I'm learning there really isn't." She smiled and changed the subject. "Have you been doing your homework?"

"You mean Googling my father so I don't have to talk to him about his background? Yes."

"Well, good. Whatever it takes." She sighed. "Have you been feeling okay?"

"You're worried I'm gonna freak out and have another panic attack?" I pointed my index finger. "Hey, there's another P to add to your public speaking list. Panic!"

Her expression remained serious. She didn't seem to appreciate my humor. "Seriously, have you had any more?"

I shook my head.

Noelle nodded and lowered her voice. "I haven't been able to stop thinking about what you told me about your mom. I'm just...really sorry it's happening."

"Me, too, Noelle." My voice softened. "Me, too."

She looked down at her shoes. "And I promise to keep it to myself. I wish there was something I could do."

"Just having you here this summer is helping," I said, surprised at my admission. But it was true. "I'd been dreading coming to the island this year. School is my escape. I wanted to stay in California and not join my parents here for the summer. But I couldn't do that to Mom. Believe me, if it weren't for her, I wouldn't have come." I exhaled. "But...I was wrong about how things would be. I thought I was gonna have to keep pretending everything was fine a hundred percent of the time, that I wouldn't have anyone to talk to. But I don't feel like I have to pretend when I'm with you. And that feels good."

*Jesus. That was a bit much.*

Noelle's eyes glistened. "I'm really glad you feel like you can trust me." She chewed her lip and caught a look at the time. "Shit. I'd better go. I'm meeting him there. I'm already late."

I reluctantly hopped off the bed. "Have fun, grease monkey."

She flashed me a smile before disappearing down the stairs.

Rather than go to my room, I returned to Noelle's bed and stared up at the ceiling, wondering why I felt so damn out of sorts.

• • •

At least I didn't have to worry about her with James. He wouldn't hurt a fly. This situation could have been a lot worse. She could've been messing around with that Xavier douche. So, this was a good thing, I told myself.

That said, I couldn't seem to stop looking over at Noelle and James after they came back from their dinner and joined everyone else on the beach. They were across from me, so I couldn't hear what they were talking about. I attempted to read lips, but that wasn't working either. I finally made my way over to them and played nice. "How was dinner?"

"It was delicious," Noelle said. "And miraculously, I don't have grease pouring out of me."

"Grease?" James looked confused. "What?"

"Never mind." She laughed.

"You two make a cute couple," Bree said, clinging to my arm.

Jesus, I hadn't even noticed that she'd followed me over here.

James smiled, and even in the darkness, I could see Noelle blush.

Noelle didn't strike me as someone very experienced in the dating arena. I often wondered how experienced—or inexperienced—she really was. I also wondered about myself and why I seemed fixated on Noelle and her date with James. Did I feel protective of her, or was it something more? I couldn't quite figure it out. But she'd been on my mind all night.

"We should go to the rocks," Bree suggested.

I stayed silent as James looked over at Noelle. "Want to?"

"What's that?" Noelle asked.

"It's this rocky area that's kind of hidden where people go for privacy," he explained.

She shrugged. "Sure."

I gritted my teeth. *Fuck.*

There was only one reason you went to the rocks, and that was to hide behind them to make out or have sex. Bree and I had been there together countless times. It used to be exciting, but I was just biding my time with her this summer. She seemed to only want the same thing—a fuck buddy—but that was getting old. There wasn't any mental stimulation or deep conversation. I'd never needed those things in the past, but they seemed to matter lately.

After we made our way down to the rocks, I found myself distracted by the fact that James and Noelle had disappeared. As Bree and I situated ourselves in our own hiding place, she noticed my inability to...focus.

"What's wrong?" she asked, stopping our kiss.

"Nothing," I said, pulling her close and kissing her harder so she didn't see the look on my face. Also, now I could look behind her in peace to see if I could spot Noelle and James.

She started to pull down her pants, but I stopped her. "Not tonight, okay?"

A look of shock crossed her face. "Why not?"

"I don't have a condom," I lied.

I couldn't exactly say I wasn't sure I could get it up. The only time I ever had trouble in that department was when something was upsetting me.

"It's okay. I'm on the pill," she said.

"I don't go bareback. Sorry."

Bree looked as if I'd just told her that her cat died. "I can run home and get something."

"Actually, I just want to chill tonight. I've got some things on my mind."

Bree pouted. "Is everything okay?"

"Yeah. Nothing terrible. Just some...stuff going on at home."

She brushed her hand along my cheek. "You can talk to me, you know."

It didn't feel natural opening up to Bree like it had with Noelle. Then again, the issue right now *was* Noelle, if I was being honest.

"Do you mind if we just take a walk?" I asked.

She shrugged. "Sure."

After a few minutes of wandering through the rocky area, I finally spotted Noelle and James. They were talking and laughing. I let out a sigh of relief. That seemed innocent enough. I had no idea if they'd been messing around before, and it wasn't any of my business, I supposed.

When Noelle spotted me, she stood up. "Oh, hey. I was gonna head back to the house."

James looked bummed. "Already?"

"Yeah." She turned to me and winked. "Some of us have to get up and run in the morning."

"I should walk you back," I said.

"No." She shook her head. "James is going to."

My chest tightened. "Oh. Okay." Grinding my teeth, I looked over at him. "Thanks."

"No problem. I've got her." He smiled over at Noelle.

*He's got her. Perfect.* I swallowed what felt like bile in my throat.

# CHAPTER 8

## Noelle
*Past*

**ARCHIE SEEMED ESPECIALLY** quiet during our run this morning. Sure, we'd agreed not to talk while we were actually jogging, but he didn't say anything when he came out to meet me, either. He just started running, and I followed.

At first I'd chalked it up to him being out late last night. Maybe he was just half asleep. But we'd been jogging for nearly an hour now, so the air should've woken him up.

When we stopped to take our usual break at the top of the hill, he remained silent.

"Is everything okay with you?" I asked.

"Yeah. Fine," he panted. "Why?"

"You don't have much to say. Normally, I have to scold you to keep you quiet during our runs."

"I'm good," he said curtly.

"You sure?"

"Yeah. Let's go back to the house. I've got shit to do."

*Okay...*

As we started our trek home, I decided maybe he was just in a crappy mood for no reason. That happens sometimes. We all have bad days.

When we entered the house, he went straight upstairs to shower without greeting anyone in the kitchen.

After a half hour, he came back down, all dressed up for his internship. He tried to sneak out without saying anything, but I caught up with him.

"Hey," I called from the doorway. "Don't forget. We have a session tonight," I added in a low voice, not wanting his father to hear.

He scratched his chin. "We do? I would've forgotten."

My heart sank. *He forgot?* "Um...yeah. We do. After dinner."

"Okay." He nodded. "I'll be there."

• • •

I spent the rest of the day anxious—and confused. I tried to keep myself busy by going to a local farmer's market, but I mostly ruminated there as I picked fresh strawberries and petted the goats.

My date last night with James had been a lot of fun. We seemed to get along really well, and I did find him attractive. When we went to the rocks, he even gave me the most amazing kiss. But I remembered thinking about Archie in the middle of it, which was unsettling—and so dumb, considering what Archie had likely been doing with Bree at that moment.

I was attracted to Archie in a different way than I was to James. James was sweet, classically good-looking, and a seriously good guy. Archie, on the other hand, was heart-breakingly handsome and made my knees weak whenever he was around. He was also unattainable. That made any feelings I had for him futile. I was pretty sure Archie looked at me like some younger cousin he needed to protect.

That night at dinner, I realized I'd been looking forward to seeing Archie, but he never showed, not even in his usual fashionably late manner. That made me wonder if he planned to skip our session tonight, too.

After supper, I went up to my room and surfed the net for a bit. At one point, I heard Archie showering. Then about ten minutes later, there was a knock at my door.

Archie was dressed in black joggers and a fitted T-shirt, looking totally fuck-hot and smelling amazing. A piece of wet hair fell over his eyes, and a waft of his scent traveled over to me, putting my body on alert.

"You weren't at dinner..."

"Yeah. I stayed at Rodney's law office late."

"Have you eaten?" I asked.

"I picked up a sub on the way home." He cracked a smile.

I was instantly relieved that he seemed less on edge than earlier. "So, the big question... Did you do your homework?"

He moved to the corner of my bed. "I did."

My pulse reacted. Today was the longest I'd been apart from him in a while. My body had apparently missed him. I cleared my throat. "Wonderful."

Archie opened his notebook and showed me a long list of points he'd jotted down about his dad. Over the next hour, we constructed an outline of everything in chronological order and together began writing his speech. The plan was that eventually, he'd recite it over and over until he was almost bored with it.

After the hour was up, I nodded. "I think we made a good dent in things tonight. Your father has a pretty impressive background, I have to admit."

"Yeah." Archie fell back on my bed and stared up at the ceiling. "Impossible to measure up to all that."

"I can see why you'd think that. But you're your own person. Regardless of how he makes you feel, you don't have to measure up to anything."

He sat up. "It would be nice if *he* felt that way."

"Was your dad always tough on you, even when you were younger?"

He shook his head. "Something happened years ago, to me, that changed him."

Dread filled me, and I didn't want to prod him. Instead, I just waited.

"There's something you don't know about me," he said. "No one knows, actually, because my parents don't talk about it."

My stomach sank. "What is it?"

He looked up at the ceiling again and expelled a long breath. "I may have to bring Fred out for this one."

"Okay, *Fred*. Tell me. What happened?"

He met my eyes. "If I tell you, I need you to promise not to mention it to your parents. It's not something my family talks about with anyone."

"Okay." I nodded. "I promise."

"I was sick when I was a kid. I had leukemia."

My mouth went agape. "Oh my God. I had no idea."

"I know. Like I said, they don't talk about it. My father was just starting his career back then and was under a ton of stress. My parents nearly went bankrupt paying for an experimental treatment that wasn't covered by insurance. But the drugs worked." He shook his head slowly. "I think that's part of why my dad pushes me so damn hard. Almost like... 'We saved your life, Archie. Now don't waste it.'"

I blinked incredulously. "How can they not have told my parents about something so important?"

"Well, they didn't know your parents back then, and very few people know. My parents basically pretend it never happened." He seemed to think for a moment. "Actually, it's more my father who won't let my mother talk about it. It's his coping mechanism, I guess. There's still a lot of unresolved trauma from that time that they haven't dealt with. I don't know if it's a form of PTSD or what, but my mother says my dad was never the same after, even though I went into remission."

It was hard to imagine that this strong, virile guy in front of me had ever been sick like that. "But you're okay now? You never had a relapse or anything?"

"No. I'm absolutely fine. I mean, you always live with that fear, right? That it could come back. But the doctors said with the kind I had, there was a good chance it wouldn't ever return."

"That must've been hard for you...to go through that."

"Honestly, I was so young that I don't remember a lot of it clearly. Probably a good thing."

I stared off for a bit to process this. "Well, for the record, I'm really glad you're okay."

"Me, too."

Something occurred to me. "You said your dad changed after that. Do you think him being so harsh toward you is a protective mechanism?"

"You mean, like, he's afraid to love me because he could lose me?" He nodded. "It's funny, my mother had a theory similar to that once. But since he won't talk about it, it's hard to know what's going on in his head."

I nodded, still trying to absorb everything. "Sorry... I feel like I need a minute."

"Take your time. I totally threw that on you. Or Fred did."

"I'm glad he told me."

He rubbed his eyes. "Okay, I'd like to go back to Archie now. Let's change the subject. How was your date with James? I didn't have a chance to talk to you, since he hogged all your attention last night."

Surprised at his choice of topic, I shrugged. "It was good."

Archie raised a brow. "Just good?"

"What do you want me to say?"

"Did he kiss you?"

My eyebrows jumped. "I don't have to answer that, do I?"

"I think you just gave me the answer."

My face felt hot.

He pointed at me. "Damn, you're turning red."

I touched my cheek. "Am I?"

"It's cute, actually."

"Why?"

"So few girls—at least the ones I know—get embarrassed about such things. Nothing is new anymore. Everyone's done everything, tried everything."

I swallowed, feeling seen yet embarrassed. "How do you know I haven't done everything?"

"I don't know for sure. I'm just going off your reactions. I could be totally wrong." He paused. "But...am I right?"

"I don't have to answer that."

"No, you don't. But then I just make assumptions, which isn't any better for you." He stared at me with a mischievous grin. "Alright. I'll stop pushing."

The room went quiet for a bit. A part of me wanted him to know the truth so I could get his opinion on my situation. It had been weighing on me. I mean, the guy just told me he'd had cancer, for Christ's sake.

"I haven't had sex yet," I blurted. "Is that what you wanted to know?"

Archie's expression turned serious. "Okay. There's nothing wrong with that."

"Most everyone I know has," I added.

He shrugged. "So what?"

"So what? I'm about to start college, and I'm a freaking virgin, that's what."

"That doesn't make you weird. You're just waiting for the right time."

"I don't know why I just admitted that. I think you made me feel like I could tell you anything after the cancer thing."

"Cancer makes you want to talk about sex?" he teased. "It makes you horny?"

"No. But it makes *you* seem vulnerable, I guess. Like it's safe to tell you stuff."

"Cancer will do that." He laughed. "You know what sucks? Because I don't talk about it, I can't even use the cancer card to my benefit. Do you know how much ass I could get if I went around telling everyone I'm a survivor?"

"More than you get already? I doubt that. You have no trouble getting laid."

"Whoa. Here comes judgy Noelle again. You think I'm a manwhore or something?"

"Yeah. That's exactly what I think. But I don't blame you. Every girl on this island has had her eyes on you from the moment you arrived. Maybe you don't even notice because you're glued to Bree."

"Bree's just a shield."

"A shield to what?"

"I don't want to meet anyone new and invite drama into my life this summer. So Bree is a cover in that sense."

"Does she know she's being used?"

"I don't think she cares. We're using each other. But I guess that should serve as a lesson to you—if you let a guy walk all over you, use you for meaningless sex, he will."

I knew they'd been having sex, but this was the first time he'd said it. That burned a little.

"You're warning me against guys like you..."

He scratched his chin. "I guess I am."

"But James isn't like you."

Archie tightened his jaw. "He's not. At least I don't think he is."

"Maybe I should have sex with him. Get it over with."

He drew in his brows. "Why would you want to do that?"

"I don't want my first time to be at BU. I don't want that complication. The first time isn't pleasant, from what I hear. It just seems like something I might want to get over with so I can enjoy any sexual experiences I have at school."

"The first time isn't pleasant for some girls...but you shouldn't just waste it, either."

"When was your first time?"

"It was that girl in high school I told you about who cheated on me. I was sixteen."

"Was it special?"

"At the time, I thought it was."

"Until she showed her true colors?"

"Yeah. I mean, the first time is easier for a guy, you know? It certainly didn't hurt—just the opposite." He chuckled. "After that, though, she started changing. Then when I found out she'd messed around with my friend, I went balls to the wall—started dating half the girls in school. Kind of never stopped."

Growing anxious, I asked, "Do you think you will... stop someday?"

"Stop having sex? Never." He laughed.

"That's not what I meant."

He arched a brow. "Like settle down, you mean?"

"Yeah. With one person."

"I don't know. That's not something I really envision for myself."

I swallowed. "Really..."

"Yeah. Just being honest. I don't see myself settling down or having kids."

"Okay."

"That's something you want?" he asked. "A family and all that?"

"Of course. I mean, way down the line, you know?"

"Yeah." He nodded. "That's cool. Good for you."

The tiny glimmer of hope that had dwelled deep in my subconscious, the same one that had been planning my wedding to Archie a decade from now, had just been destroyed.

"Are you headed down to the beach?" I asked.

Archie grimaced. "Not feeling it tonight."

As we sat in silence for a bit, an ache remained in my chest. Was I still reeling from Archie's cancer news? Or the fact that I'd confessed my lack of sexual history to him? Or was it something more? He'd given me the biggest reason ever not to get my hopes up. Not wanting to settle down or have kids was a dealbreaker for me. His feelings could change over time on that, but I couldn't waste time developing feelings for someone who, as of now, intended to play the field for the rest of his life. That was a recipe for heartbreak.

Archie interrupted my thoughts. "You want to skip the beach tonight with me? Stay home and watch a movie?"

*Boing!* Just like that, my stupid hopes were up again. That didn't take long. "Won't Bree miss you?" I asked sarcastically.

"I could invite her to come over, too."

He must have noticed the look on my face.

"I'm just kidding, Noelle."

"Well, I had no reason to think you'd be lying."

"I wouldn't be able to relax with her around," he said.

85

I nodded. "A movie sounds good. But where should we watch? Our parents hog the television downstairs in the living room at night."

He flashed a devilish grin. "I got a better idea."

"What?"

"You'll see. Give me like half an hour." Archie stood and abruptly left.

Butterflies swarmed in my stomach as I putzed around the room and waited for him to come back.

About twenty minutes later, he texted.

**Archie: Come out to the yard.**

I descended the stairs and went out back.

My eyes widened when I saw what Archie had set up on the lawn: a movie screen. A projector was hooked up to his laptop.

"How the hell did you put all this together so fast?"

"Magic." He winked.

"Seriously..."

"The previous owners left all this equipment in the garage. How cool is that? I saw it the other day when I was in there working on one of the bikes."

"No freaking way. This is amazing."

He pointed to a blanket on the grass. "I brought snacks, too."

There was a basket filled with plastic Easter eggs in pastel shades.

I laughed. "Easter eggs?"

"Those people left behind so much shit. I found two huge bags of these giant eggs. They must have had an Easter egg hunt or some shit here. So I filled them with surprises for you."

"Should I be scared?"

"No. It's just snacks."

I bent to grab one and opened it. There were a handful of gummy bears inside.

"Are these edibles?"

"Believe it or not, those are normal gummy bears."

I pretended to be disappointed. "Damn."

"Are you looking to get high? Because that can be arranged."

"I'm not. I've never done that, actually."

"Ah." He flashed an evil grin. "Lots of ways to corrupt you this summer."

That statement went straight to my loins, of course.

We were laughing when Archie's mom interrupted us.

"What's going on out here?" she asked.

He turned and straightened. "Hey, Mom. We're about to watch a movie. Wanna join?"

She smiled. "How fun!"

Then she turned to me. "Have we met?"

I glanced over at Archie in confusion, but it hit me what her question might have meant. "It's Noelle, Mrs. Remington."

Before she could respond, my mother came out.

"There you are, Nora! You had us worried for a moment. We couldn't find you."

Nora smiled. "They're watching a movie."

My mother surveyed the lawn. "Pretty nice setup you have out here."

"Archie found the equipment in the garage."

Then Archer came out of nowhere. "Archie's resourceful when he wants to be," he announced. "It's getting him motivated that's the issue."

No way I was going to let him berate Archie tonight. "I think he's *quite* motivated," I defended. "Archie has gotten up at the butt crack of dawn to go running with me, which is not easy when you're on summer vacation. And he goes to that internship, too. He's one of the most motivated people I know."

Archer chose to ignore me, instead reaching for his wife's hand. "Come on, Nora. We're about to start the card game."

When the three of them left the yard, Archie shook his head. "You didn't have to respond to him."

"Did I embarrass you?"

"No. It just falls on deaf ears—a waste of your energy."

"I meant what I said. And he doesn't even know you're spending extra time with me to combat your public-speaking fear."

"Let's keep it that way." He took a deep breath in and exhaled. "Anyway... We should watch the movie."

"Okay," I said, feeling emotional.

I hated that Archie's dad had dampened the mood. I chose not to bring that up, nor mention the fact that Nora hadn't known who I was. I didn't want to upset Archie further when we were supposed to be having a fun night.

We agreed on a suspense film on Netflix, and I settled on the blanket next to him, conscious of his proximity with every second that passed. One or two inches closer, and my leg would touch his. I longed to know what that would feel like. Let's face it, I longed to know a lot more than that—what his *mouth* would feel like on mine, for starters. It didn't help that his amazing smell kept taunting me. I might have appeared to be watching the movie, but my brain was focused on other things.

In a sick twist of fate, the movie included a graphic sex scene with the two main characters naked on top of each other. I somehow felt outed, as if the movie gods had read my mind and decided to play out my thoughts on screen.

Archie remained stoic and unfazed—either he really was, or he was a great actor. Just when I was about to squirm from the awkwardness, a little voice came from behind us.

"Boobies!"

Archie and I turned around in unison. *What the hell?* We had company. There were two little kids standing there. They couldn't have been more than ten years old.

"What the fuck?" Archie grumbled, scrambling to shut off the movie.

"Don't say fuck!" one of them shouted.

"Who are you?" I asked.

"We live next door," the girl said. "We're twins."

"You shouldn't be out here."

"Why not?" the boy asked.

"Isn't it past your bedtime?" I asked.

"No," he said. "Our mom said we could play outside as long as we stay in the yard."

Our yards were back to back, but technically these kids weren't on their property.

"What are your names?" I cleared my throat, still rattled.

"Henry, and that's my sister, Holly," the boy said.

"Can we watch a movie with you?" Holly asked.

I turned to Archie for guidance. He simply shrugged.

"Uh...sure," I said. "We'd better put on something else, Archie."

Archie pulled up the children's selections. They gathered around the computer to provide their input and chose a Disney movie.

Just like that, my evening had gone from rated X in my head to rated G in reality.

# CHAPTER 9

## Archie
*Present*

**I CLUTCHED MY** chest as the pavement seemed to sway. "I think I'm having a panic attack."

Noelle placed her hand on my shoulder. "I know, Archie. It's okay."

She did know, didn't she. In fact, this was like déjà vu. I made my way over to the large rock. "I need to sit for a minute."

"Yes, of course."

So much for a peaceful weekend away. But I'd always known today was gonna be hard. I just hadn't expected to lose it *this* fast. Until a month ago, I hadn't had a panic attack in years. But they were back in full force lately. The difference was, in the past, it hadn't always been easy to pinpoint the cause. But now I knew exactly what was causing my anxiety and stress. The news I was withholding from Noelle had been weighing on me since I arrived on the island. It was now or never.

The sun caught her eyes as she stared at me with great concern. Noelle had never looked more beautiful. Her brown hair was longer than I remembered. I yearned to run my hand through it. Not to mention, the fucking tank top she'd put on left nothing to the imagination. *Is she trying to kill me?* I'd hoped not to feel so attracted to her during this trip. That would've made everything easier. Instead, I was more attracted to her than ever. That was bittersweet—and definitely inappropriate—given what I was about to unleash.

She took my hand, and a warm feeling came over me. No one else in this world made me feel as safe as Noelle. I could always be myself without judgment. It seemed like everything was going to be okay, no matter what was actually happening in my life. We'd only been together in the same place a limited number of times through the years, but I instantly felt that comfort again whenever I was around her. While she always made me feel like I could tell her anything...this? *This* was a tough one.

I took a deep breath. "Mariah's pregnant."

She moved away suddenly. "What?"

I wasn't sure how else to say it. "I'm having a baby."

Noelle just kept blinking. I waited for her to say something.

"I know it's a shock."

"Um...yeah." She looked away and exhaled. "It is." She finally turned back to me. "It wasn't planned?"

"God, no."

"Then...how did it happen?"

I raised my brow. "You need me to spell it out?"

"You know what I mean, Archie."

Nodding, I sighed. It was hard to admit how stupid I'd been.

"I wasn't careful once...in part because I believed I wasn't capable of having kids."

She frowned. "Why would you think that?"

"I was led to believe that was a strong possibility from a young age—because of the cancer treatments I had when I was a kid. The doctors told my parents to expect that I might not be able to have children. So I had it in my head that kids would never be in the cards for me." I shrugged. "Clearly, I beat those odds. Turns out I'm just fine in that arena. But the bottom line is, I was careless one time when I was drunk, and that's all it took."

She wiped her palms on her Spandex. "Apparently..." Noelle blew out a long breath as she gazed up at the clear blue sky. "I think I might be the one having the panic attack now." She looked over at me. "This is why you're getting married."

I wouldn't use the term *shotgun wedding*, but there was no denying that this matrimony would not have been happening so soon if the current situation were different.

I nodded. "It's why I asked her to marry me. I wanted to do the right thing."

Noelle's chest rose and fell as she looked into my eyes. "Do you even love her?"

My answer was a copout. "I care about her."

"That's not what I asked."

Feeling my panic kick back up a notch, I said, "Honestly, I need to try." I stared into the bright morning sun. "I never thought I'd be a father." I sighed. "I never thought I'd have the opportunity to be a better dad than mine was to me. I don't know whether I even have it in me... But I owe it to my kid to try to give him or her the kind of life they deserve."

"So you *do* want this marriage...for that reason."

The detailed answer would've been too complicated, so I simply said, "I do."

Noelle nodded. "I get it, Archie. That's all you need to say."

Running a hand through my hair, I examined her eyes. "What are you thinking, Noelle?"

She stared out at the road for a moment and shrugged. "I guess I'm thinking...that it finally makes sense—why you decided to get married. At least it makes *some* sense now. I'd been trying to wrap my head around the whole thing."

As much as she tried to seem accepting of my news, her mannerisms, the way she was breathing, told me she was still in shock. "Noelle, the look on your face is confirming exactly why I chose to wait until today to tell you. I needed that one day of normalcy before this."

"I'll get over the shock eventually." She shook her head. "I'm...happy for you. As long as *you're* happy. I've always believed in you—you know that. Look at your career as an example. You can do anything you put your mind to. That includes being the best dad ever."

"All those lessons from you in public speaking, and I ended up choosing a profession that doesn't require much talking at all, huh?"

"That's the beauty of it. You followed your heart."

We shared a smile. The tension in the air was still thick, but Noelle's beautiful smile brought me some comfort. It made me feel all sorts of things, actually, most of which I needed to bury. "I'm so lucky I have you, Noelle."

She turned away slightly, as if my words, which were meant to be kind, somehow hurt. I understood, though.

I'd always had a special place in my heart for Noelle, but I held my feelings there too tightly, never allowing them to matriculate into real life. I never felt good enough for her and never wanted to hurt her in a way that might ruin our friendship, which was more important to me than anything in the world. I had so few people in my life I could depend on, and she was at the top of that list.

Things would always be complicated between us, though—because of the decisions I made that one summer, because of my own inability to resist temptation. If only it didn't still feel like yesterday.

# CHAPTER 10

## Archie
*Past*

**THE SUMMER WAS** going by way too fast. I couldn't believe it was already the middle of July. The internship had turned out to be great, despite my dreading it in the beginning. I learned a lot from Rodney, who had way more patience with me than my father did. Rodney would have me sit in on his client meetings and then discuss them with me after to see what questions I had about his process. He never made me feel stupid for asking too many questions.

I hadn't seen much of Bree lately and had been spending more time with Noelle. I really enjoyed Noelle's company, and I could always be myself around her. The vibe this summer had been unexpectedly perfect, and I didn't want anything to ruin it. And that included a girl I'd been seeing back in California who I'd promised could come visit me on Whaite's Island. That plan no longer seemed to fit with my current routine.

When Heidi called to tell me she was making arrangements to fly out at the end of the month, I knew I had to break the news as gently as possible.

"Hey, so I was thinking…" I said. "It's probably better if you don't come. Things aren't great with my parents. And the house is a bit crowded."

That was partly true.

"Are you serious?" She sounded pissed.

"I'm sorry. I just don't think it's a good idea anymore."

"I don't even know what to say. I was really looking forward to it." She paused. "Have you been seeing someone there? Is that what this is about?"

"Do you really want to know? I thought we agreed not to talk about that stuff."

"You know what? Forget I called. Forget the whole thing, Archie."

"Look, I'm really—"

She hung up on me. *Wow*. I'd expected her to be mad, but I didn't think she'd react *that* badly. I probably deserved it, though.

"Who was supposed to come?"

I turned to find Noelle standing at the entrance to my room. She'd overheard. I couldn't lie to her, even if this made me look like an asshole.

"That was…Heidi."

"Heidi?"

"Yeah. She's a friend from school."

"A *friend*, huh? She was supposed to stay with us?"

"She's someone I was seeing this past semester," I admitted. "Before I left, I stupidly mentioned that if she wanted to come hang out for a week, that'd be cool. But I've thought better of it since. It doesn't seem like the right decision anymore."

Noelle pursed her lips, looking like she had something to say.

I let out a nervous laugh. "You have thoughts. I can tell."

"Nothing." She plopped down on my bed. "I just don't know how you do it."

I narrowed my eyes. "Do what?"

"Manage it all—a side piece here, a girl waiting in the wings back in California."

"They're not my girlfriends."

"I know. But it's still...work. Isn't it?"

"You are *so* judging me right now, Benedict."

"I'm not." She chuckled. "I swear. It's just curiosity."

She had me pegged as a gigolo. "You want to know the truth?"

"What?"

"I didn't want her to come because lately I've really liked just hanging out with you. If she came, she'd disrupt that."

She proceeded to blow off my answer. "Yeah, right."

My eyes met hers. "I'm serious, Noelle." *What the fuck are you doing?* I needed to backtrack because it was starting to sound like I was *insinuating* something. *Am I?* "It's, like, no pressure when I'm with you. I don't have to worry about what I say, what I look like...what I smell like."

Her tone was bitter. "No one to impress. I get it."

"That's not what I meant. I just mean I'm comfortable. And I'm loving this summer because of it. I don't want anything messing with that. Heidi would've definitely disturbed the peace."

Her expression softened. "I like hanging out with you, too. If you'd told me that before I came here, I wouldn't have believed it."

PENELOPE WARD

"Not sure if that's a compliment or not."

"It is." Her cheeks turned pink.

That reaction reminded me that I needed to be careful. If Noelle started to catch feelings, I was going to be in trouble. I didn't want to ruin what I had with her. So I created a distraction by bringing up the most depressing subject I could think of. I'd been talking a lot about it with Noelle lately, so it wasn't totally out of left field.

"My mother's getting worse."

Her eyes widened. "Did something happen?"

"Just more of the same." I shook my head. "I don't know what to do. It's hard when I know soon I'm not gonna be around her every day. Some days I think maybe I should take some time off from school, but I know she wouldn't let me do that. It would stress her out even more."

Noelle expelled a long breath. "I want to say something to make you feel better right now, but I'm a firm believer that you shouldn't say things just to say them when you don't know shit about what it's like to be in someone's shoes. I'd like to tell you everything's going to be fine. I just don't know."

"I appreciate that. I don't need smoke blown up my ass."

She placed her hand on my arm. "I can't promise you that everything's gonna turn out perfectly. But I promise you can always call me if you need to talk."

When she removed her hand, I was quite aware of how much I'd enjoyed her touch. I cleared my throat. "I can't believe how fast this summer is flying by. I'm not ready to leave."

99

"Neither am I."

"Who knows what it's gonna be like next summer—if we'll even be here, depending on how Mom's doing."

Noelle frowned. "I couldn't imagine not getting to spend the summer with you all again."

"Buying this house was kind of bad timing," I said.

"Or good timing, depending on how you look at it. Your mom has had her moments this summer, but she seems to be enjoying herself."

"That's true. That part does make it all worth it."

Between these confusing feelings for Noelle and being down about my mother, I came up with what seemed like a brilliant idea.

"Wanna get drunk?"

"That was random." She laughed. "Are you serious?"

"Yeah. Dead serious. We've never gotten drunk together. We can't have this summer pass without one drunken evening."

"Am I missing something? We've been a little drunk at the beach together."

"Yeah, but we've never had a drunk movie night here."

"That sounds like fun. But, um, hello? Not sure we can get away with drinking here while our parents are home."

I wriggled my brows. "Sure we can."

"How?"

"We'll be discreet." I winked. "I've got an idea."

• • •

"What the hell?" Noelle looked down at the handful of plastic Easter eggs I'd arranged on the grass.

"I told you I'd figure it out."

"What is inside those eggs this time?"

I winked. "Why don't you open one and find out?"

It was amusing to watch her open the Easter eggs, each filled with a mini bottle of liquor. Because the eggs were the larger kind, the bottles fit perfectly. I'd made a special trip to the one liquor store I knew from experience would take my fake ID. Thankfully, I wasn't too far from my twenty-first birthday, so I wouldn't have to risk criminal charges to get booze for much longer.

We put on a movie, and egg after egg, buzzed slowly grew into full-on hammered. Thankfully, our parents hadn't come out to check on us once, and I made sure to place each empty bottle back inside the egg it came from.

"It's a good thing Holly and Henry aren't around tonight," I said, laughing.

"Great point." Noelle hiccupped. "I hadn't accounted for the possibility of them."

After the movie finished, we lingered on the grass, looking up at the night sky and enjoying our pleasantly fucked-up state. I sensed our parents were already in bed since the lights on the second floor had gone out. Then our conversation took an interesting turn.

Even in the darkness, I could see Noelle's cheeks turning redder than I'd ever seen them. She kept fidgeting and looked like she was ready to burst.

"What's up?" I finally asked.

She opened and closed her mouth a few times and then shook her head, seeming to think better of it.

"Noelle, what's going on? You're acting weird right now."

She hiccupped again. "I'm drunk."

"I know. But still..."

Then she blurted, "Are you attracted to me?"

*Ohhkay.* I must have blinked fifty times without saying anything. Her question had stunned my drunk ass into silence. Of course, I was attracted to her. But admitting it was a slippery slope. The only solution was to stall. "Why are you asking me that?"

"We spend a lot of time together, and you've never... tried anything. I was just wondering if that was because you don't find me attractive."

*Fuck.* "We're friends. Why would I try anything even if I...*wanted* to?"

"I'm not saying you should. I'm just curious whether you find me attractive."

I wasn't sure if being drunk right now was a good thing or not. On one hand, it made the awkwardness of this conversation easier to bear. On the other, I wasn't completely sure what was going to come out of my mouth. "You realize you're backing me into a corner, right?"

Her eyes were hazy. "Why is that?"

I somehow managed to articulate my point. "If I tell you I'm not attracted to you, you'll hate me. And if I tell you I *am* attracted, it will make things weird between us."

She nodded. "You're right. I shouldn't have said anything. I guess weird things just come out when you're drunk."

"Actually, the *truth* comes out when you're drunk." I paused, my own curiosity getting the best of me. "What's the real reason you asked that question?"

"I thought if you were attracted to me...you'd maybe want to...have sex with me before the summer ended."

The Earth felt like it was starting to spin faster. I was pretty good at handling booze, so I suspected it was just the normal reaction I would expect to have, you know, when Noelle randomly suggested we fuck.

*Jesus.* "I wasn't expecting that," I said.

"I know you weren't." She exhaled. "My suggestion... It's not what you think."

"What other way is there to think about it?"

Noelle licked her lips. "I wanted to know if you would take my virginity...so I don't have to go through that with someone else. Since you're so experienced, I figured maybe you wouldn't—"

"Fuck no." I sat up. "That's not happening."

She waved her hands. "Never mind. Forget I said anything."

Crickets chirping were the only sound for several seconds.

I should've let sleeping dogs lie, but I couldn't help myself. "Seriously, why would you want me to do that?"

Noelle stood, brushing grass off her jeans. "I just figured it wouldn't be a big deal to you. You'd be doing me a favor."

"You want me to pop your cherry, and you think it would mean *nothing* to me?"

"Look. I'm obviously drunk. I just said what I was thinking. I regret it. Can we drop the subject?"

"Yeah. Sure." I rose and started to pace, feeling equal parts enraged and turned on. I directed my energy toward cleaning up the Easter eggs and the rest of the mess we'd made.

We didn't speak of this again for the rest of that night, and we each retreated to our own rooms.

• • •

The next morning, I forced myself to get up to run, only to find Noelle wasn't waiting outside.

For the first time ever, she'd overslept—either that or she was intentionally avoiding me, and for good reason. She'd put herself out there last night, and I'd shot her down. I could've handled that better.

Today I could see things more clearly, and that meant I looked like even more of an asshole for my abrupt reaction to her brave and vulnerable request. Even if she was drunk, that took a lot of courage. Deep down, I knew I'd been defensive because I *did* like Noelle as more than a friend. It was fucked up for her to have assumed she meant so little to me that I could just screw her and forget about it.

But I guess I hadn't given her reason to believe I had true feelings. Yet I felt so much for Noelle that I could hardly breathe around her sometimes. We'd developed a strong connection this summer. And while I was attracted to her, it was so much more than that. Experiencing more than just physical attraction to someone was new for me. But my feelings for her couldn't go anywhere because I would never be the kind of guy she needed. Crossing the line with Noelle would mean losing her as a friend—something I wasn't ready to risk.

Even so, I couldn't stop thinking about what she'd proposed. I'd gone to bed hard, unable to sleep, so goddamn horny. I wanted to give her what she'd asked for and more. I just didn't want the guilt that would be associated with it. I didn't want to go back to school with any regrets hanging over my head, and I didn't want to do anything that would risk being unable to face her next summer.

As I pounded the pavement alone, my thoughts went from sensible to anything but. I started to think about all the things I could teach her, all the ways I could make her come. Had anyone even made her come before? What was so wrong about giving in to a friend's request for a little sexual education? I shook my head. *Are you fucking crazy, Archie?*

Given all of the dirty thoughts in my head, it was unfortunate that I ran right into her as I returned to the house. Noelle was waiting for me at the side door by the kitchen. She held a mug of coffee in her hand and looked as hungover as I knew she was.

My breathing was heavy as I stood there, dripping sweat. "Where were you?" I asked as I took my earbuds out.

Her eyes were red and a bit sunken. "I overslept. I'm sorry."

"I get it. We drank a lot last night."

"I'm surprised you got up on time," she said.

"Well...I was hoping to talk to you." Glancing toward the dining area to make sure our parents couldn't hear, I lowered my voice. "Things got weird last night."

She nodded. "Yes, they did. And I need to apologize."

"No. You—"

"Yes, I do." She looked over her shoulder. "I know you just came in from a run, but can we take a walk?"

"Sure."

She set her coffee mug down before we stepped outside. We went just far enough that we were no longer within earshot of the house. Then we stopped and faced each other on the side of the road.

Noelle looked down at her feet and zipped her hoodie all the way up. "I'm embarrassed about what I said to you."

I placed my hand under her chin and brought her face to meet my eyes. "Be real with me, Noelle. Was it the alcohol talking? Or was that something you'd thought about when you weren't drunk, too?"

She hesitated. "I'd thought about it...but I never would've mentioned it without the liquid courage."

"I'm sorry for the way I reacted. I feel really protective of you, and ironically, I also feel like I'm at the top of the list of people you need to be wary of. You know my track record. I don't fucking trust myself with you, even when you're not *asking me* to have sex."

Her breathing quickened. "I guess... I'm just confused. I obviously value your friendship and care for you deeply. But I've never had a guy friend like you—someone I'm also...attracted to." She shook her head. "I don't want you to think I was trying to exploit you by asking you to have sex with me."

Closing the space between us, I said, "I don't think that."

"But the lines have a tendency to get blurred," she continued. "When we're hanging out, sometimes I notice you staring at me, and I can't tell if you're lost in thought or if it's something more. So I thought maybe..."

I swallowed. *Busted.*

She sighed. "I often think about what it would be like...to be with you. I have no clue whether you're even attracted to me. I know you don't do relationships, so I wasn't trying to insinuate anything more than just..." Noelle looked down at her feet.

She was being so honest right now. I owed her the same. "Noelle, I think you're beautiful. Truly. My reaction last night had nothing to do with a lack of attraction. Your face, your body have definitely been in my mental spank bank multiple times this summer. I never would've admitted that before last night. But I feel more comfortable being open about it now, since you put it all on the table. I still think it would be a bad idea, though—if we went there."

She nodded almost frantically, trying to zip her hoodie up again, though it wouldn't go any farther. "Totally. Like I said, I'd thought about it but would never have suggested it if I weren't drunk."

"You're not drunk right now, though. Be honest. What if I'd said yes last night? Would you still want to go through with it today, now that you're sober?"

Her face reddened as the seconds passed without a response. "Yeah. I would."

"Fuck," I muttered. "Okay. I was kind of hoping you'd say no."

"Why? It's not gonna change anything anyway. You said it would never happen. So now I have to work on making things not awkward between us again. That will probably take years."

"Why would you want to waste your first time on me?"

She looked out toward the ocean. "Because I trust you—not necessarily with my heart or as a boyfriend, but as a friend I trust you. And I feel like I could..."

"What?"

"*Learn* from you—without feeling stupid for my lack of experience. I feel like you'd have my back, if that makes sense. I wouldn't feel unsafe having sex with you as a learning experience."

I let out a shaky breath. "You want me to *teach* you how to have sex?"

"No," she muttered. "I mean...not if you don't want to."

I should've put a stop to this conversation. But instead, I was listening. I was aroused. My body was here for it, even if my conscience wasn't. "I'm not saying I wouldn't want to do that for you, Noelle. But this is about what's truly best for you. Messing with *me*? Complicating our relationship? It's not a good idea."

"You're right. It's a *very bad* idea. But you asked me to be honest about what I would want, and I answered. Sometimes what we want is a bad idea."

My eyes fell to her lips, and suddenly all *I* wanted was to devour them. But my brain still tried to resist it. "Okay." I let out a long breath as I placed my hands on my hips. "Then it's settled. It's a bad idea. And we'll just forget about it." I looked into her eyes. "Okay?"

Noelle spoke under her breath. "Yeah."

"Okay." I forced a smile.

As we walked back to the house in silence, I sensed this conversation was far from over.

# CHAPTER 11

## Noelle
*Past*

**AFTER MY CONVERSATION** with Archie this morning, I had to talk to someone, so I'd called my friend Ashley to fill her in. I'd just finished telling her how I'd made a mess of my relationship with him. Running a hand through my hair, I paced. "I can't believe I blurted that out last night."

"Well, you could've told him you didn't remember saying it. Why were you so honest the next day?"

"I guess I still wanted him to consider it." I covered my face. "What the hell is wrong with me?"

"You're horny and hot for him, and you don't know what to do about it."

"Yeah, but shouldn't our friendship matter more to me than wanting to have sex with him? I don't want him to think I was trying to use him. I just wanted the experience—with him. Even if nothing more came of it. But I still shouldn't have said anything."

"Well, you did. You can't take it back. So own it. Don't avoid him. Just try to work your way back to how things were without doing anything else to make the situation weird."

"Yeah. I plan to try. Summer is half over. I don't want to waste this precious time. He really does mean a lot to me. I'm just afraid I ruined everything."

"Here's an idea," she said. "Maybe try to focus on something else for a little while."

"Like what?"

"It sounds like you started the summer hanging out with all these different people—until you became obsessed with Archie. You need a breather, I think. Go flirt with someone else."

Maybe she was right. I needed to break the cycle.

• • •

That night, I headed down to the beach alone—without checking in with Archie first. I'd had to force myself to act in a way that went against what I really wanted. Although avoiding him wasn't difficult after the awkwardness of this morning. *A break is necessary*, I told myself.

Even though nothing had been happening between James and me, I made a point to go right to him at the beach, immersing myself in conversation. I tried to be interested in everything he had to say. And when Archie showed up later, I didn't look in his direction even once. *It's for the best*, I told myself.

At one point, James asked if I wanted to take a walk. We were just starting down the beach when Archie's voice came from behind us.

"Noelle, I need to talk to you for a minute."

I turned and cleared my throat. "I was just taking a walk with James."

"I get that. But I need to talk to you first."

"Okay." I shrugged and looked at James. "Do you mind?"

"No." James turned to Archie and lifted a brow. "Everything okay?"

"Yeah. I just need to talk to her about something. In private," he added.

"Okay, man." James turned to me. "I'll be over by the clam shack when you're done."

I smiled. "I'll come find you."

As Archie and I took off down the beach, he was silent. The soothing sound of the ocean waves massaged some of the tension in the air.

"What's going on?" I asked.

"What are you doing?" he demanded. "You're not even into him, and you know it."

Surprised by his tone, I said, "How do you know that?"

"Because you're into *me* right now. You're throwing yourself at him to spite me because I shot you down."

"Mighty confident in ourselves, are we?"

He shut his eyes. "Alright, look, that wasn't the way I wanted to approach things. Even if it's fucking true." Archie sighed. "That came out all cocky, and that wasn't my intent."

"Oh really? Because I'm pretty sure you're a cocky fucking bastard when you want to be," I quipped.

He ran his hand through his hair. "Noelle..."

I tilted my head. "What did you need to speak to me about?"

"I have a preposition for you..."

"A *preposition?* Like in or under...or over?"

He shook his head and gritted his teeth. "Fuck. I'm nervous, alright? I obviously meant *propo*sition."

*He's* nervous? "Oh." I laughed. "That's definitely more exciting than a preposition."

Archie rolled his eyes. "I've been thinking about our talk this morning."

I got goose bumps. "Okay..."

"You've done so much for me this summer. I want to pay you back in probably the only way I know how. I'm not good for much. But I'm definitely good for what you need."

"This is the spin you're putting on things now? I don't want to be a mercy fuck, Archie. Jesus!"

"You wouldn't be." He placed his palm on my shoulder, causing my nipples to stiffen. "It's a two-way street, Noelle." Archie removed his hand. "Look, I've been turned on thinking about showing you things. I don't know that taking your virginity is a good idea, but I'd love to at least... explore things with you. Even if we don't have sex."

My heartbeat accelerated as I swallowed hard. "What does that mean?"

"It means we see where things go, but we have to set some ground rules."

"Like..."

"Anything sexual that might happen between us ends after this summer. Sex complicates shit. I don't want to lose you as a friend just because we...experimented a little. It has to be over when we go back to school."

I nodded. "That makes sense." *That makes no sense. But I'm going with it.*

"Also..." He pointed in the direction James had gone. "You don't mess around with that dude over there or anyone else as long as we're experimenting."

"You're making me sound like a science project, Archie."

"I'm trying to be more dignified than calling it hooking up."

"Okay. Understood." I licked my lips. "What else?"

"I guess I have to understand what I'm dealing with. So I need to ask you some questions."

Trying not to let my excitement show, I straightened my posture. "Okay."

"I need you to be completely honest with me."

"Alright."

"You've kissed guys, I assume, but what else have you done?"

I wracked my brain, although there wasn't a whole lot to remember. "My high school boyfriend felt me up and down."

"So you've been fingered."

"Yes."

"No one's ever gone down on you?"

A shiver traced my spine. "No."

"Okay." He let out a shaky breath. "Have you ever given head?"

"Never."

"Given a hand job?"

I'd forgotten that. "Yes."

"So, just those three things?"

"Yes. That's what I've done. But that's it." Bracing for his answer, I asked, "Is it worse than you thought?"

He scratched his chin. "I didn't know what to expect, but you're definitely inexperienced."

"Does watching porn count?"

"Not really. No."

"Well, I'm well-versed in all types of porn. I've watched a lot of weird shit—like bookookie. So nothing will surprise me."

He cackled. "Bukakke?"

"Yeah. Whatever. I've seen it."

"Watching something and doing it are two different things, Noelle."

"Maybe."

"Look at me and promise something," he said. "Promise me that if we do this, it's not gonna change our friendship. That's a dealbreaker for me."

There was no way crossing this line wouldn't change our friendship forever. We were kidding ourselves if we believed otherwise. But I'd do almost anything to experience more with him. Even if it meant lying. Even if I knew it would change things. I only hoped it wouldn't destroy us. "I promise."

He nodded hesitantly, looking about as secure in this as I felt. "Okay. I think we've had enough discussion on the matter for tonight."

"What's the next step?" I asked, once again trying not to seem too eager.

"I haven't figured it out. I'm not rushing into anything, though. I guess we'll know when the moment feels right. I have to take things slow with you because I kind of feel like your eyes are bigger than your mouth here." He chuckled. "You might think you want certain things but not really know what you're in for. I won't try anything unless I'm a hundred percent sure you're ready."

"Makes sense," I said, though he was wrong. My

mouth definitely felt ready. Every part of my body felt ready for him.

"Go back to James if you want," he said. "But don't let him touch you." He leaned in. "And let *me* know when you're ready to go home. I'm walking you, not him."

His words, and the way he said them, gave me chills. Even if it was just all part of the "experiment" to come, I loved that he was acting jealous and possessive right now. It was a huge turn on.

I returned to the spot next to James. He didn't mention taking a walk again, which was just as well. As he and I chatted, I couldn't stop looking over at Archie: his handsome face, his large hands, his big, strong muscles. He was all I could think about.

Later, when Archie walked me home, we didn't talk about what we'd discussed. I prayed he didn't come to his senses and change his mind about it.

Once we started, I wouldn't be able to keep my feelings in check. But if I let him know I couldn't compartmentalize, he'd never go for it. So I vowed to put on my acting hat and make believe. I had to pretend what he was offering was just about the experience, nothing more.

As I headed upstairs to my room that night, a mix of excitement and nervousness like I'd never felt before coursed through me.

• • •

The following morning was business as usual. I dragged my ass out of bed to find Archie already waiting for me outside at ten past 6 AM.

"You're late," he scolded.

"Sorry."

We took off down the road, an unspoken tension in the air. Archie wasn't making eye contact, seeming pre-occupied. I didn't bother asking what was on his mind, because I knew: he was probably thinking better of everything.

When we returned to the house, his parents' car was gone, which was unusual for this time of the morning.

"Did your parents go somewhere?"

"When I got up, I saw them all leaving. They're headed to Ogunquit for the day."

I swallowed, realizing we would be alone in the house. "Oh. That's right. My mom mentioned they might go. I didn't know that was today."

I walked over to the coffeemaker and fumbled with the pods before popping one in. The machine gurgled as it processed the coffee.

"You want some?" I asked.

"No. I don't drink coffee. But you know that."

My question was dumb. He'd mentioned countless times that he didn't drink coffee. I'd even teased him about being crazy for not liking it. But I wasn't thinking—because we were alone, and that was *all* I could think about right now.

"Oh yeah. That's true." I cleared my throat. "Well, I couldn't survive without coffee." As I waited for the machine to finish, he startled me with a question.

"Do you want to shower?"

"You can go first. I'm gonna drink this."

He didn't move. "I meant...with *me.*" His eyes seared into mine.

I turned to him, suddenly all too aware of his big, sweaty, masculine frame. Every nerve ending in my body buzzed. There was only one answer. "Yeah." I gulped.

He stepped away. "I'm gonna go upstairs. Why don't you meet me when you're done with your coffee."

*Coffee? Who could think about coffee at a time like this?* I tried to remain calm. "Okay."

After he left, I looked out the window and opened my mouth in a silent scream. *Holy shit. Is this really happening?* I had never showered with anyone in my life. And knowing what I knew now—after that accidental glimpse of him the first day he arrived... This was going to be no ordinary shower.

I took a deep breath. I was nervous, but more than anything I was aroused, tingling all over, excited for what was to come. I chugged some of the coffee before heading upstairs. With every step I took, my heart beat faster.

I entered the bathroom to find Archie shirtless and leaning against the counter. He still had his shorts on, but I could see his erection straining through the material. And now my heart started beating out of my chest.

"You look like you're ready to jump out of your skin, Noelle." He chuckled.

"I do?"

"Yeah. Relax. Nothing crazy is going to happen. This is just gonna be a shower." His glassy eyes fell to my breasts. "Maybe a little touching."

A relieved breath escaped me. He had no idea how much I needed that assurance. I'd made a decision to have sex with Archie this summer, if he allowed it. I was ready, but I also needed some idea of when it might happen so

I could mentally prepare. It was good to know he wasn't rushing into anything right now. Maybe I wasn't *quite* ready to jump in head first, despite how turned on I was.

Archie reached for the lever and started the water before returning to lean against the sink. The bathroom filled with steam as we stood there looking at each other. Then he lowered his shorts, followed by his boxer briefs.

*Holy...* Salivating, I gulped as I stared down at his huge dick. The tip glistened with precum. The muscles between my legs contracted. He was aroused—aroused by me. And that made *me* aroused. As if I needed a reason besides his perfect body and beautiful face. A piece of his hair fell over his forehead as he stood before me, unabashedly naked.

Then he disappeared behind the shower curtain.

Heart racing, I stood there for a few moments until I heard him say, "You gonna come in?"

"Oh." I shook my head. "Yeah."

I lifted my shirt and slipped my sports bra over my head. In the mirror, I could see a sheen of sweat covering my chest. Thankful that I'd shaved last night, I took off my shorts and looked down at my neatly groomed pubic area, hoping he'd like what he saw. Technically, he'd already seen it, albeit briefly. So I shouldn't have been that nervous, right?

*Why the hell am I so nervous, then?*

He interrupted my thoughts as he spoke from behind the shower curtain. "You don't have to come in, if you don't want to."

"I do," I insisted. Moving the curtain aside, I stepped into the steamy shower.

Archie looked like carved stone in a rainstorm as the water poured over his tanned body. I also appreciated the up-close look at the tattoo on his upper arm, an animal's face with an intricate design around it.

I traced my finger along his muscle. "This is a wolf?"

"Yeah. Our football team in high school was the Wolf Pack."

My eyes trailed down the length of his body before traveling back up to meet his stare.

He pushed the water back off of his forehead. "What are you thinking right now?"

*That I want to lick you, but I don't want to make a fool of myself.* "I'm nervous, but I'm excited."

"I'm a little nervous, too, and I'm not used to that." He put my hand on his chest. His heart beat rapidly.

"Wow," I whispered.

"Yeah." He chuckled.

That was a gamechanger. Somehow it was the one thing that managed to calm me down.

But I was now so calm that I didn't realize I was staring down at his massive dick.

"See something you like, Noelle Simone Benedict?"

"Apparently." I smiled. "And you're huge, by the way."

"I'm *hard*. Because I'm looking at you. *You're* doing this to me."

*Oh. God.*

As his gaze moved down my body, I got chills, despite being under the hot water.

Archie grabbed a sponge and squirted some body wash onto it. He began rubbing it over his chest as he continued to take me in.

He added more soap. "Can I wash you?"

I nodded.

He then began slowly rubbing the sponge over my body, sliding it along the contours of my neck before lowering it. As he circled around my breasts, I bent my head back. He wasn't even actually touching me. If this felt good, I couldn't imagine what it would feel like when his hands were on me.

He slid the sponge down my torso. When it landed between my legs, I froze.

"This okay?" he whispered gruffly.

"Yes. Please don't stop."

He gently washed between my legs as I felt arousal pooling. He stayed in that spot for a while, looking into my eyes as he worked the sponge.

He knelt and moved the sponge down my legs. When he'd finished, he stood and pressed his naked body against mine.

"Is it okay if I kiss you?"

"Please..." I panted, yearning for it.

Archie took my lips with his and let out a deep breath into my mouth. I felt my body come alive in a way it hadn't ever before. My legs felt weak as I arched my neck, and he groaned as he finally thrust his tongue inside. I moved my tongue faster to capture every bit of his taste. My clit throbbed as I raked my hands through his hair. My fingers then slid down his back, and I couldn't help but squeeze the hard muscles of his ass.

"Fuck," he muttered. "Don't touch me there."

That felt like a punch to the gut. "I'm sorry."

He stopped kissing me for a second. "No. It wasn't

bad—just the opposite. It felt too good. I'm trying to pace myself." He took my mouth again hungrily.

As the water poured down over us, I closed my eyes, allowing myself to get lost in this moment. We were in our own little world. My heart rate hadn't calmed a single bit, and I knew I was already too far gone to ever recover from this. His cock pressed into my abdomen as we continued to kiss voraciously. I wanted to feel his girth in my hand. "Can I touch you?" I asked.

He ignored me, instead lowering to his knees. His eyes turned hazy as he reached up to cup my breasts and massage them. My breathing became heavier as he slid his hand down and slowly sank three of his fingers inside me.

Archie continued to stare up at me as he moved them in and out. When he used his thumb to massage my clit, I bent my head back. I'd been fingered before, but no one had ever bothered to bring me to orgasm. It felt like that was exactly what Archie was trying to do.

"I want you to come for me like this, Noelle," he said huskily. "Okay?"

"Uh-huh," I breathed.

The back of my head met the shower wall as I imagined it was his cock moving in and out of me. It took under a minute. I focused on the sound of his breathing and the knowledge that he was turned on by this as I felt my climax rising to the surface.

"You're all I fucking want lately," he whispered, sinking his fingers in deeper.

That totally undid me. My legs shook as an intense sensation tore through me. My voice echoed through the bathroom as I orgasmed.

A few seconds later, I came down from it to find Archie leaned against the tile. He gripped his cock and stroked himself roughly as he stared at me with a look of hunger in his eyes. My gaze fixed on the smooth skin over his hard dick as his palm rubbed it. Watching him jerk himself off was the sexiest thing I'd ever witnessed. Well, it *was* the sexiest thing—until he came. Nothing beat the sight of his hot cum spurting out. Some of it hit me, landing on my stomach, which was a pleasant shock. I loved how that felt.

Even though I'd just climaxed, I was already so turned on again.

"Sorry about that," he said as he wiped his hand along my abdomen.

"Are you kidding? I loved every bit of that."

"You're dangerous, Noelle." He flashed a mischievous grin. "Let's get your hair washed."

My nipples stiffened as Archie turned me around to face the wall. I pressed my hands against the tile as he slowly massaged shampoo into my hair. It was ecstasy, especially the feeling of his cock brushing against my ass. The whole thing was erotic as hell.

Archie rinsed the soap out of my hair and turned me around to face him. I watched as he shampooed his own hair, noticing that his dick had grown hard again—or maybe it never went down.

I wanted so much more than he'd given me but had also chosen to let him take the reins. I didn't want to push things or seem as desperate as I felt right now.

He turned off the water, slid open the shower curtain, and reached for a towel. He handed it to me then grabbed his own.

After we'd dried off, he cupped my cheek and brought my lips to his one more time. I savored the taste—it felt like forever since he'd kissed me, though it had only been minutes.

"Go get dressed," he whispered over my lips.

Archie then disappeared into his room, leaving me standing in the bathroom, far from sated. I was dying for more.

If our shower was a sign of how slowly he planned to take things, I wasn't sure I'd survive the torture.

# CHAPTER 12

## Archie
### *Past*

**IN THE FEW** days since the hot-as-fuck shower I'd taken with Noelle, I'd done a 180 and not laid a hand on her. Things had felt more intense than I'd anticipated under the water that day, so I'd decided to step back. Noelle hadn't brought it up, but I'd caught her staring at me a time or two, as if trying to figure out why I'd become so distant.

We were in her room working on my bumbling-idiot training again when she finally decided to ask.

"Why haven't you touched me since the shower?"

I didn't want to tell her the truth—that I couldn't trust myself. "I didn't realize there was a timeline on touching you," I said, trying to seem nonchalant.

"Seriously, Archie?"

"Okay. Full disclosure." I paused. "The shower? It was fucking amazing. That's why I need to take a step back. I don't want to lose you as a friend, and I feel like I will if I take things too far. Staying in control was harder than I anticipated. I have so few true friends, Noelle. And I consider you one of them."

She crossed her arms and looked away from me. "You're worried I'm gonna catch feelings."

*Actually, I'm more worried I'll be the one to catch feelings at this point.* But I went along with her version. "Yeah..." I lied.

Her mouth curved down. "Well, I'm not. I...haven't. The shower didn't change anything for me, if that's what you're worried about. I need you to not treat me like I'm fragile. But the bottom line is, if you don't want to continue what we started, we shouldn't." She exhaled. "I'd just been looking forward to what came next."

It killed me that she thought I didn't want to go further with her. I felt myself weakening, too curious to stop. "What were you *hoping* came next?"

"I'm not gonna say it out loud."

"Why not? I thought we could tell each other anything."

"We can. But not when it comes to whatever *this* is."

After a tense moment, I walked over to her desk and picked up one of those plastic Easter eggs that seemed to be all over the house now. I grabbed a blank sticky note and placed it inside before closing the egg.

I handed it to her, knowing this idea would pave me a path straight to hell. When I got there, I'd explain that I was serving time for corrupting the perfect daughter of my parents' friends.

"What's this?" she asked.

"Popping your cherry isn't on the table right now. I want to make that clear. But if there's anything else you want, write it down and put it in here. That way you don't have to say it."

Her eyes widened. "Now?"

"You don't have to do it now. Whenever."

She looked down at the egg. "Okay." She tucked it away in her desk.

Miraculously, we were able to resume working on my speech after that. I got up and read from the notebook where I'd completed a rough draft detailing my father's rise to the top. Archer Remington had started from humble beginnings in New Jersey, born the son of a shoe repairman. As the middle child of five, he felt unseen at times and always worked hard to excel—yada, yada, yada. I ended with a lie about what a great father he was and how he'd been a huge inspiration to me...*of what not to do.*

When I looked up at the end, Noelle smiled. "You did great."

"You mean, I can read? That's basically all I did—not really the same as giving a speech."

"No, but it's a start. The goal is for you to get so sick of this speech that you know it like the back of your hand."

"As well as I know the palm of my hand?"

She scrunched her nose. "I don't get it."

"It was a jerk-off joke."

"Oh." She laughed. "Okay. Well...we can be done for today. Unless you can think of anything else you *haven't* touched?" She flashed an impish grin.

My fists tightened as I stopped myself from reaching over and kissing her senseless. Goddamn, I needed a breather. "I'll catch you later," I said as I got up from her bed and practically fled the room.

Downstairs, I found my mother sitting alone in the kitchen.

"Where is everybody?" I asked.

She turned to me and smiled. "They went to the Summer Lights festival."

"You didn't want to go?"

"I wasn't feeling up to it." She stood and headed toward the living room. "Come sit with me."

My stomach sank. "What's going on?"

"I had a rough day." She sighed. "I forgot a lot of stuff that happened yesterday, and your dad got frustrated with me. That's why I told him to get out of the house."

I reached for her hand. "It's not your fault, Mom."

"Have I forgotten a lot when it comes to you this summer, too, and not realized it?"

I didn't want to depress her by admitting how much I'd noticed. "Not the important stuff."

That was the truth. Most of her slip-ups were minor things, with the exception of the time she hadn't seemed to remember Noelle.

"I haven't had a lot of time alone with you," she said.

Guilt crept in. That was my fault. "I know. Dad's always around, so I tend to avoid you because of that. It's not because of you. Anytime you need me, you know I'm here."

"I want to say some stuff to you while my mind is clear, okay?"

My throat felt tight. "Okay..."

She turned to face me. "There are some things you need to know," she said. "And I'm not sure I'll get many other opportunities this summer to address what's going on. Because, like you said, he's always around."

"Talk to me, Mom."

She came right out with it. "Your dad is having an affair."

It nearly broke my heart to have to confess. "I know."

Her mouth fell open. "How?"

I couldn't lie to her. "He was in the shower one day while I was home over Christmas break. I jumped in to use the bathroom and saw a message pop up on his phone. I realized he was getting ready to leave and go see her, even though he'd told you another story. So...I followed him."

My mother's eyes watered. "You saw her?"

I'd never wanted to physically harm my father until this moment, when I saw tears in my mother's eyes. It made me want to go upstairs and rewrite that entire speech, focusing only on the fact that he was a lying, cheating bastard.

"I'm sorry, Mom. I should've told you. But I didn't know how." I fought my own tears. My voice shook. "I don't know why he's doing this."

"It's okay. It's not your responsibility to know."

"It's just...you're going through so much already. I didn't want to hurt you more by telling you he was cheating."

"Please don't feel guilty." She sighed. "Look... I don't know how much longer I'm going to be able to have these kinds of conversations with you. So I need you to listen to me."

I reached for her hand. "You have all of my attention."

"You don't need to do anything to please him. You're perfect just the way you are, and whatever you decide to do with your life will be right if it makes you happy. You owe him nothing."

I drew my brows in. "Are you saying you don't think I should go to law school?"

"I am saying you should go to law school if that's what *you* really want, but otherwise it's not too late to change your mind."

"He'll make my life miserable, Mom." I didn't add that if something happened to her, he'd be all that I had. That was part of my fear of disappointing him.

"He would make you miserable for a while," she said. "But there's no life more miserable than living out someone else's dream and not your own." Mom squeezed my hand. "Just know that I will be proud of you no matter what you decide."

I placed my hand over hers. "That means a lot. Thank you."

"Maybe you should out him for his behavior at that award ceremony."

My eyes went wide. I freaking loved that she'd suggested that. "Should I?"

"No." She smiled. "But that would be something, wouldn't it?"

I shook my head. "I'm dreading that stupid speech. If it weren't for Noelle, I don't know if it would be happening."

"Why? What's Noelle doing?"

I'd told Mom about my idiot lessons with Noelle, but she didn't remember. "She's working with me on my fear of public speaking and helping me write the damn thing."

"Wow. She's becoming a good friend, huh?"

"Yeah, she is."

My mother tilted her head. "Or is she something more?"

I felt bad not being honest about the complicated feelings I had for Noelle. But what was I supposed to say? *We took a shower together the other day, and it got complicated. I fingered her, and then she watched me come?*

"No. Nothing's going on there. She's just a friend."

"Well, I wouldn't blame you if you liked her."

Mom and I talked for a few more minutes and then turned on a movie to watch together. For lots of reasons, this moment felt important to me.

Soon after the film ended, Noelle's parents and my dad came home from the lights festival. I decided to head upstairs.

It seemed Noelle hadn't gone to the beach tonight; I could see the light on beneath the door in her room. When I got to my room, the plastic Easter egg I'd handed her earlier was sitting on my desk.

My heart raced as I opened it to find the sticky note folded inside.

I took a deep breath in and read it.

• • •

At 6:15 the following morning, Noelle was waiting for me when I strolled out.

She pointed to her watch. "You're fifteen minutes late."

"I am. Sorry."

"You didn't go out last night. I'm surprised you overslept."

I'd been up all night thinking about her note, debating whether to sneak into her room before morning. But the bedrooms in the house were pretty close together. If I'd gone into her room, there was a good chance someone would've heard. That probably saved me.

She might've been expecting me to acknowledge the egg, but I chose not to.

"Ready to go?" I asked.

She stretched. "Yeah."

We took off down the gravel road, and neither of us said anything until we stopped for a break at our usual halfway point.

"I left something in your room last night," Noelle said.

My eyes darted to hers. "I know."

"You didn't say anything...so I wasn't sure if you saw it."

"I saw it," I answered.

I was being a dick. But talking about it wasn't going to get us anywhere, especially since I still felt guilty whenever I pondered the various ways I could *educate* Noelle.

When we got back to the house, our parents were having breakfast. I almost jetted upstairs like usual, but after last night, I decided I owed it to my mother to give her more of my time, even if that meant spending more time with my father, too.

So I got a bowl of cereal and took a seat. My presence at the table didn't go unnoticed.

"It's so nice to have you with us for breakfast." Mom smiled.

"It's about time you graced us with your presence in the morning," my father added.

Noelle got her coffee and sat in the chair across from me.

Dad buttered some bread. "Rodney says you've been doing a pretty good job. He's having you sit in on some client meetings and conduct research, I hear."

"You've been calling him to find out how I'm doing?"

"We text. I was curious as to whether he saw potential in you."

"He doesn't criticize my every move, and he shares his knowledge, rather than constantly needing to challenge me or set me up to fail."

My father went quiet. The entire table did.

Noelle changed the subject. "Ashley's coming next week."

"Oh, that's right," her mother said.

"This is your friend from home?" I asked.

"Yeah." She looked over at me. "She's coming for a week."

*Damn. A week?* That was probably a good thing. It would keep some space between Noelle and me.

"Well, that's exciting," my mother said. "We'll have the spare room downstairs ready for her."

Throughout the rest of breakfast, I stole glances at Noelle from across the table. She did this thing where she licked her lips after taking a sip of her coffee, and every time, my dick twitched. The sheen of sweat over the cleavage coming out of her tank top turned me on, too. *Everything* about her turned me on lately, and it'd been worse than ever since she left me the egg.

After breakfast, our parents announced that they were leaving for a farmer's market about a half hour away. I tried to act casual about that, but alarm bells sounded in my head. Noelle and I were going to be alone again. I didn't trust myself, not with how damn horny I felt this morning.

It didn't help that as our parents prepared to go, Noelle lingered in the kitchen. I suspected she was waiting for some direction from me once we were in the clear.

My heart raced the moment I heard my father's car start. It sped up even more as I heard the sound of the engine disappearing down the road. I knew what I was about to do.

"Go upstairs and get in the shower," I told her. "I'll meet you there."

"So demanding..." she teased.

"I thought that's what you wanted."

"It is."

Noelle's eyes sparkled as she got up from her seat and went upstairs. I took a few minutes to find my bearings in the kitchen before following her, urging myself not to let my current level of desire push me into a decision I'd regret.

Once upstairs, I found the bathroom filled with steam. I took off my shoes and socks. My dick was rock hard as I lowered my shorts and kicked them aside before sliding open the shower curtain.

Noelle was soaking wet, her beautiful, naked body covered with soap as she lathered her breasts and looked at me with a come-hither grin.

*So going to hell.* I wanted to do so many things to her right now. I didn't know where to begin. But I knew I had to start with her wish. "Of all the things you could've chosen..."

She bit her bottom lip and smiled.

"Get on your knees," I demanded.

She did as I said and looked up at me.

My cock bobbed in excitement. "You've really never done this before?"

"Never."

"Take it slow. There's no art to it. You'd be surprised how easy guys are when it comes to getting head."

The next thing I knew, she'd wrapped her little hand around my shaft and taken me all the way into her mouth, probably as deep as I could fit.

*What the fuck...* I wasn't expecting that right off the bat.

As she moved her mouth over my cock, I decided not to direct her. She didn't fucking need it. The fact was, I'd lied. Not all blowjobs were the same. Some weren't as good as others. But this one? It was phenomenal. She was a natural. But I would be keeping that to myself. I didn't want her overly confident and sharing her talent with anyone else right now. This was all mine.

Threading my fingers through her hair, I couldn't help but push my cock deeper down her throat. I loved the moan she made as I did. I nearly came but managed to stop it.

A moment later, she looked up at me. It was so goddamn sexy that I could no longer contain anything. I let myself go, shooting my cum down her throat and giving her every last drop.

Just like she'd asked me to in her note.

# CHAPTER 13

## Noelle
### *Past*

**ASHLEY BEING HERE** had left me almost no time to spend with Archie, and he'd also been giving me space I hadn't asked for. I wished he'd chosen to hang out with us more. My ankle had been bothering me, too, so he and I weren't even running together. Now that August was upon us, the clock was ticking down the days until I'd no longer get to see him.

I'd told Ashley everything about what had happened thus far between Archie and me. She was my only real confidante, and I trusted her not to give anything away. Although I'd definitely noticed her looking between Archie and me at dinner.

One morning after Archie left for his internship, Ashley made him the topic of our conversation. "So, you're basically playing it calm and trying not to let on that you like him so he keeps messing around with you?"

"Pretty much."

"That's a good way to get hurt, Noelle."

"I know, but showing my true feelings will scare him away, and I don't want to lose the opportunity to have this experience. I care about him as a friend and can understand him not wanting anything more with me right now. We both have too much going on, and we live on different coasts. It wouldn't work, even if he were the boyfriend type."

"Okay..." She sighed. "I see."

"Are you judging me?" *Now I sound like Archie.*

"No, I swear. I just don't want to see you get hurt. I don't understand how this situation can possibly end any other way."

While I was definitely in danger of that, I was way too horny to stop what was happening. We had so little time left here on Whaite's Island, and I needed more. Since our last encounter in the shower, I had replayed that blowjob so many times in my head—the way he'd seemed to come apart when I sucked him, the salty flavor of his cum. I couldn't believe I'd swallowed it all. That was the point of my request, though, which I must have been nuts to write down on that piece of paper. But the graphic nature of my Easter egg submission was necessary to prove I was serious about our experiment. I wanted to try it *all* with him, and this summer might be my only chance.

• • •

Later that night, I took Ashley to the bonfire. It was the first time I'd been to the beach in a while, and there was a reason for that. *Bree.*

Archie and I had never discussed what had happened between them since our arrangement began. But I assumed nothing was going on since he'd asked me not to mess around with anyone else. She wasn't hanging on to him tonight like she used to, yet she stayed very close, and that made me uneasy.

*More like territorial.*

My handling of this situation was precisely why I could never be Archie's girlfriend. My jealousy over other women throwing themselves at him would kill me.

Ashley and I mostly chatted with James. In fact, Ashley and James seemed to be getting along especially well. They were both pre-med and enjoyed the same kind of alternative music. Archie came over and chimed in on our conversation a couple of times, but I couldn't read him tonight. This entire week, I'd had no idea what he was thinking because I'd barely spoken to him.

Then all hell broke loose—at least in my head.

Bree whispered something in Archie's ear, and he followed her down the beach. They were headed toward the rocks, where I now knew people went to make out—or worse.

Ashley saw me looking at them. She flashed me a sympathetic look but didn't say anything about it since James was right there.

My blood boiled for several minutes until jealousy finally broke me. I had to know. "Ash, I need to leave for a few. Wait for me here?"

She likely knew exactly why I was leaving, so she didn't question it—not that I stuck around long enough for her to say anything before I took off. All I could think as I trudged through the sand was whether the sexual stuff Archie and I had done was just foreplay for his time with

Bree tonight. He didn't want to have actual sex with me, but he'd had it multiple times with her. I hated the horrible, burning jealousy running through me.

I had no right to claim Archie, but he'd requested that I not be with anyone else while we were trying things. I certainly expected the same of him, even if I hadn't specifically said it.

To my surprise, before I got to the rocks, I spotted Archie and Bree walking back toward me.

"Where are you going, Noelle?" he asked as they approached.

I placed my hands on my hips. "I went to...to look for you."

"Why?"

Bree shook her head, seeming pissed, and took off, leaving Archie and me alone.

I turned to watch her walk away before facing him again. "What's wrong with her?"

"Why were you looking for me?" he repeated. "You thought I took Bree to the rocks, didn't you?"

I blew out a long breath as my blood pressure began to return to normal. "Yes."

"I told you I wouldn't be messing around with anyone but you."

"Actually, you didn't. You told *me* not to mess around with James, if I recall. But you promised me nothing."

"Well, that should've been understood." He narrowed his eyes. "You don't trust me."

"Why should I? You're not my boyfriend."

"No, but I'm your friend, and I wouldn't do anything to hurt you." He looked out toward the water. "Bree wanted to know why I'd been avoiding her. I hadn't formally talked to her about not seeing each other. I finally told her straight out that I wouldn't be hooking up with her anymore."

"Oh." I swallowed. "Well...it makes sense now why she didn't seem happy."

He ran a hand through his hair. "She was more upset than I expected. Maybe she was hanging on to some feelings I didn't know about. Anyway, it's done." He reached out and cupped my cheek. "I didn't mean to upset you. It's kind of cute that you were jealous, though."

"Between not running together and Ashley being here, I feel like I haven't seen you this week. Then that happened. So I got a little rattled."

"You can always come see me. I'm not hiding from you. I was just trying to give you some space to hang with your friend." He leaned in. "I've missed the fuck out of you, actually."

Goose bumps peppered my skin. I wanted him to kiss me.

He looked past my shoulder. "Where *is* your friend right now?"

"I told her I'd be back. I left her with the group."

"Text her and see if she's okay with you being gone for half an hour."

I nodded and texted Ashley, letting her know all was well and I would be gone for a bit. She sent me a winky face, which told me she'd figured out who I was with. I asked if she was okay without me, and she responded that James was keeping her company. I wondered if she liked him and hoped something might develop between them, especially since all hope was gone for James and me.

Archie took my hand and led me down the beach and over to the rocks. He situated us in the perfect hiding place and ran his finger gently along my arm. "I loved how open you were about what you wanted in that note."

"You certainly delivered on my request."

"Believe me, *you* were the one who delivered. That was the best damn blowjob I've ever had. I don't know if it's because I knew it was your first time or if you were just so damn good at it, but I can't stop thinking about it." He narrowed his eyes. "Are you sure you'd never done it before?" He shook his head before I could answer. "Forget it. I don't want to know."

I laughed. "It was definitely my first time."

He sat back a bit, and I leaned my head against his chest.

"If I had an egg right now—which I don't—what would you write in it?"

I looked up at him. "I want to grind against you while you kiss me."

"That's it? Or are you holding back?"

"Maybe a little," I admitted. "But you've told me a certain thing is off the table."

"Well, even if it weren't, we wouldn't be having sex here." He chuckled. "Can I tell you what I want right now?"

"Please tell me." I smiled.

"I want you to sit on my face, and I want to eat you out until you scream—give you oral as good as you gave me." He groaned. "But we can't do that here, either."

"I thought that's what this hiding place was for."

"Yeah, but I want you completely naked. That's too risky here. People creep up all the time. So we'll have to wait until we have the house to ourselves." He exhaled. "When is your friend leaving?"

"Two days."

"Okay...we'll figure it out. In the meantime, come here." Archie lifted me over him.

Through my shorts, I felt the heat of his engorged cock throbbing under me. Gyrating my hips, I pressed into him, my clit rubbing against the bulge in his jeans. I loved how warm he was between my legs, as if he'd been heating up the entire time we'd been talking.

When he took my mouth with his, I let out the longest breath. It felt like it had been forever since we'd kissed. Hungry for more, I moved my hips faster, wanting to feel every inch of him. Archie wrapped his hands around my ass to guide my movements. He pushed himself harder against me, and I felt like I could come at any second. This was the most intense thing I'd experienced thus far. Going down on him had been great because I knew I was giving him pleasure. But this? The pressure against my clit, feeling like I was so close to him being inside me? It was the sweetest torture yet.

I began slowing down and pressing harder against him, readying myself to come. His eyes smoldered in the darkness, his breathing turning erratic.

"Come on my cock," he rasped. "I can tell you're ready."

Those words were all it took. The muscles between my legs contracted, and my vision blurred as my head bent back. It was the most intense climax I'd ever had.

I'd been expecting him to come, too, but he hadn't. Instead, he panted, looking conflicted.

"Why didn't you come?" I asked.

"I didn't want it to get on you."

"That's pretty funny considering your pants are soaked from *me* right now."

"Just didn't want to chance anything."

"Let me go down on you," I said.

His eyes were glassy, filled with desire. "Are you sure?"

"Yes."

"Fuck..." he breathed. "I'm too weak right now to refuse." He unzipped his jeans and took his beautiful, hard cock out. It was wet at the big, round tip. My mouth watered as I took him down my throat. I released him immediately as a tease.

"Goddamn it," he groaned. "You give the best head."

As I moved up and down, I savored the experience. The first time, I'd been a little nervous. And the water in the shower had washed away some of his taste and made things a little slippery. Now I could taste everything, feel every bit of the friction of his silky skin against my tongue. I loved this blowjob even more than the last. I also loved the way he gripped my hair and guided me over him. The first time, he'd seemed to want to let me explore at my own pace. But now? He was showing me exactly how *he* wanted it.

"I'm gonna come." His voice shook. "In or out?"

"In," I muttered as best I could.

He let out a loud groan and warm liquid filled my mouth. I didn't slow my movements—just the opposite. I took him faster and deeper with every spurt of salty cum.

I wanted more. So much more. My clit was throbbing, ready to grind on him again. I felt like a sex-crazed fiend.

It was probably good he'd chosen to take things slowly because I would've let him have my virginity if he'd been willing to take it right now. I felt so ready. Yet I also recognized taking it was a responsibility he didn't seem eager for. On some level, I knew that was because Archie truly cared about me. That was one of the only things I felt sure of lately.

He tucked himself back in. "That was so fucking good, Noelle. Thank you."

"Thank *you*." I grinned.

"You seem to like doing that."

"I do."

He smiled. "I could stay here all night, but you shouldn't leave your friend alone any longer."

"Yeah," I sighed. "We should go back."

I started to get up, but he pulled me back down, giving me one last amazing kiss.

*I am so screwed.*

I was falling.

I knew it. And I was willing to take the fall.

That's all there was to it. I'd take getting hurt just to experience being with him.

When we returned to Archie's group of friends, Bree was nowhere to be found. Just the way I liked it.

Ashley flashed a knowing smile. "Everything good?"

"Everything's great."

Archie's hair was all messed up. I couldn't imagine what I looked like right now.

"I figured, considering how long you were gone." She winked.

My face must've been a dead giveaway. "I'm sorry I left you. Do you hate me?"

As we stepped away from the rest of the crew, she lowered her voice. "Of course I don't hate you. You've given me your undivided attention this entire time. I knew you were itching to hang out with him. I don't mind at all, you know, if you leave me for a bit while I'm here." She looked over toward James, who was talking with a couple of guys. "Anyway, I'm enjoying James's company. He asked if I wanted to hang out tomorrow morning. Would you be okay if I did? I know you and he—"

"There was nothing between him and me, Ash. I told you—we only kissed. And while I enjoyed it, I kept thinking about Archie. So I am totally okay with you hanging out with James—or more. You need to have fun while you're here."

"Cool. Thank you." She smiled.

I smiled back. Maybe bringing Ashley into the picture was my way of paying James back for the short time I'd strung him along while I was obsessed with Archie Remington.

But, *oh*! Ashley was going out with James *tomorrow morning*. That meant I'd be free to hang out with Archie, even if we likely wouldn't have the house to ourselves.

After Ashley said goodnight to James, we prepared to head back to the house.

"Ash and I are going home," I told Archie.

"I'll walk with you guys."

"You don't have to…"

"No, I was waiting to walk you back. I'm ready to go."

A shiver ran through me, but I warned myself not to get carried away by Archie's sweet gestures. Ultimately, he was going to crush me.

# CHAPTER 14

## Noelle
*Present*

**IT WAS OUR** last evening at the beach house before Archie and I flew back to our respective cities tomorrow morning. Not only was it our final night here this weekend, it was most likely our final night here *ever*. The house would be sold before we could get back here. A cloud of sadness hung over me.

We'd taken our dinner out to the backyard, as it was the perfect evening to sit outside. The moment should have been relaxing, but tension remained in the air after Archie's revelation earlier, and he still seemed mentally exhausted from his panic attack. I was definitely still in shock about the news he'd dropped—that he was going to be a father.

I'd had no idea that all this time Archie had believed he might not be able to have children. So in that respect, this was good news. I was trying to be happy for him, but I didn't get the impression *he* was totally happy. Despite our complicated history, first and foremost, Archie was my friend. So as much as I needed comforting right now, I knew it was my job to comfort *him*.

"It's all gonna be okay, Archie," I told him.

"Promise me I'll never lose you, Noelle."

My heart nearly broke. It was a perfectly fair request from someone I was sure loved me *as a friend* and had no idea how devastated I was at the moment. I didn't want to lose what we'd had these past several years, yet I knew things would never be the same.

Still, I acted as if his fear was unwarranted. "Why would you think that?"

"Because my life is about to shift in a major way. I don't want you to feel like there won't be a place for you in it."

That was exactly how I felt—like everything was about to change, leaving me behind. Normally, I could run to Archie whenever I needed him. How was that going to work with a wife and baby in the picture? No way would Mariah be okay with me constantly emailing her husband or dropping in unannounced to visit.

I kept thinking about how close I'd come to telling Archie how I truly felt about him. I'd considered bringing it up tonight, our last night at the beach house—until his confession, of course. What if I'd blurted out my feelings for him before he'd had a chance to tell me he was having a kid? That would've fucked things up so badly. At least now it was just me fucked up, keeping my romantic feelings inside for eternity. He didn't know what I'd almost done, and that was a blessing.

"A lot *is* about to change," I finally said, feeling hollow inside. "We'll no longer have this house in common. And you're gonna be really busy and lacking sleep in the near future." I chuckled. "But I'll always be here if you need me, no matter what and no matter where I am."

"Speaking of that... Do you see yourself doing this much traveling forever?" he asked.

I set my plate on the lawn and shrugged. "Until there's a reason not to. If a family is in the cards for me someday, maybe I'll take a different job in the industry. But until then, I don't see a reason to settle down."

Archie shook his head. "It's weird how the roles have reversed, huh? Back in the day, I used to say I'd never settle down. Now look at us."

"Yeah," I muttered. *Look at us.*

I could've admitted how envious I was of Mariah and how badly I *did* want to find the right person and settle down. But life didn't always bring you what you wanted. Just like it had granted Archie something he didn't feel ready for.

"Long time no see!"

*Huh?* I turned to find two teenagers walking toward us. It took me a second to realize they were Holly and Henry, the Disney movie twins, all grown up.

I stood and reached out to hug our old neighbors. "Oh my goodness, look at you guys. I hardly recognized you! I can't believe you remembered us."

"Well, Dawn, the realtor, is a friend of our mom," Holly said. "She told us you guys were here and asked if we remembered you. That's what tipped us off."

Archie stood and clasped hands with Henry. "Never thought you'd be big enough to beat my ass."

"No more movies on the lawn?" Holly smiled.

We chatted with them for the next several minutes. They told us stories of some of the wild parties renters had thrown here over the years. It seemed our old home had turned into quite the party house for college students and the like.

"What are you guys up to tonight?" I asked.

"We were just heading to the beach to meet up with friends."

Archie and I shared a knowing smile.

"I guess that's still all there is to do around here at night, huh?" I said, bursting with nostalgia.

Holly nodded. "You guys should come!"

I shook my head. "Not sure we'd fit in down there anymore."

Archie looked over at me with a gleam in his eye. "I don't know. Might be fun. Wanna go for old times' sake?"

That sounded a bit crazy, but it might have been exactly what we needed after this tense day. I shrugged. "Why not?"

We walked with Holly and Henry down to the beach and joined the swarms of teenagers and college students converging on our old stomping grounds. We were still in our twenties, but Archie and I seemed ancient compared to them.

Unlike the kids who had to smuggle their alcohol in Gatorade bottles, Archie and I legally bought beers from the clam shack and took them down to a spot on the sand.

I stared at his profile as he looked out toward the ocean, once again noticing how Archie was even more heartbreakingly handsome at twenty-eight than he had been seven years ago. I hated that my body never stopped reacting to him, especially when he was physically close like this.

He sipped his beer and looked around. "I don't think I realized how much I needed to be back in this place, to connect with that carefree feeling I had before everything changed." He shook his head. "Even if it's not real anymore, it feels good to bask in the memory of it, you know?"

"Yeah," I whispered. Except I wasn't basking. I was *drowning*. Drowning in the nostalgia of that summer. And drowning in the pain of how it had ended.

*Suffocating.*

• • •

Mixing alcohol with nostalgia, it turns out, is not always the wisest choice.

When Archie and I returned to the house that night, we didn't know what to do with ourselves. Neither of us was tired enough to sleep. But the alcohol from the beers at the beach and the wine he'd opened once we got back home was going to my head fast. I could no longer be trusted with my words.

Archie took out the chocolate cake he'd made earlier and placed it on the counter. We both began eating it—with our bare hands. It was a mess, and I likely had chocolate all over my face. *So this is how it ends, huh? I suppose it could be worse.*

"I had so much fun tonight," he said with his mouth full. "You?"

"It was awesome. Reminded me of the old days." I licked chocolate off the corner of my mouth.

Archie's eyes fell to my lips. "Seven years ago sometimes feels like yesterday, and other times like forever ago, doesn't it?"

When I felt my eyes starting to well up, I knew that was my cue. I never wanted to leave Archie's side, but I needed this weekend to be over before I lost it in front of him. "Anyway, we'd better go to bed," I told him. "We both have early flights in the morning."

I hopped down from my stool and rushed over to the sink to wash my hands. I hadn't intended to make eye contact with him again because I didn't want him to notice my eyes. Then again, he was a little drunk, too, so not sure how perceptive he would be.

Then I felt his presence nearby.

"I have so many regrets," he said from behind me.

I turned to face him and swallowed. "Regrets about what?"

He had chocolate cake on his face, but somehow he'd never looked hotter.

"Everything," he whispered. "With you." He paused. "What we did and what we *didn't* do. The way that summer ended. Everything."

"Why are you bringing this up now?"

"Because I'm fucking drunk, I guess. I don't know." He pulled on his hair. "You look so goddamn beautiful right now." His eyes were hazy as he murmured, "It hurts to look at you."

My tears felt ready to fall. I couldn't let that happen. "Keep that shit to yourself," I muttered.

"We never talk about it, Noelle. We talk about everything else except the massive elephant in the room—the things we did that summer, what almost happened be-fore—"

"Stop." I sniffled. "You're only bringing it up because you're drunk. This is not a healthy way to discuss any-thing."

"Maybe." Archie leaned against the center island and placed his head in his hands. He went silent for a long time. "You were with Shane for like...forever. I thought you were gonna marry that guy. And I thought you were happy. I never thought you'd break up with him." He looked down at the floor. "I kept waiting and..."

*Waiting? He was waiting for things to end between Shane and me?*

"I'm sorry..." He shook his head. "You're right. I need to stop."

Nothing good could come of two people with a ton of unspoken baggage trying to work things out while drunk. I could've poured out all of my feelings. I could have chosen to complicate his already-complicated life—turned it into a goddamn soap opera. But I loved him too much. *I loved him.* So I wouldn't do that.

"Goodnight, Archie. Get some sleep."

I left him standing in the kitchen next to a chocolate cake that looked like it had been ravaged by wild animals.

Then I went to my room and cried myself to sleep.

• • •

After a quiet breakfast together the next morning, Archie and I waited for our respective rides to show up. We were flying out of different airports—him from Portland and me from a smaller, closer airport since my flight was only a commuter one back to New York.

From the road outside, we both took one last look at the beautiful house.

Archie finally broke the ice. "I apologize if I said anything weird or out of line last night. I drank too much. Everything is hazy this morning. I just remember feeling nostalgic and emotional. I'm sorry if I got carried away."

My stomach twisted. "You didn't do anything wrong."

He nodded as his eyes lingered on mine. "You'll be there, right?"

"Where?"

"The wedding. You'll be there?"

*Oh.* The question felt like a jab to my heart. I took a deep breath. "Of course. I wouldn't miss it."

"That means the world to me."

*You mean the world to me, Archie. You really do. I know you're gonna be an amazing dad. And I'm not going to stand in the way of that.*

A car pulled up, and I received a text. A sinking feeling came over me. "That's my ride."

I didn't want to leave him. I wanted to stay in this house forever, without a care in the world and go to the beach every night and then come home and fuck Archie's brains out. In that perfect world, there would be no Mariah, no baby. Nothing but Archie and me and this island. Our happy place. I wanted to go back to that fateful day before everything changed.

I shook the delusional thoughts from my head. God, I was losing it. I lifted my hand. "Well...bye."

Archie's eyes were red and a bit sunken, marring his beautiful face just a bit. I couldn't remember the last time he'd looked so sad.

"Oh. I almost forgot..." He bent to take something out of his bag. "I sketched this of you last night."

My heart filled with bitter joy as I looked it over. My hair was a mess, and I had smudges on my face. The caption read, *Drunken Chocolate, AR*.

"Holy shit. Is that what I looked like?"

"Yeah." He laughed.

"I didn't know you still drew."

"I don't typically." He flashed a sad smile. "Anyway, it's a snapshot of the grand finale of our weekend. I wanted to remember it." He reached out to take it back. "I'm keeping this one, though, okay?"

When he took it, he also pulled me to him. My heart pummeled against his chest, and I knew he could likely feel it. If there were ever a moment that I'd blown my cover, it was now.

"Have a safe trip back," he whispered in my ear, sending shivers through my body.

"You, too."

He took my hand and brought it to his mouth, placing a gentle kiss on my knuckles. It was the most intimate thing he could have done at the most inopportune time.

Forcing myself away, I got into the Uber.

Even looking his worst, Archie was painfully handsome as he stood on the curb with his hands in his pockets, watching me leave.

When the car began to move, I blew him a kiss and waved. I knew I'd see him again soon enough—at the wedding—but in so many ways, this was goodbye. My head knew it. My heart just hadn't caught up yet.

# CHAPTER 15

## Archie
### *Past*

**IT WAS A** week and a half after Noelle's friend Ashley had gone back to New York. Our parents hadn't left the house for any great length of time recently, and I was this close to booking a room somewhere just to be alone with her. The summer would be over in a couple of weeks, and I was obsessed with the idea of living out my fantasy of going down on Noelle. Since when had this thing become about what *I* wanted?

That night, I woke up, feeling something move beside me in bed. It freaked me out for a second...until I realized it was Noelle.

"What are you doing?" I asked groggily.

"I can be quiet," she whispered. "I figured I'd take a chance."

"I'm glad you did." I got up carefully. "Hang on. Let me lock the door."

The one good thing about having this bathroom between us was that it would serve as an escape route if someone ever needed to quickly disappear. *Why didn't I think of that before?*

When I returned to the bed, I hovered over her on all fours and teased, "Is there a specific reason you came in here?"

She bit her bottom lip. "I was going a little crazy."

"Me, too." I sighed. "They're always here."

"I couldn't wait any longer," she said.

"What in particular were you waiting for?" I asked, raising an eyebrow.

"To act out the fantasy you told me about at the beach."

Practically shaking with how badly I wanted to taste her, I slid Noelle's panties down and without further ado, lowered myself until my face landed right between her legs.

I licked my lips. "Spread your legs for me."

After she did, I took a moment to appreciate the beautiful sight, barely visible in the darkness. Thank goodness for the moonlight through the window. My mouth watered in anticipation, and I felt goose bumps forming on her legs.

"Are you cold?"

"No. Just excited."

My tongue ached with the need to taste her, but first, I wanted her totally naked. "Take your shirt off," I ordered.

I watched as she slipped her T-shirt over her head. Unsure where to begin, I went straight for the gold, lowering my face to her beautiful mound and pressing my mouth against her opening. My dick was ready to explode. She was already wet.

"Damn, Noelle," I spoke over her skin. "You're so ready."

Her fingers threaded through my hair as she writhed under me. I began to massage her clit with my tongue. Then I pulled back and circled my thumb over it before sticking my tongue gently inside of her, eventually moving in and out with growing ease.

Her legs were restless around me. I needed to slow down so she could savor this—so *I* could savor this. I moved back, rubbing her arousal over her clit before lowering my mouth yet again, this time sucking and licking even more voraciously. After several seconds of devouring her, I knew I needed more, so I stopped and whispered, "Let's switch places. I want you to ride my face."

Her eyes widened as she smiled and moved out from under me. I lay back as she positioned herself directly over my mouth.

Wrapping my hands around her ass, I pushed her down on to me and went to town on her swollen clit as I groaned into her. Her breathing became labored, and I knew I was hitting her sweet spot even better in this position.

When Noelle's legs began to shake, I figured she must have been close. I pressed my mouth harder against her and spoke against her flesh.

"Come on my mouth," I urged.

I felt a spray of something hit my face and almost laughed out loud. Not even a few seconds later, I felt the pressure of her bearing down. Reaching up, I covered her mouth as she panted into my palm while she came. Eventually her movements slowed, and she moved to my side and lay facing me.

Ready to explode, I tucked a piece of her hair behind her ear. "I'll be right back," I said, excusing myself to the bathroom.

I didn't trust myself to put my dick anywhere near her right now, so I rubbed one out real quick to take the edge off as I looked at myself in the mirror, turned on by the sight of her arousal all over my face.

"Did you just go in there to jerk off?" she asked when I returned.

"I did."

"Why? I could've helped."

"I know, but I don't trust myself tonight," I said. "By the way, you need to add a talent to your repertoire for Miss America *Scholastic*."

"What?"

"Squirting."

She covered her mouth. "Oh my God. Did I?"

"Pretty sure that's what I felt. It was fucking amazing."

"Not sure that qualifies as a talent..."

"It does in my book." I wrapped my arm around her, pulling her close and bringing her into a kiss.

"Do I have to go back to my room?" she asked.

"Not if you're quiet."

We lay in silence for a bit, Noelle gliding her fingers along my chest. "If you could do anything with your life, what would it be, Archie?"

I ran my teeth along my lip. "I would probably be a chef..."

Her eyes went wide. "Really? I thought you'd say art-ist."

"That's a close second, but I love to cook more than anything."

"You've never mentioned that."

"It calms me, and I love the idea of creating some-thing that gives people pleasure."

"You're good at giving pleasure."

"Why, thank you." I sighed. "Anyway, I never cook around my dad because he likes to chastise me. But when I'm alone, I do some serious damage in the kitchen."

Noelle patted my chest. "You need to make me some-thing before we leave."

"If I ever get the kitchen to myself, I will." I gently grabbed her ass. "What about you? What's your dream job?"

She shrugged. "I just want to travel and tell stories."

"Well, you're headed in the right direction. I have no doubt that you will."

"I hope so. I'm excited to see where life takes me," she said.

"You're very optimistic. I'd love for some of that to rub off on me." And then my mind went to the gutter at the thought of anything rubbing off of her on to me. Especially since I could still taste her on my lips.

She ran her fingers through my hair. "So much in life is about how you look at it, Archie. If you dread something, that negative energy will impact the experience. If you try to make the best of it, always look for the good in things, you'll have a much better time."

"That's sort of how I feel about this summer," I said. "I was dreading it at first, but then you gave me a reason to look forward to every day."

"Aw..." She wrapped her hand around my cheek and leaned in for a kiss. Noelle spoke over my lips, "I think it's my turn to make you come again."

That would've been really fucking awesome, but the sound of someone getting up to use the bathroom put a stop to that real quick. I froze and whispered, "As much as I hate to say this, I think you should go back to your room before we get caught."

"You're right." She frowned. "But I don't want to."

"I don't want you to, either. Maybe we'll get the house tomorrow and I can cook for you. I heard my dad saying something about renting a boat again. As long as my mother goes with them, that means we'll be alone."

Her eyes brightened. "Oh man, I hope so."

I pulled her in for one last kiss and noticed an unfamiliar feeling in my chest. Despite my best efforts to deny it, Noelle was becoming more to me than I was ready to admit.

• • •

The following day, we got our wish. Our parents rented that boat for the day, and they left early in the morning, leaving Noelle and me alone. This might have been our last chance to take advantage of it, so I called in sick for my internship.

I'd ridden one of the bikes in the garage to the market and picked up groceries to make lunch for Noelle and me. She now leaned against the counter, watching me dice garlic, and it was probably one of the most enjoyable moments of my entire summer.

Earlier today, when I'd asked her what she wanted me to make, she'd said, "penne a la vodka." When I asked her why, she said she had no freaking idea why she'd blurted it out, especially since she'd never tasted it before. That made me laugh, so I absolutely had to figure out a way to make it. I guaranteed that when I got through with it, my penne would become her new favorite meal.

And carefully following an online recipe, I'd managed to pull it off.

The aroma of garlic and tomato sauce filled the air. After plating the penne, I poured the creamy red sauce over each dish.

"That looks and smells so amazingly good." She clapped her hands. "I can't wait to devour it."

I couldn't wait to devour *her*.

We took our food outside and ate in the sunshine. Taking advantage of our parents not being around, we drank wine as well.

"What time did they say they were coming back?" Noelle asked.

"My father mentioned that they wouldn't be home until after dark." I took a sip of my cabernet. "Still not long enough for me."

After we ate, I called up some Jimmy Buffett on my phone. That seemed to fit the current vibe. As "Margaritaville" rang out, Noelle made an announcement.

"I want to have sex with you."

I nearly spit out my wine. Now anytime I heard "Margaritaville" for the rest of my life, I knew I'd think of what she'd just said.

"That was really random of me, but I feel ready, Archie."

Her tone was confident. Noelle *did* seem ready. I just didn't know if *I* was. In the physical sense, yes. But not in every other sense.

"There's a problem, Noelle..."

"What is it?"

"It's not just you. I want it, too. A little too much. That's why I think maybe we shouldn't. It would complicate things."

Frustration crossed her face. "Why do you think I'm so fragile? I'll be fine. And I *want* you to want it. That's what I've wanted this entire time."

I reached for her hand. "I've wanted you from the very beginning. This has never been about not wanting you. I want you so fucking much. I just...don't want to end up hurting you. That's been my hesitation all along."

She nodded. "I understand if you'd prefer not to. I don't want you to think sex is all I want from you. It's not. I've enjoyed every moment we've spent together this summer and won't forget any of it."

"Me neither," I said.

This day had been perfect. If there was ever a moment for us to go all the way, this was it. I felt myself weakening fast.

"Let's go upstairs and see where things lead," I finally said, knowing full well where that would be.

I turned off Jimmy Buffett, and we left our plates and headed inside. This was no time to be doing the damn dishes. Noelle took my hand and followed me up the stairs. We went into her bedroom, and I took my time taking off her clothes while she undressed me.

We lay down together, totally naked, and just kissed. *Slowly.* It was the most sensual kissing I'd ever experienced. I wanted to savor this, but with every second that passed, I became more certain we weren't going to be able to stop this time.

We began to kiss more intensely as I slid my rigid cock against her abdomen. I loved the feel of her bare skin against mine.

"Jesus. I need to be inside you." I looked down into her eyes. "You really want this?"

"I do," she murmured.

Burying my face in her neck, I whispered against her skin, "Okay."

Without breaking the kiss, I reached over to my pants where I'd conveniently placed a condom this morning—just in case. I was about to rip it open when my phone rang.

Ignoring it, I tore the condom wrapper and sheathed myself as Noelle watched my every move. We fell together onto the bed. I hovered over her as she looked up with wonder in her beautiful green eyes. *This is really happening.*

The phone finally stopped ringing, only to start again immediately.

"Who the fuck is that?" I muttered, finally looking over at the caller ID.

*My mother.*

I got an odd feeling—especially since she'd called two times in a row. So I answered. "Mom? What's up?"

Her words were all jumbled together. I heard bits and pieces.

*Hospital.*

*Your father.*

*Heart attack.*

The room started to spin.

*Couldn't save him.*

*Died.*

*Died.*

*Died.*

*Dead.*

I looked over at Noelle's concerned face.

*My father is dead.*

By the time I hung up, I felt like I'd been transported someplace else. Every shred of the joy I'd been experiencing just seconds earlier was gone.

"My father had a heart attack." Dazed and confused, I forced the words out. "He...died."

Noelle shot up, covering her mouth with a shaking hand.

And just like that, summer ended.

My life as I knew it ended.

# CHAPTER 16

## Noelle
*Present*

**MY HOTEL IN** Sonoma, California, wasn't the closest one to the wedding venue. But that was intentional. I was not interested in running into anyone from the event. The hotel I'd chosen was a few miles away, located next to a gorgeous winery. It was the perfect hiding place for me this October weekend.

This was the night before Archie's wedding, and I'd decided to drown my sorrows alone in the hotel lounge with a word game on my phone and a couple of glasses of wine. Or at least that was my original plan. Then I made a friend.

Her name was Veronique. She was here at the hotel in Sonoma decompressing after a breast cancer diagnosis. Her husband had offered to take the kids so she could have a weekend away to clear her head and think about treatment options. Her situation certainly put my problems in perspective. Sure, I was here to watch the man I loved marry someone else, but that didn't compare to cancer.

When she found out my situation, Veronique begged me to tell her the full story to take her mind off things. Recalling everything for an unbiased stranger turned out to be therapeutic for me as well.

I told her the whole story of the first and only summer Archie and I spent together, and I'd just gotten to the point when everything came to an abrupt end—the moment we found out Archer Remington had died.

Veronique leaned in. "So what happened after that?"

"It was surreal. Archie and I jumped into my parents' car and met everyone at the hospital, where his dad was lying there dead." I shook my head. "Archer was such a powerful man. It was hard to believe he was gone." I looked away. "The worst part was knowing what it would do to Archie."

"The guilt?"

I nodded. "I knew in my heart that it was the beginning of a really tough road for him. He and his father had never gotten along. But deep down he loved his dad, despite all the strife. All I wanted was to be able to help him. I remember offering to go back to California with him and his mom for a while, but he wouldn't hear of it. He insisted I couldn't miss school. My parents and I did fly out to California with them and stayed for the wake and funeral." I shut my eyes. "The sad thing? That speech he'd written about his dad? It became the eulogy. When he delivered it in front of all of those people, he pretty much read straight from the paper, only looking up a few times. And when he did? He only looked at me. No one else." I felt a tear roll down my cheek.

"Wow," she breathed. "And then after that, you had to leave..."

"Yeah." Emotion swelled my throat. "I had to start classes. I'd already missed my first day at BU to be there for the funeral. Those first few weeks of college were a blur. Archie was on my mind almost every moment of every single day."

Veronique ran her hand along the stem of her glass. "Did he go back to school after that?"

"No. He took more than a year off to look after his mom. She'd insisted he go back for his last year, but he refused. He'd gone from preparing for law school to not knowing what the future held. Eventually, he transferred to a school closer to home for his senior year."

"Did you ever visit him?"

"The summer after freshman year, yeah."

"Did anything happen between the two of you?"

Now we were getting to a sore spot. I took a sip of my wine. "We emailed back and forth, but we never brought up the subject of us. Then during my trip out there, a year after his dad died, Archie apologized for everything that had happened—or *hadn't* happened—between us. He wanted to make sure I knew that all he could be to me was a friend. He said I shouldn't wait for him for any reason."

"Were you...waiting?" she asked.

I exhaled. "Yeah. I think I was. I was holding out hope. And I was heartbroken that he'd closed the door on us. If he hadn't told me to move on, I might've waited forever."

"Do you think he was really uninterested, or was it just...life at the time?"

I looked at the flames dancing in the fireplace in a corner of the bar. "I think he was overwhelmed. The thought of owing me something or having to worry about me wanting to pick up where we'd left off was too much pressure. Once he clarified things, we became closer than ever—without the added pressure of a romantic relationship."

Veronique tilted her head, the light from the fire reflecting in her hazel eyes. "Really... I find that odd."

I nodded. "Strange, isn't it? After that, Archie emailed me even more, kept me apprised of everything. It was a surreal time for him. He had responsibilities he'd never anticipated. And I was happy to be there for him." I took a breath. "After my summer visit when Archie put me permanently in the friend zone, I met Shane—my first boyfriend, I guess you could say. We were together for several years but broke up fairly recently—earlier this year."

"I see." Veronique nodded slowly. "And by that time... Archie was with this woman he's marrying."

"Exactly."

"Do you think Archie would've changed his mind about the two of you if you hadn't been with Shane all those years?"

My heart felt heavy. "When Archie and I were last together at the house on Whaite's Island—this past August to prepare it for sale—I got the impression that some of those old feelings were still there. We were drunk one night, and he alluded to waiting for me to break up with Shane. That confused me. It made me wonder if he'd pushed me away for my own good and not because he didn't have feelings for me." Looking over at the fire again, I added, "Anyway, it's all a moot point now, isn't it? Considering the reason I'm here in Sonoma."

"When is the wedding?"

"Tomorrow. About twenty minutes from here."

"Wow." She shook her head and chuckled. "I give you credit for showing up."

"I have to. For him. I promised to always be there for him." I lifted my hands. "And so, here I am."

"Please tell me you have a killer dress."

I managed to laugh. "Oh, you know it."

"What are you hoping for next...after this weekend?"

I blew out a breath. "I'm hoping I can finally move on, that tomorrow will wake me up to the fact that Archie and I are over. I almost *need* to see this wedding happen to believe it."

Veronique sighed. "I hope you don't mind me saying... This is like a real-life soap opera."

I chuckled. "Well, glad I could take your mind off things for a bit."

"You did. I can't thank you enough for sharing your story with me." She leaned in. "Listen, I'm feeling a bit tired, so I'm going to head up to my room. But if you have any time before you go back to New York, I'd love to have breakfast or something before you leave. I'll be here until Monday. I don't think I can go home without hearing about this wedding."

The idea of getting to see her again made me happy. "We can absolutely do brunch on Sunday morning. That would be amazing. I feel like meeting you tonight was a gift, Veronique. Telling the story really helped clear my mind."

"The pleasure was all mine." She patted my arm. "Take care of your heart tomorrow."

• • •

Shortly after Veronique went to her room, I headed back to mine to have a pity party for one. Aside from that lovely stranger in the bar, there was no one else I'd felt comfortable sharing these feelings with. I wished I could talk to Archie tonight. But since that wouldn't be appropriate, I pulled up some of our old emails. I'd favorited certain ones over the years so I could find them easily.

Noelle,

This is a bad dream I can't wake up from. It's been three weeks, but it feels like three years. My mother's mental state is not good. There's so much paperwork and shit we have to figure out. My dad didn't have as much money saved as we thought. Anyway, I don't want to burden you with all that shit.

I want you to know how much it meant to me that you came out to California and missed the start of school to be here. I hope you have a kickass year—don't let the nightmarish way this summer ended put a damper on that. I also hope you don't mind if I write to you from time to time. I feel like you're the only one who understands what I've been through. It's just too much to open up to anyone else right now and have to rehash it. I hope I'm not depressing you. Because that would suck.

Enough about me. What's going on with you? Tell me all about BU.

xo

Archie

I scrolled down to my reply.

Archie,

Please don't ever feel like you have to hold back with me. I can't be there for you in person, so it makes me really glad to know you feel like you can count on me for venting.

It all seems surreal to me, too. I have to be honest, I've had a tough time focusing since school started. I've been thinking about you a lot, thinking back to the good parts of the summer. My heart is still on Whaite's Island. Actually, that's a lie. My heart is with you. I'm sure things will get easier once some time passes.

BU is okay so far. There's not really much of a campus. It's basically like living in the city. So not a lot different than home. But I don't mind that. I'm a city girl at heart.

Write back soon, Archie. Anytime you need me. Day or night. Okay?

xo

Noelle

The next email I'd saved was from about a year after his dad died.

Hi Noelle,

I wanted to let you know that I'm not going back to Ford to finish my last year. I'm transferring to a state school closer to home in Irvine, and I'll be starting in the spring. I'll be commuting. It's for the best. I can't leave Mom. Her memory is getting worse by the day. She needs me here, even if she'd be the last to say so. It is what it is. I know I'd regret it forever if I left her.

I've started seeing a therapist. It's been a long time coming. Ironically, I could've never done it when my dad was alive because if he'd found out, he would've accused me of being weak. Oh the irony... Now I have to see a shrink because of him. Not just because of his death, but because of the fucked-up feelings of relief and freedom I sometimes feel now. I loved him, but it wasn't simple. I don't think I could ever admit this to anyone but you. I know you understand what I mean and won't judge me.

So...is there anything you want to tell me? I happened to see your Facebook photos the other day. You don't need to spill if you don't want to, but I'm curious. Who's that guy?

Talk to you soon.

xo,

Archie

I read what I wrote back to him.

Hi Archie,

Wow. Not returning to Ford was a big decision. I'm proud of you for making it, even though I know that must have been hard. You're the best son to your mom. She'll be so happy to have you around, even if she tries to convince you she doesn't need you there.

I'm so glad you're seeing a therapist. It can never hurt. And I totally understand what you mean about the relief part of your dad not being around. It's completely possible to love someone and also be relieved that certain parts of them aren't here anymore. Your relationship with your dad was complicated. Just because someone isn't around doesn't erase the pain they caused. I feel like wherever your dad is right now, he sees things differently. He sees his mistakes. He sees you for who you are—not who he wants you to be. He appreciates you taking care of your mom. He's proud of you. Just like I am.

Okay…so I guess I have to explain the last thing you pointed out. His name is Shane. We've been dating now for a little over a month. I guess you could say he's my boyfriend. He treats me really well, and we have a good time together. I was going to tell you about him. But I suppose those photos he tagged me in beat me to it.

What about you? I know you don't have a lot of time, but are you seeing anyone?

xo,

Noelle

I remember adding that last part like it was yesterday, the courage it took to ask the question when I really didn't want the answer. I'd been happy with Shane at the time, but things had still been new; and I'd still been very much in love with Archie. I'd felt raw as ever when I wrote that email.

And it had taken him a full week to write back. That had been a terribly long wait.

Noelle,

Thank you for your kind words about my dad. You actually made me tear up. That's pretty fucked up, considering I haven't cried this entire time. But the thought of him seeing things differently now is a comforting one, a different perspective. That's why I love you. You make me see things in a different light.

Okay. Wow. Boyfriend. Well...I'm glad he's treating you right. Make no mistake, if he ever doesn't, I don't care what I have going on out here, I will get someone to stay with Mom and will be on the next plane to Boston to kick his ass. I mean it. LOL. Does he know about me? About our friendship? (Hopefully nothing "else?")

It's funny you asked whether I was seeing someone. I hadn't been until a few weeks ago. Things are a lot different for me now that I'm spending more time with Mom and no longer the "big man on campus" at Ford. But I did go out to a bar with my high school buddy Marcus one night and met a girl. Her name is Fallon. She's cool, and we've hung out a couple of times. It's still new.

Write me again soon, okay?

xo,

Archie

That email had been *a lot*. I'd analyzed the sentence, *That's why I love you*, endlessly. Archie had never used the word *love* toward me before. And he'd never used it since. It wasn't romantic love he meant when he wrote those words, and maybe he'd just meant it in a casual way—like when people say "*gotta love her*."

I remembered my angst at learning he was dating someone new. He'd ended up dating Fallon for over a year. Even though I was supposedly happy with my new boyfriend at the time, the jealousy had hit me like a ton of bricks. She got to pick up where he and I had left off.

*Where we'd left off.*

It was always a strange feeling, like a pause button had been pressed on that summer with Archie. A part of my heart was still stuck there in that moment before we got the call about his dad. In a way, my heart might always be stuck there in that bedroom on Whaite's Island.

The next email I'd saved was the hardest to reread. My response to it might have been the biggest mistake of my life.

Noelle,

I made a decision today. I'm going to culinary school. It's what I've always wanted to do, so fuck it. Nothing in my life has ever gone to plan, so what does it matter if I fail at this? At least I'll enjoy the process. So, that's that. I'll keep you posted.

Is Shane still behaving? I don't need to get on a plane anytime soon, do I? Which reminds me... God, I miss you. Do you think you'd be able to come out here for a visit? It's no big deal if you can't. I just figured I'd ask. I'd love to see you. It sucks that I can't leave Mom long enough to take a trip out east. I would if I could. Please know that.

Speaking of Mom, she isn't doing well. Her memory just keeps getting worse and worse. At least I'm getting help. The home health aides are awesome. I couldn't do it alone. And I couldn't do any of it without being able to vent to you, either.

Also...Fallon and I broke up. That whole thing went on way longer than it should've. She wanted more from me than I could give right now. There isn't much more to it than that.

Write back soon.

xo

Archie

My hand shook a little as I moved the cursor down to my response, still angry at myself for being so self-absorbed that summer.

Archie,

Holy crap! Culinary school. That's a huge deal. I'm so happy you decided to bite the bullet. It's what you've always wanted to do, and I, for one, cannot wait to reap the benefits of that! So proud of you.

I'm sorry about your mom not doing well. You're doing the best you can, and I hope you realize that. I will continue to pray for her.

Okay…wow on Fallon. It was about a year you guys were together, right? I'm not saying this to be funny, but that was the longest relationship you've ever had, yes? Anyway, I'm sorry to hear that you decided to end it. But you know what you need right now, and it doesn't make any sense to waste someone's time if you can't give them what they need as well.

And I miss you, too. I wish I could come out there. But I just found out I got an internship at ABC News. It's full time, and I won't have the ability to travel for a while. I'm so sorry. Maybe I can work something out in the fall or winter? We'll make it happen.

I'll be in touch soon!

xo

Noelle

I stared at that email, wondering what might have happened if I hadn't been with Shane, hadn't gotten that internship, and had instead gone out to spend some of that summer with Archie. I'd never know.

I moved on to some of the more recent emails. There was one from earlier this year where I'd told him about my breakup with Shane. Archie had already gotten involved with Mariah by then, but I'd yet to meet her.

Hey Archie,

Good news—or I'm hoping it is. I've been assigned to do a story out in California. I was hoping we could meet up, at least for dinner, while I'm there. It feels like forever since I've seen you. I'll email you dates as soon as I have them.

How's your mom doing? Are you still getting the help you need while you're working at the restaurant?

Also…are you ready for this? Shane and I broke up. It's a long story. I'll tell you more about it when I see you.

xo

Noelle

I scrolled down to his response.

Noelle,

Holy crap. Was not expecting that news about you and Shane. I'd assumed you'd be with him forever. What was it, like five years? What the hell happened? I think this one might warrant a phone call. And you KNOW how much I hate talking on the phone.

But…you're coming out here? That's fucking awesome!! Just let me know when, and I'll make sure to take the appropriate time off. I guess you can finally meet Mariah. She's been curious about you. I'm sure you can read between the lines of that one. It'll be good for her to meet you, though.

Thanks for asking about Mom. Things have been the same for a while now. But I consider stable a good thing, and I do still have some help.

If you want to talk, I'm here. I'm curious about what happened. I can't wait to see you.

xo,

Archie

That was the last email I'd saved.

The trip out to California had ended up being hard, particularly meeting Mariah, who was beautiful and smart and all the things I'd hoped she wouldn't be. Yeah, that trip was painful. But not as painful as tomorrow would be.

# CHAPTER 17

## Noelle
*Present*

**I'D NEVER COUNTED** so much in my life. Who knew that simple counting could be a coping mechanism? I counted through almost the entire ceremony, stopping at a hundred and starting from the beginning again.

Somehow, I'd made it to Archie and Mariah's reception without truly *feeling* anything. One thing I had going for me? I looked good, if I did say so myself. I'd chosen a pink Oscar de la Renta floral lace minidress for the occasion. It was covered in embroidered daisies that popped off the dress in 3D. It was the ultimate everything-is-just-dandy statement.

I'd been assigned to a table of random friends of Archie's from the restaurant. It felt like the right placement for me, a person who had no clear role in his life anymore. Even if I was hurting inside, I made sure to keep a permasmile on my face, so no one could see through me.

Aside from waving at me when he'd spotted me in the church, Archie and I hadn't communicated at all. They didn't do a receiving line after the ceremony. Instead, the happy couple was whisked off to take pictures until they reemerged at the reception.

I made it through the meal, making small talk with the people at my table. I'd also survived Archie and Mariah's first dance. The moment I lost it, however, was when Archie and his mom danced. I wasn't sure Nora knew what was going on. That was the only moment I'd deemed worth my tears today.

A little while after dinner, I headed to the bathroom for a breather, but when I entered,

Mariah was trying to squeeze out of a bathroom stall, impeded by the size of her massive ballgown.

If I could've walked back out without her noticing me, I would have. But she spotted me right away. *Commence fake smile.* "Hey, Mariah."

"Hi, Noelle." She looked at my outfit. "I love your dress! It's so...flowery."

I looked down at myself. "Thank you."

"Are you having a good time?"

*If you count wanting to vomit every half hour and obsessive counting a good time, sure.* "This wedding was...perfect," I told her. "Truly. And you look absolutely beautiful."

"Thank you for coming."

"I wouldn't have missed it."

She finally got free and made her way over to the mirror. She ran her hand along her brown hair before rubbing a bit of smeared mascara off her eye. "I know you're very important to Archie."

"Well...he's important to me, too," I told her, resisting the urge to flee.

"I have a confession." She turned to face me. "When Archie and I first met, I felt a little threatened by you."

*Get me out of here.* My heart began to race. "Oh... That's silly."

"I mean, I guess it's natural to be jealous of your boyfriend's female best friend." She smiled. "Especially when she's as pretty as you."

"Aw, well..." I looked down at my Pepto-Bismol pink heels.

"I don't feel that way anymore," she clarified. "I'm much more confident about everything now."

*Well, yeah, you trapped him, so...*

Ugh. I couldn't help my thoughts. "Good." I smiled.

*Nod and smile.*

*Nod and smile.*

"I hope we can be friends, too," she said.

*Nod and smile.*

"I would love that."

*One...two...three...*

She looked around to make sure no one was listening. "He told me he let you know about..." She lowered her voice. "Our baby."

I swallowed. "Yes."

*Four...five...six...*

"We just found out it's a girl."

*Wow.* I willed myself not to fall over. "Really..."

"Yeah. I told him not to say anything to anyone yet. But I'm just so excited."

"That's...amazing." My chest constricted. "So amazing."

"Well, I'd better get back out there. I hope you're enjoying yourself." She left before I could tell another lie.

A moment later, I exited the bathroom in search of some air. Archie was having a baby girl. He was *already* a dad. *My* Archie. A mix of joy and pain overtook me as tears welled in my eyes. I'd finally reached my breaking point.

I'd just stepped outside onto the veranda when I heard his voice behind me.

"Noelle?"

I turned and tried my best to put on another fake smile. "Hey."

"I've been looking for you," he said.

"I'm sorry. I needed some air. My allergies have been acting up."

"Do you need something? I'm sure somebody here has something you can take."

"No." I sniffled. "I have...some stuff at the hotel."

"I haven't had a second to talk to you."

"Well, you're in high demand today." He looked so handsome in his white tux that I had to look away for a moment.

"What did you think of everything? I had nothing to do with the planning, but..."

"Everything was perfect. Truly. And I'm so honored to be here."

"It means everything to me that you are." His expression turned serious. "But I wish you'd be honest with me."

"What are you talking about?"

"You don't have allergies, Noelle. I've known you for a long time, and you've never once mentioned fucking allergies."

*Shit.* "You got me." I wiped the corners of my eyes, feeling ashamed. "I just got a little emotional, that's all." I looked up at the darkening sky. "I ran into Mariah in the bathroom, and she told me you guys are having a girl."

"Oh...okay." He scratched his chin. "She did, huh? She told me I couldn't tell anyone, and she ended up telling you. That's interesting. I kind of wish she hadn't done that. I wanted to tell you myself."

"It doesn't matter. The news is still amazing." I patted his arm. "Congratulations, Daddy. I can't believe you're gonna have a daughter."

He shook his head. "I know. The universe has finally figured out a way to get back at me for all the shit I pulled when I was younger. I mean, how the hell am I gonna handle a girl?"

"I have to say, it is kind of funny." I chuckled. "But you'll manage."

Our eyes locked for a moment.

"Are you sure you're okay?" he asked.

"I'm fine, Archie. Weddings have a way of making people emotional. Finding out you were having a daughter... That was powerful, too. Not in a bad way. Just makes me realize life is moving on, you know?" I looked toward the entrance. "You should go back to your party."

"I want you to know something first, Noelle." Archie took a few steps forward. "Looking out at the guests at the church today—the bride's side versus the groom's side—it was pretty pathetic, wasn't it? There were so many more people on her side. I don't have a big family. I don't have a lot of people I can count on. My mother is mentally gone, and my father is physically gone. You've been my family for so long. I know we have a complicated history. I haven't forgotten that, even if I don't talk about it. You could've blown me off after the way I handled things when we were younger. I was so wrapped up in my own head after my dad died. But instead, you've been there for me every step of the way." He looked down and fiddled with his white-gold wedding band. "Anyway... I don't even know how to articulate it. I just want you to know that having *you* on my side of the church today meant a lot. And I truly hope I don't ever lose you."

I swallowed hard and barely got the words out, "You won't."

Archie pulled me into an embrace. I started to count again.

*One...two...three...four...*

Because being in his arms right now was downright unbearable.

He finally let me go. "That Shane bastard is a fucking fool for not doing everything in his power to keep you."

"Seriously," I urged, feeling ready to break. "You need to go back in there." *Before I fucking cry my eyes out in front of you.*

"Okay, but promise you'll come find me before you leave. Don't go without saying goodbye."

"Of course."

After he finally walked away, I opted to stay outside for a few more minutes. I breathed slowly and evenly until I felt more in control.

On my way back to the ballroom, I noticed the satiny white guest book I hadn't signed. I was a little tipsy, so it might not have been a good idea to write something that would forever be part of the couple's wedding memories. *I almost fucked your husband once. Congrats!* I smothered a snort-laugh. But this was my opportunity to write in that damn book because I wasn't going to last here much longer. I picked up the white, feathered pen.

*Archie and Mariah, I cannot tell you what an honor it was to be included in your special day. I wouldn't have missed it for the world. Mariah, I hope to get to know you better over the years. I know you know what an incredible man you married. But I'm not sure HE always knows how incredible he is.*

*When I first met Archie, I thought he was stuck up. I made assumptions about him from afar because of the way he looked and the way he acted. Once I got to know him, I realized he was a sensitive, vulnerable, and caring person. He's handled everything life has dealt him like a champion, always putting others first.*

*He's an amazing son and friend, and I know he will make an even more amazing husband and father.*

I wanted to write, *I hope you know how lucky you are, Mariah*, but settled on:

*I wish you both many years of health and happiness.*

*All my love,*
*Noelle Benedict*

I returned to the ballroom, where Archie and Mariah were dancing amidst a crowd of people. I went over to

Nora Remington and offered her a hug, making conversation with her caretaker for a few minutes before returning to my table. I sat and stole glances at Archie on the dance floor.

I was angry at my inability to feel happy for him. As much as I wanted to be joyful, I couldn't. There were still too many unanswered questions—like whether things might've been different if Mariah hadn't gotten pregnant. Would he have stayed with her? Married her? Was he truly happy? What would've happened if I hadn't been with Shane for so long? Would Archie and I have gotten together? None of this mattered, but it still haunted me as I sat in my own world while everyone else was immersed in the Cupid Shuffle.

After another half hour, I decided to remove myself from the situation. It had been a long day, and I was eager to get back to my hotel room where I didn't have to pretend to be happy. I also wanted to get to bed at a decent hour so I'd feel refreshed tomorrow when I met Veronique from the hotel bar for brunch. It was my duty to share the next episode of my soap opera.

Even though Nora had no clue who I was anymore, I stopped by again to give her a final hug. She seemed happy as she looked out toward the guests dancing.

I hated having to interrupt Archie, who was in the middle of a conversation with some guy at one of the tables. So I stood patiently to the side, waiting in the wings until he noticed. The moment he saw me, he held his finger up and excused himself.

His eyes widened as he approached. "Are you leaving already?"

"Yep."

He frowned. "Shit. Okay. When's your flight?"

"Tomorrow afternoon."

"Are you headed back to the city or to a location?"

"I'll be in New York for a couple of days before I fly out to Colorado for a new assignment."

He shook his head. "You're always on the go. It's crazy."

"I know, but it's good for me. I don't have any reason to stay in one place." I patted his arm. "Unlike you now."

"I guess that's true. You'll settle down when you're ready, though."

I shrugged. "Or never…"

He seemed understandably confused. I'd always said I wanted to settle down and have kids. I was probably just being a brat in denying that.

"Whatever makes you happy, Noelle."

*The last time I was happy, you were on top of me.*

"Let me walk you out," he added.

"Okay…"

With each step I took, I vowed to be stronger moving forward. Once I got past the emotions of this night, it would be easier to accept everything.

We stood facing each other in the vestibule outside the ballroom.

"Maybe this is no longer appropriate for a married man to admit, and I hope you don't take it the wrong way." He paused. "But you look absolutely beautiful in that dress. I know I've said this once already tonight, but Shane is a fucking idiot."

*You're not helping, Archie.* I reached up to hug him. Not because I was overly eager to do so, but because I needed a moment when he wasn't looking at my face so I could fend off the tears that wanted to fall again.

Today had been damn hard. Much harder than I'd imagined. Taking a deep breath, I managed to compose myself as I pushed back to look at him. "Go back in there and enjoy the rest of your night."

He ignored me, standing firmly in place. "Email me soon, okay?"

"I will."

"I love hearing about the crazy stories you're working on."

I forced a laugh. "This next one's a doozy. It's about a woman who claims to have been abducted by a UFO right outside her house in Boulder."

"Damn. I can't wait to watch. I watch them all, you know."

"By the time it comes out next year, you'll be on diaper duty."

"Shit. That's nuts to think..."

I stepped away. "Take care, Archie."

"Have a safe flight home."

"Thank you," I said, walking backward.

He blew me a kiss, and I could have sworn I felt it penetrate my skin.

*Goodbye, Archie.* We might always be friends, but I needed to say goodbye to the hope I'd been hanging on to—I hadn't realized how firmly until tonight. A part of me had always thought we'd end up together; that hope needed to die now.

As I walked out, I believed with every inch of my soul that Archie and I would never find our way back to each other. I thought *that* part of our story was over, that the eternal pause button from the day his father died would forever remain in place.

But I was wrong.

# PART TWO

## *FIVE YEARS LATER*

# CHAPTER 18

## Archie

**I HAD ABOUT** an hour left before I needed to get to the restaurant. Between my busy work schedule and needing to give my four-and-a-half-year-old daughter the attention she deserved, there weren't a lot of moments where I could just sit at the computer with a cup of coffee and catch up on things. But at the moment, Clancy was busy watching a kids' movie in the other room, allowing me some time to myself.

I opened my social media, and the first thing in my feed was an album of photos that included numerous shots of Noelle. Her bright eyes and beautiful smile took my breath away. Noelle had the kind of smile that lit up her entire face, the type of smile that was contagious when it was genuine. Noelle had displayed her share of fake smiles through the years, and I could always tell she was putting on a front when her smile didn't reach her eyes. My wedding day, for example.

Being there had been difficult for her, though she would never admit that to me. Things had never been quite the same between us after that day. Noelle slowed in responding to my messages and gradually distanced herself. We still kept in touch, of course, and continued to exchange emails; it just wasn't like before.

She'd come out to meet Clancy when my daughter was about a year old. That visit had coincided with an assignment that had brought her out west again. The last time I'd seen Noelle was at my mother's wake a year ago. It touched me that she'd left an assignment in Chicago to be there, even after I'd insisted it wasn't necessary.

I focused on one of the photos of Noelle in particular. In it, she gestured with her hands, talking to someone and totally oblivious that her picture was being taken. Photos of Noelle on social media were a rarity. That sucked, because I missed seeing her face. On her own pages, she mainly shared location photos or pictures of food, and rarely showed herself. She was private like that—always the one behind the camera documenting everyone else's life. The only reason I had this access was because a coworker had decided to tag her in a bunch of photos that looked like they were from some company party. Noelle probably didn't even know about it since they'd just been posted a minute ago. I laughed. She would hate me peering into her world without her knowing.

I clicked through the album to see the other shots and suddenly stopped at an image of Noelle sitting with a guy who had his arms around her. She was smiling—and it reached her eyes. My heart skipped a beat.

*This must be him.*

She'd told me in the last couple of emails that she'd been dating an older guy with kids, but this was my first look at him.

His name was Jason, and he was some sort of television executive who worked for a competing network. In another shot she sat on his lap, looking a little drunk. Or maybe she was just happy. I used my thumb and index finger to zoom in on his face for a moment. He definitely had some light wrinkles around the eyes, but he was a handsome guy. Salt-and-pepper hair and a slight beard. She'd told me he was in his late forties—more than fifteen years older than her. She'd also mentioned that his two kids were college-aged. It surprised me that she'd taken up with someone who'd already been married and had kids. One of the reasons she'd broken up with Shane was because he claimed he didn't want kids. This guy already had kids who were grown. Did he want more, or was he done? Those were questions I should've asked her, but I hadn't felt comfortable prying as much lately.

I zoomed back out and looked at her smile again. Grilling her would mean having to reciprocate on my current personal life, which I wasn't prepared to do. I wanted to make sure I didn't come off like a failure when I finally told her.

One thing was for certain, though. I'd missed Noelle's face. And seeing her smiling like that made me happy, even as it made me physically ache. I zoomed in on *his* face again.

"Whatcha doing, Daddy?"

I flinched as Clancy startled me. Her movie must have finished. I closed my laptop before turning to her. "Nothing important."

"You were looking at an old man," she noted.

I loved my daughter. She had no idea how much pleasure that comment gave me.

"It was just a friend of a friend." I laughed.

"Oh." She scrunched her nose. "You have friends?"

I bent my head back in laughter. "Of course I have friends. What are you tryin' to say, little girl?"

"I thought Uncle Max was your only friend."

Max, my business partner, was practically a member of the family. He and his wife, Sharon, lived right down the street from us.

"No. I have other friends besides Uncle Max."

Since my daughter only ever saw me going to work when I wasn't hanging out with her, it was no wonder she'd assumed I had no social life.

"Who's your *best* friend?" she asked.

At one point the truthful answer would've been No-elle. But I wasn't sure where she and I stood as of late. And Clancy had no clue who Noelle was since the only time they'd met, she was just a baby. I'd never spoken about Noelle to Clancy, since I knew it would get back to Mariah. To this day she still had a complex about my female friend. I hoped someday Clancy could meet Noelle again.

"*You're* my best friend." I tickled her.

"Can we go get ice cream, best friend?" Clancy flashed her little teeth.

*Such a manipulator.* "Trying to butter me up, huh?" I looked over at the clock. I still had a little time before I had to be at the restaurant to prepare for the dinner crowd.

She hopped up and down. "Please!"

"Sure." I sighed. "I think we can swing that."

I had a tendency to spoil my daughter lately. I think I was trying to make up for the fact that I'd let her down in the one area that mattered most. She just didn't know it yet.

When Mariah entered the room, our daughter turned to her. "Mommy, Daddy says we can go for ice cream."

"Overcompensating again, are we?" Mariah muttered.

"She and I haven't gone this week. I have a little time before work, so why not?"

"Well, it's kind of close to her dinner time, that's why." Mariah rolled her eyes. "Sometimes with you it's like having another kid."

"If you really don't want me to take her, I won't."

"No, it's fine." She turned to Clancy. "Why don't you go grab a jacket? It's cool out."

"Okay!" she said, running out of the room.

With my daughter gone, the silence was deafening.

"When are we going to tell her?" Mariah asked.

I placed my head in my hands. "I don't have the heart. You know that. If it were up to me...never."

"You're just going to keep taking her for ice cream and hope the issue disappears? It's not going to be any easier if we wait."

"I agree. But... She's too young to understand that it's not her fault." I raked my hands through my hair. "Maybe we should put it off for just a little while longer."

She shook her head. "I need to move on with my life, Archie. This situation is suffocating me."

I lowered my voice. "Is this about Andy?"

"No. He hasn't put any pressure on me at all." Mariah crossed her arms. "But I'm not happy. I think you and I need our space. We can't have that until we tell her."

Staring up at the ceiling, I blew out a breath. Mariah was right, but I wasn't ready for the drastic changes that would come from taking this step. The thought of living apart from my daughter killed me. Once we told Clancy we were getting a divorce, the next step would be for me to move out. I was in no rush to do that. But I had to respect Mariah's wishes. She had every right to her independence, especially since I was the primary reason our marriage had fallen apart.

"Okay," I conceded. "When do you want to do it?"

"This weekend."

My chest tightened as she turned and walked out.

After Clancy and I got to the ice cream shop, I sat across from her, watching as she devoured her blueberry cone with rainbow sprinkles. She didn't know what was about to hit her.

My sweet daughter was going to be blindsided by her parents in just a few short days.

# CHAPTER 19

## Noelle

JASON GAVE ME a foot rub as I filled him in on my medical appointment earlier today.

"So...I spoke to my OBGYN this afternoon, and he said if I want the best chance at conceiving, I should probably move forward soon. Even though I'm still relatively young, it only gets more difficult with age."

A couple of years ago, I'd been diagnosed with endometriosis. I was told it might complicate my ability to conceive and that the sooner I got on that, the better. I'd always hoped to have a child by thirty. Well, now I *was* thirty. I'd come to the conclusion that I needed to take matters into my own hands.

"I want to be sure you're really okay with this before I commit," I told him.

"Would that change anything?" he asked.

"No. But it makes me feel better to know you support me."

"I do." Jason squeezed my foot. "I've already told you that."

He and I'd had many heart-to-hearts lately about my desire to have a child of my own. I no longer felt the need to be married in order to make that happen. Jason had two grown kids and no interest in starting over again, and he'd also had a vasectomy years ago. That was reversible, but he'd made it clear he wasn't interested in having another child—or raising anyone else's. I had to respect that.

To be honest, maybe that worked out better for me since it removed the pressure of worrying about how our relationship might impact anything. Having a child was something I wanted to do for me. Deep down I supposed it hurt a little that he'd ruled himself out as a potential father. It would've been nice to have that option, even if it probably wasn't the best one. That said, I'd known what I was getting into when I started dating Jason. He'd always been transparent with me, which I appreciated.

When I expressed interest in seeking an anonymous sperm donor, I'd wondered if Jason would run the other way. It took a lot of confidence for a guy to accept his girlfriend having another man's child—even if the man was anonymous. But Jason was nothing if not secure in himself. He oozed confidence, which was one of the reasons he was so successful, and one of the things I found so attractive about him. Thankfully, since I'd first told him what I wanted to do, he'd fully supported my decision.

"I spoke to the cryobank people today as well," I continued. "I have some paperwork I need to fill out, but I paid the initial fee, so they gave me access to their database of options."

"What are you going for?" he asked.

I tilted my head. "What do you mean?"

"Height, ethnicity, educational background—that kind of thing."

"I'm not sure yet. Looks don't matter to me so much, as long as the baby is healthy. But the number of options they give is overwhelming. They even show you some of the donors' childhood photos. I mean, how do you choose?"

"I think it comes down to a gut feeling." He massaged my heel.

I sighed. "Yeah, probably."

As he continued to rub my feet, I looked down at my phone and noticed I'd received a new email. It was from Archie. My heart clenched. He and I hadn't been in touch as often lately. I hadn't told him about my plans to undergo intrauterine insemination. When I opened the email, my stomach dropped. I needed to read it in private.

Straightening suddenly, I pulled my feet back.

"Everything okay, babe?" Jason asked.

"Hmm?" I blinked.

"Is everything alright? You look like something upset you."

"Yeah. Everything's fine. I just need to...use the bathroom. Be right back."

I headed down the small hallway in my apartment. Closing the bathroom door behind me, I opened the email again.

Hey Noelle,

I'm sorry I haven't been in touch. There's been a lot going on, and it's time I filled you in. There's no easy way to say it. Mariah and I are getting divorced.

I know this might come as a shock since I hadn't told you we were having problems. But the truth is, there's been trouble in paradise for quite a long time. I just haven't wanted to admit it.

I don't even know where to begin. We told Clancy tonight, and I feel like such a failure.

You and I haven't spoken on the phone in ages, but this is all too much to write. If you have time to talk tonight or tomorrow evening, I'm around.

I hope everything is going okay with you. I saw a photo of you recently on Facebook, and you seemed really happy. It was so nice to see your face.

Hope to talk to you soon.

xo

Archie

When I returned to the living room, my boyfriend asked, "You good?"

The shock was likely written all over my face, so I had to be honest. "I got an email from my friend, Archie. I've told you about him."

"The chef out in Cali?"

I nodded. "He's...apparently getting divorced. I had no idea. He had to tell his daughter tonight. He wants to talk on the phone to give me the details. Archie never wants to talk on the phone, so I know he must be upset. He asked if I had some time to call him."

"You want some privacy?" Jason asked.

"No. Stay. I just wanted you to know why I need to hop on the phone for a bit."

Jason grabbed his keys from the coffee table. "I'll head out. It's just as well, babe. It's late, and I told Jay I'd stop by and take a look at his car before tomorrow. It's giving him some trouble."

Jason's kids, Jay and Alexandra, both lived about thirty minutes away in New Jersey, where Jason also had a house. He often jetted back and forth between my apartment in the city and the suburbs.

"Are you sure?"

"Positive. Go give your friend a call." Jason wrapped his arms around me and placed a firm kiss on my lips. "I'll bring you breakfast in the morning."

After he left, I picked up the phone and dialed Archie, my heart racing more with each second.

His voice sounded strained when he answered on the third ring. "Hey, Noelle."

"Hi."

"I didn't think I'd hear from you so soon. This is a pleasant surprise."

"Is now a good time?"

"It's perfect, actually. Clancy's already in bed, and I'm otherwise alone."

"That was some email you sent me."

"I know. I'm sorry for not mentioning anything sooner. I felt like I owed it to my daughter to make sure she was the first to know."

"I understand." I nodded. "How did she take it?"

"Well...she cried. And I feel like a monster."

I lay back on my couch. "What happened, Archie?"

"What happened?" He let out a long exhale into the phone. "That's a really fucking good question. It probably can be summed up like this..." He paused. "I married someone I wasn't truly in love with because it felt like the responsible thing to do. By the time I realized I couldn't make myself fall in love with her just because she'd had my baby, we were already married. I refused to give up, not wanting to fail my daughter, yet all the while failing as a husband and pushing my wife away through lack of affection and intimacy. So while I wasn't technically the one to end my marriage, I all but forced her into the arms of another man who gave her *exactly* what she needed. Mariah insisted on a divorce so she could be with said man because I would've continued to stick it out for my daughter, while my wife and I remained miserable."

*Jesus.* I'd really been out of the loop. I'd never loved Mariah, but my heart broke for her and for Archie. My voice trembled. "I feel like a terrible friend that I didn't know any of this."

"Please. I intentionally hid it from you because I was ashamed."

"I'm so sorry, Archie."

"As we speak, my wife is at her boyfriend's house while I stay home with our sleeping kid."

*Oh man.* "God...I'm..." I shook my head. "Wow."

"How the fuck did I get here, Noelle?"

I took a deep breath in and exhaled. "You made the decision you felt was best for your child, and you tried."

"Did I, though? I couldn't even fake it after a while. Clearly I didn't try *that* hard."

"Archie, you're human. We all make mistakes."

"This was a pretty damn big one." He sighed. "I'd always known I wasn't cut out for marriage. I should've known better, and now my daughter has to pay for my poor judgment. It might've been better if she hadn't had her parents together from the start."

"You're perfectly capable of being a good dad to her, even if you're not married to her mom. People make it work all the time. In fact, you'll probably be a better dad without the added pressure of a marriage you weren't happy in."

A few seconds passed. "As always, you're very wise, my friend. Thank you for being here when I need you, even if I haven't been the greatest friend lately."

"I've been distant, too," I told him. "I thought I was doing the right thing by giving you space."

"Space from you is not something I've ever wanted," he said.

His words gave me pause. Before I could overanalyze them, he spoke again.

"You've always been the type of friend where things pick up right where they left off, no matter how much time has passed."

*Not exactly.* We were never able to pick up from that one moment in time I seemed to be stuck in when it came to Archie.

"Where will you be living?" I asked.

"I'm gonna start looking for a place this week. Clancy will live here with Mariah, and we'll work out an arrangement amicably so she can stay with me some of the time. That's the one good thing about this. Mariah and I are on pretty good terms." He sighed. "I don't think I'll be okay for a while, though. Not after seeing my baby cry tonight."

Pain gripped my heart. "Do you still see a therapist?" I asked.

"No. I stopped years ago."

"Maybe it would be a good idea to go back. There are a lot of feelings to work out here."

"I think you might be right." He let out a long breath. "God. It's so good to hear your voice. I've missed the calming effect it has on me."

I closed my eyes, angry at my foolish heart for leaping so easily whenever he complimented me. Old habits died hard, no matter how many times I'd tried to kill them over the years. As much as I cared about Archie, he'd closed the door on a romantic relationship with me years ago. He'd made decision after decision that created more distance between us. I was finally in a good place after the trauma of watching the man I'd pined for marry someone else. Little did he know, I'd been to therapy myself through the years—in part to get over *him*. I needed to continue to keep my feelings in check for my own well-being.

"I saw those photos of you and Jason that your coworker tagged you in," he said.

"Oh...I wondered what you were referring to in your email because I knew I didn't post anything."

Archie cleared his throat. "Things seem to be going well with him?"

"Yeah." I picked some lint off my pants. "We've been together about nine months now. It's a nice, low-key relationship. No expectations. Just mutual respect. We have a really good time together."

After a moment, he said, "Well, that's good. I'm happy you're happy."

There was a lot I hadn't told Archie—namely my plans to have a baby on my own. But it wasn't the appropriate time to drop that bomb. Tonight was about Archie, not me. I'd send him a message about my news when his mind was clearer.

"You'll get through it, Archie. I know you will. Your daughter will be better off in the long run, having two parents who are happier apart than they were together."

He sighed. "I hope so."

Archie and I spent about an hour on the phone catching up. Among other things, he told me he was in the process of getting his mother's house ready to be sold. He was currently letting a friend of hers stay there.

"I can't thank you enough for making time for me tonight," he said.

"I told you I'd always be there for you. That's the way it works with us."

"I hope you know I'd do the same for you," he said. "I feel like you've always had your shit together, so I've never been able to prove that. My life has taken some crazy turns, but in the midst of everything, you're always on my mind, Noelle. Even if I don't always reach out."

It was so good to catch up, even if the circumstances weren't exactly joyful. I hadn't realized how much I'd missed Archie until tonight.

But as soon as I had the thought, a voice of warning sounded in my head.

*Be careful, Noelle. You've come so far. Don't ruin it.*

# CHAPTER 20
## Archie

**AFTER A REALLY** rough stretch, things were finally looking up in my life.

A couple of months after breaking the divorce news to Clancy, I'd settled into a new normal, purchasing a small home down the street from the house where my daughter still lived with Mariah in Irvine. My place wasn't fully furnished yet, but it was a work in progress. The one room I'd managed to complete was my daughter's, as I tried to make the best of the situation, letting her pick out the colors and breaking the bank on all new furniture and décor—anything to lighten the blow of her having to live two separate lives thanks to my mistakes.

Because I worked at the restaurant on weekends, I had my daughter two weekday evenings at my place and visited her every chance I got when I wasn't working on Saturday and Sunday mornings. We'd sometimes have breakfast or lunch together on those days before I had to head into work.

I'd asked Mariah not to let Andy move in with her for at least a year. Thankfully, she hadn't argued. I'd been lucky that my soon-to-be ex-wife was a fairly reasonable person. I supposed I should also feel lucky that she'd found someone to share her life with. This divorce would've been inevitable whether she'd met Andy or not. At least she wasn't hurting so much anymore, so I didn't have to feel any *more* guilty for not loving her the way she deserved.

Then a few days ago an email had hit my inbox, knocking the wind out of me in the process—more like turning my world on its axis. The funny thing was, I'd been thinking about Noelle more than usual even before that message. Now that my life seemed to be on even ground again, I'd finally had time to think about all the things I'd been missing. I'd been pondering finally going to visit her, which was long overdue. I'd even looked at flights to New York.

But since reading her message, I'd been in an almost frozen state, unable to form a response. Normally, when I had such a dilemma, I'd write to Noelle and get her advice. But how was I supposed to do that when the subject of my dilemma was Noelle herself?

One Sunday afternoon, with an hour to go before work, I finally bit the bullet and picked up the phone to call her. Any more time without responding might make her think I was judging her or something, which wasn't the case at all.

She answered after a couple of rings. "Hey, Archie."

"Hey, you."

There was a brief pause. "I take it you got my email."

"I did." I swallowed. "I have to be honest. I opened it a couple of days ago. I wasn't sure how to respond."

She laughed nervously. "That's not very encouraging."

"No, no, I was just a little shocked. You'd never even hinted at this. I had no clue it was something you'd been thinking of doing."

"I know. I kept it to myself."

"I'd always imagined you getting married and having kids the traditional way. But there's nothing wrong with doing things unconventionally, if that's what you really want."

"Well, life doesn't always make it possible to get to your dreams the way you've imagined."

"I get that—totally. Especially with what you told me about the endometriosis. I obviously had no idea you were going through that, either." I hesitated. "Noelle, please know I respect whatever decision you make. I just wonder...if you've thought this through. Thirty is still pretty young."

Her tone became a bit defensive. "Just because I've only now told you about it, doesn't mean I haven't been considering it for a long time. Believe me, this decision was not one I made lightly."

My chest felt tight as I tugged on my hair, but damn, she had a good point. "The guy you're dating is okay with this?"

"Our relationship is not what you'd consider traditional. It works for us, though. And he *is* fine with it, but this is my choice, not his."

"Of course," I agreed, though I didn't really understand.

Sure, Jason already had kids, but if he cared about Noelle, why the hell would he want her using a stranger's sperm to have a baby instead of offering his own? That made me not trust this guy, even if he had his reasons. It told me he didn't plan on sticking around forever. It made me want to strangle him. But I couldn't tell her that. And it wasn't like the idea of her having *his* baby made me comfortable, either. So, not sure what I was even rooting for here.

"You know I'll always support you, Noelle," I told her. "I just feel protective when it comes to you. That's all this is about. It's not judgment, only protectiveness."

"Well, you have a daughter to protect now. You don't need to protect me."

*Ouch.* I shut my eyes. "You don't need me, but I'll always *want* to protect you. Nothing will ever change that." Pulling on my hair, I paced. "When is this supposed to happen?"

"Well, I haven't..." She hesitated.

My body stilled. "You haven't what?"

"I haven't been able to settle on a donor. I don't know why the decision is so difficult for me. It just seems so... big."

*Maybe it's difficult because it's not meant to be.* I took a deep breath. "I have a favor to ask."

"What?"

"Don't make any decisions until I come out there. I'm planning a visit soon—in the next couple of weeks, if that works for you. Maybe I can go through the choices with you and help you decide."

"Wait... You're coming here?"

213

"I'd like to." I chuckled. "Is that good news or bad?"

She laughed. "It's very good news. I never thought you'd be able to."

"I've been meaning to come see you for a while. I need to get away from the grind. The last trip I took was my goddamn honeymoon. All these years you've been the one to come visit me because of various shit going on in my life. It's about damn time I return the favor." I sighed. "You don't have to go out of town for work, do you?"

"I've been doing more in-house production stuff lately. I haven't field produced or traveled in a while. So I'll be here."

"Alright." I resumed pacing. "I'm serious about this. I'll look into flights tonight, and I'll email you the dates. Text me your address again. I'll book a room near your place."

"You don't need to do that," she insisted. "You can stay here."

"Your apartment is small, from what you told me, and I'm not sure your boyfriend would appreciate me staying there, either. Don't want to cause trouble, you know?"

"Whatever you prefer. Just know that you're welcome."

"Thanks."

After we finished our call, I pulled up flights and booked my ticket.

• • •

The following Thursday, my daughter watched eagerly as I packed my clothing into the suitcase. I had an early flight to New York City tomorrow morning. I'd be dropping Clancy off at Mariah's after she and I had dinner together tonight.

She bounced on my bed. "Daddy, when are you coming back?"

"Monday. I'll only be gone for a few days. I wouldn't be able to go longer than that without seeing you."

"Why are you going to New York again?"

"To visit an old friend, someone who's very important to me. You met her once, but you were too young to remember."

Her eyes were like saucers. "What's her name?"

"Her name is Noelle."

"What's her last name?"

"Benedict."

"Like eggs benedict? What you order from the diner?"

"Yup." I laughed. "Just like that."

"Where do you know her from?"

"Remember we were watching that movie once and I pointed out that big house by the water and said it looked like the one Nana Nora and my dad used to own on the island in Maine?"

She nodded. "Yup."

"Noelle was there, too. And we became really good friends one summer. Even though our lives took us in different directions, we've always stayed friends. And it's been a long time since I've seen her."

"You miss her?"

I chuckled. "I do."

Looking down at my daughter's sweet face, a heavy feeling settled in my chest. I thought about what Noelle would miss if she never had a child of her own. My daughter meant more to me than anything in the world. Even though she'd been unplanned, I couldn't imagine life without her now. Noelle deserved to experience what I'd been gifted with. I shouldn't have questioned her decision to make that happen, especially since I couldn't relate to her feeling that she was running out of time and might not be able to have something she'd dreamed of. Having a child wasn't something I'd known I wanted until it happened to me.

Over the last few days, I'd tried to dig further into what was *really* bothering me about Noelle's choice to use a sperm donor. I'd asked for guidance from above—which I almost never did—on how to handle this feeling of urgency inside me. But I was still waiting for that much-needed clarity.

My daughter interrupted my thoughts. "Is Noelle pretty?"

"She's very pretty."

"Pretty like Mommy?"

I smiled. "Yes. Just like Mommy." *Except prettier.* I ruffled her hair. "But you know what?"

"What?"

"It's more important to be beautiful inside than outside. You know that, right?"

She nodded.

Noelle was definitely that, too.

The past several years had been one big blur since my dad died. Between the shock of that, my mother's illness, switching career paths, the surprise pregnancy, getting married, becoming a father, I hadn't fully grasped what

I'd lost when it came to Noelle Benedict. I'd blocked out the questions about what might have happened between us if things were *different*. Almost every decision I'd made until now was because I felt I had no choice. My life had been ruled by obligation, not by my own wants and needs. If it were a matter of what *I* wanted, I would've chosen Noelle a long time ago.

As soon as I had that realization, the strangest thing happened. I looked down at the floor in my bedroom and could hardly believe my eyes. I got chills.

"Daddy, what's wrong?" Clancy asked.

Lying on the floor was one of those plastic Easter eggs like the ones Noelle and I'd toyed around with during our summer together. But it wasn't even close to Easter.

I bent and lifted the egg. "What is this, Clancy?"

"My Easter egg! You found it! I was looking everywhere for it." She held out her hand.

"You were?" I squinted. "Where did you get it?"

"I found it on the ground outside. I was gonna put pennies in it."

My heart sped up as I stared down at the purple egg. Everything seemed clearer.

*Am I crazy?*

*This is crazy, right?*

*But is it truly crazy if it feels right?*

I'd just gotten the sign I'd asked for.

# CHAPTER 21

## Noelle

**I STOOD IN** the airport waiting for him, unsure why I was so nervous. I'd readied myself to see Archie many times in the past, but it had never felt like this.

When he finally came into sight, my heart beat faster. His gorgeous face curved into a smile the moment he spotted me. I lifted my hand in a wave and hopped excitedly.

"Wow," he said as he dropped his duffel bag. He opened his arms wide and hugged me, my body melting into his as I became instantly drunk on his scent.

"It's so good to be here," he said. When he let go of me, he smiled. "Look at you. God, I've missed you."

My heart wanted to burst out of my chest. I'd somehow known it would feel like no time had passed, that I'd still have the same reaction to Archie I always did. I was right. And I was fucked. "I am so freaking happy you're here," I said. "What do you want to do first?"

He lifted his bag and threw it over his shoulder. "Show me everything—where you live, where you like to eat. Honestly, it doesn't matter what we do. I just want to spend time with you and let loose." He sighed, running a hand through that beautiful mane of golden-streaked hair. "I needed this break."

"You got it." I smiled. "Did you check another bag?"

"No. I didn't want to waste any time. Packed everything into my carry-on."

I laughed. "Impressive." I pointed him toward the exit.

"So...am I gonna get to meet Jason while I'm here?" he asked as we walked.

*Thankfully, no.* That would've been uncomfortable. But timing was on my side. "He, uh, had to go out of town this weekend. He promised his daughter a trip to look at grad schools out west, so ironically, he's headed to where you came from as we speak."

"Ah. Alright. I assumed I was gonna meet him. No biggie."

"Next time."

"Well, I won't complain about getting you all to myself." He winked.

We stopped at Archie's hotel first so he could check in and drop his bag. I then gave him the quintessential New York experience. We walked through Central Park and got pizza in Little Italy. I'd suggested a Broadway show, but he said he'd prefer to spend time talking to me than watching a performance. So, after strolling around the city, we had a late dinner in Chinatown and pretty much closed out the restaurant as we reminisced about our summer together and reflected over the past decade. The way he beamed when he talked about Clancy made my ovaries want to explode. I never dreamed Archie Remington would be a father, let alone a damn good one. He hadn't had the best example in his own father, but it seemed he'd learned from his dad's mistakes. He encouraged his daughter to be whatever she wanted to be.

We skirted the issue of my insemination plans most of the evening until Archie brought the subject up, just as we were about to say goodnight.

"We need to talk more about *you* tomorrow," he noted as we stood outside my building.

"What exactly?" I asked, knowing damn well what he was referring to.

"Operation turkey baster."

I laughed. "It's a little more high-tech than that."

"I wanted to keep things light tonight, but seriously, let's talk about it tomorrow."

"Okay..." I forced a smile.

Having spent time with Archie again, I looked forward to going through the donor options together. With Archie's help, I might actually be able to come to a decision and move forward on this.

Archie's hotel was only a couple of blocks from my apartment, so he'd said he'd walk there. "I don't feel like leaving you right now," he confessed as he lingered. "This weekend is going to fly by too fast."

A piece of his hair fell over his forehead in the way that always made my heart flutter. I almost asked him to come upstairs and hang out more, but then thought better of it—especially now that I realized every shred of my attraction to him was still here. I wasn't a hundred percent sure I could trust myself. I'd fallen into old feelings tonight and needed to be careful not to let nostalgia mar my judgment.

"Any idea what you want to do tomorrow?" I asked.

"Again, it doesn't matter to me as long as we're hanging out together." He grinned. "Today was so much fun."

"I was thinking we'd go to a diner for breakfast and explore the city some more."

"That sounds like a plan." He looked into my eyes, his expression turning serious. "Then we should go back to your place and talk—after I make you dinner."

"You don't have to cook for me."

"I do. At least once while I'm here. There's this gourmet market I scouted online. It's not too far from here. We'll have to hit that."

After Archie and I parted ways, I had trouble relaxing that night in bed. I just wanted tomorrow to come so I could see him again.

• • •

The following day, after a breakfast of waffles and bacon at one of my favorite greasy spoons, Archie and I walked around the city, got coffee in the afternoon, and went to that gourmet market he'd told me about.

Archie had insisted on making me whatever I wanted. I chose crab cakes and zucchini fries. Not sure where I got that combo, but it just sounded good, and Archie certainly delivered. The crab cakes with homemade tartar sauce were to die for, and the zucchini fries were crisped to perfection.

After dinner, we took our glasses of wine over to my sofa. He sat next to me, and for the first time all day, I sensed a shift in the mood.

Archie put his wine down and rubbed his palms on his pants. "I feel like I gave you the impression that I was scrutinizing your decision when you told me about your baby plans..."

"It did seem like you might have thought it was a bad idea."

He nodded. "I don't know what it's like to be in your shoes. But I *do* know what it's like to be a parent. It's a huge responsibility, but a joy—an experience I would never want you to miss, if it's something you want. So, of course, if there are no other options, you should absolutely take advantage of what science has made available." He hesitated. "But if there *is* an option to have a partner in this, you deserve that. You deserve for someone to have your back. As much as my relationship with Mariah is still a work in progress, parenting is a lot easier because we have each other."

I shook my head. He was losing me. That was nice in theory but not always realistic. "I already explained that it's not an option with Jason." I sighed. "And yes, okay, while I secretly hoped he might change his mind and decide he wanted to be part of this, I respect his decision."

Archie looked into my eyes. "Do you see yourself with him forever?"

I felt a bit like the walls were closing in. "I don't know. But that's the beauty of it. I don't need to know in order to make this decision."

Archie just stared at me, his mouth opening and closing as if deciding whether to say something. Sweat formed on my forehead. I worried he was about to try to talk me out of this.

I cleared my throat. "Did you...want me to log into the cryobank site? You said you'd help me look through the donors, give me your opinion."

Archie ignored my suggestion. "Can I ask you something?"

"Yeah..."

He looked down at the sofa, then back at me. "Did I hurt you?"

"What do you mean?"

"I've never asked you that question. And I want to know if anything I've ever done...or *not* done...has hurt you."

I swallowed. How could I answer this honestly? "There have been times I felt hurt by you, yes. Although I don't think it was ever your intention to hurt me."

He blinked rapidly. "When?"

Feeling my throat close up, I didn't want to admit it. But I also didn't want to lie. Archie had no idea how hard I'd worked to get over him. "When I came out to visit you the summer after your dad died, and you told me we shouldn't continue what we'd started on the island. At that time, I had strong feelings for you, though I'd never admitted them. And I didn't tell you then because you were going through a lot."

His stare was incendiary. "You don't think I knew you had feelings for me? Of course, I did." He paused. "But do you know why I pushed you away, Noelle?"

I shook my head.

"There was no way I was gonna take you down with me. That was a rough time. I needed to be there for my mother. I knew I was stuck in that situation for a very long time. I didn't have a whole lot of choices. But I *could* choose not to hold *you* back. So that's the decision I made—not because of a lack of feelings for you, but because I cared about you too much to drag you down." He closed his eyes a moment. "I never meant to hurt you."

It felt like the room was swaying.

When I didn't say anything, he continued. "Time was never on our side. I know it's too late for me to change the past. Even if you weren't currently with someone, I still don't think I'd be the right man for you. And I would never make a promise to you I couldn't keep."

My head spun. "I'm not sure where you're going with this..."

"It's always been hard for me to figure out where we fit into each other's lives. You're my friend, but you're so much more." He reached for his wine and took a long sip, as if he really needed it to continue. "I want the absolute best for you. And you should be creating a life with some-one who cares about you. Who respects you. Someone who knows how amazing you are. And someone who will have your back and your child's back if, God forbid, any-thing were ever to happen to you. You and I, we don't have big families..."

Now I was *really* confused. "What are you saying, Ar-chie?"

"I'm saying just because you can do this alone doesn't mean you should *have* to. I don't think you should have a baby with an absolute stranger." The room went silent. "I think you should have a baby with me."

*What?* My mouth fell open. The shock was so pro-found that I could hardly form a sentence. "With you..."

"Yes." His eyes burned into mine. "And before you think that I've lost my mind, I've been thinking about this from almost the moment you told me your plans. I know what I'm doing, Noelle. I was never great at anything besides, well...maybe cooking and drawing, before my daughter came along. I might've been a shitty son according to my dad and a shitty husband according to Mariah, but I think I'm a damn good father. I wouldn't mind having another child. Moreover, I would love to have one with you, to share that experience with you." He paused. "I could be as involved—or uninvolved—as you'd want me to be."

I shook my head. "I'm sorry. I'm just...confused. I don't even understand how you think this could logistically work. There are so many reasons it couldn't."

"I actually can't think of one." He shook his head. "Not a single one."

The passion in his eyes was palpable. He seemed so confident and determined. *Is he insane?* "How would this even...happen?" I asked. "What are your expectations here?"

"I'd give a sperm sample. You know, just like your donor would've." Archie's face reddened as he held his palms out. "I should've clarified... I wasn't insinuating that we do it the old-fashioned way. I'm guessing your boyfriend wouldn't go for that."

"But you live in California..."

"I do."

I just looked at him, unable to process.

"Here's what I propose." Archie straightened his posture. "You said most of your work is online these days—writing copy and digital editing?"

"Uh-huh," I said, staring blankly at the wall.

"You could do it anywhere? Would they let you?"

Still in a daze, I muttered, "Probably. I don't know. Maybe."

"What if you came out to Cali for a while? Only temporarily. We could find a fertility doctor out there, try to make it happen. And then whatever you wanted after that would be cool. You could go back to New York or—"

"You make it sound like a business transaction." I finally looked at him again.

"It can be whatever you want it to be."

I stood and paced for a minute. He hadn't thought this through. "Suppose this did happen." I turned to face him. "I conceived your baby. You wouldn't want to live apart from your child. I know you. It would mean me having to relocate. I don't know if I'm ready for that. Not to mention, I have a boyfriend here." I resumed pacing. "So it wouldn't work, Archie. I really appreciate it, but—"

Archie got up and put his hands on my shoulders to stop me from moving. A shiver ran down my spine. "Look at me," he said as he lifted my chin to meet his eyes. "You have my word, Noelle, that I will never pressure you to live anywhere you don't want to live. We could draw up whatever legal papers you need. If you decided to move back to New York, that would be okay. I'll deal. You'd be the primary caregiver. This would be *your* child. But at least he or she would know their dad, even if I lived far away."

Once again, I noticed the intensity in his eyes. Archie was dead serious. Oh my God. *He's serious.* That scared the absolute shit out of me. I took a step back. "This sounds very complicated, as much as you're trying to simplify it. I can't imagine why you would want to do this."

"You can't imagine why I would want to have a child with you? Noelle, you're such an important part of my life. Why *wouldn't* I want to do this for you?"

The emotions pummeling my chest were too much. I both loved and hated him for throwing this curveball. I shook my head. "I'm sorry, Archie. I...can't take you up on this. You're just coming off of a divorce, for Christ's sake. It's not even final yet. Even if you were my only option on Earth, I couldn't do that to you. It's not fair. Please don't be offended by my reaction. I appreciate your offer. But I just...can't."

On top of everything else, having this man's baby would dredge up old feelings I'd worked so hard to overcome.

"Okay." Archie looked down at his feet. "The offer still stands, if you change your mind. But I understand your hesitation, and I respect your decision." He nodded. "No hard feelings, okay?"

I took a few steps toward him. "I will never forget that you wanted to do this for me."

A look of melancholy crossed his face before he scrubbed his hand over it. He'd either regretted offering or was disappointed in my answer.

This was messing me up inside. Deep within my soul, I wanted nothing more than to have Archie Remington's baby. But I wanted *everything* with Archie. That irrational piece of my soul didn't want him to impregnate me because he felt sorry for me. It wanted him to love me. And bearing his baby would kill me if that weren't the case. Because it would only make me love *him* more.

• • •

Two weeks after Archie went back to California, I was still consumed by thoughts of his proposal. I'd shut down Archie's offer in front of him, but it was alive and well in my head, taunting and torturing me.

On a rainy Wednesday afternoon, I was supposed to be going through b-roll for an upcoming piece on mail-order brides, but I couldn't concentrate.

I regretted the way his New York trip had ended. The tone for the rest of Archie's stay had shifted after that Saturday evening. After previously saying he hadn't wanted to waste his precious time with me, the next day he'd suggested we go see a Broadway show after all. I think we'd both needed a distraction from the tension in the air.

When I'd hugged him goodbye at the airport that Monday morning, the lingering regret nearly paralyzed me. I'd lacked the ability to articulate my feelings, but I'd been overcome with appreciation for him and didn't want to let him go.

Since then, I remained conflicted, going through every donor option in the cryobank database again. Not a single one felt right. I was beginning to think maybe this wasn't going to happen for me. I couldn't bite the bullet. I kept waiting for *it*—a feeling of comfort. Of love. Of excitement. That *right* feeling.

As shocking as Archie's proposal had been, beyond logistics, I hadn't really imagined what accepting it might be like. I wouldn't allow myself to visualize it for even a second because I was scared that would make me want it enough to consider it.

Yet for some reason on that rainy Wednesday afternoon, sitting at my desk and staring out at the busy city street, raindrops pelting my window, I closed my eyes and let myself visualize what it would be like to have a baby with Archie.

*Just this once.*

I saw myself pregnant, massaging my belly.

I saw Archie rubbing my back.

I saw Archie holding my hand during the birth.

I saw what I imagined our baby would look like, with Archie's almond-shaped eyes and sun-kissed hair.

I might not have trusted Archie with my heart, but I trusted *him*—as a human, as a father, as a friend. As someone who would never desert me.

Taking Archie up on his offer felt scary. But when I immersed myself in it, it was the only scenario thus far that felt *right*.

After that I couldn't imagine anything else.

• • •

"I have to talk to you about something," I told my boyfriend a few nights later at dinner. My heart pounded, and my palms were sweaty; I couldn't hold it in anymore.

Jason set his fork aside. "You alright?"

"There's been something weighing on me. It's time I told you."

His forehead wrinkled. "Talk to me."

Over the next several minutes, I confessed everything—from Archie's proposal to my doubts about using an anonymous donor.

For the first time probably ever, my cool and confident boyfriend showed a look of true concern. Despite knowing all about Archie's visit, he hadn't seen this coming any more than I had when Archie dropped the bomb.

"I'm gonna be honest with you, Noelle. That would be harder for me to stomach than you getting sperm from a stranger."

"I know. I can absolutely understand why you feel that way."

Jason gnawed at his bottom lip, looking contemplative. "At the same time, I can't in good conscience stop you if it's what you really want. I care about you a great deal. And I'd love to continue to see where things go with us. I don't have the right to keep you from something I can't give you myself."

I let his words sink in. Well, it wasn't that he *couldn't*. It was that he didn't want to. He didn't want to be tied down. That was exactly why I couldn't let him be the deciding factor in this. I had to do what was best for *me*, even if I owed him an explanation first.

"So you would accept this, if I decided to take Archie up on his offer?" My body stiffened as I braced for his answer.

He reached for my hand. "I would." He hesitated. "As long as you can promise me there's nothing more to it with this guy."

"There isn't." I swallowed.

That was a lie, of course. Because despite Archie's good intentions, in my heart there would always be something *more* when it came to him, even if it was one-sided.

That night after Jason left, I picked up the phone, called Archie, and never looked back.

# CHAPTER 22

## Archie

**EVEN AS I** opened the door to let Noelle into my mother's house, it didn't quite feel real.

"Here it is, your new home for a while," I told her.

Noelle had arrived in California last night. After I got her from the airport, I'd brought her to my apartment and cooked her a late dinner. We'd stayed up talking—going over the itinerary of appointments, among other things. I'd insisted on her taking my room while I slept in Clancy's.

So this morning was the first time she was seeing the house she'd be staying in while she was here.

It had worked out well that I still hadn't sold Mom's place. At the moment, it was a dumping ground for all her old things. Unfortunately, Noelle wouldn't be living alone. I'd been letting my mother's friend, Roz, stay here free of charge, aside from utilities. Roz had helped me a lot with Mom over the years. When her landlord had recently sold the house she'd been renting, I'd told her she could live here until I sold the place. But I was glad she wasn't home at the moment so I could show Noelle the house in peace.

Noelle looked around. "Wow...okay."

"It's still pretty cluttered."

"It's got character." She turned to me and smiled. "It's perfect. Truly. It feels like a real home, you know?"

After my father died, my mother and I had sold our old house and downsized, moving into this slightly dated property together. There were a lot of heavy memories here, all the times I'd struggled to take care of her while balancing school and work. Having Noelle's vibrant spirit brighten up the place for a while made me happy. I still couldn't believe she'd changed her mind about my proposition, but from the moment she'd called to tell me she'd had a change of heart—about a month ago—I'd started getting her bedroom ready.

I gestured down the hall. "I'll show you to your room."

I'd put new bedding in my mother's old room and spruced it up.

As Noelle stepped through the doorway, she dropped one of her bags. "Oh my God, Archie. It's so nice in here."

"I might've gotten some help from an eager little girl. She enjoyed picking out the purple bedspread."

"That's so sweet." She ran her hand along the soft comforter. "What have you told Clancy about me?"

"Just that you'll be living out here for a while, and I'm giving you a place to stay. She knows you're an old friend of mine and is excited to meet you. She obviously doesn't remember the first time when she was a baby."

"I can't wait to meet her." Her expression changed. "What have you told Mariah?"

I sure as fuck hadn't told her the truth. I'd be putting that off for as long as possible. Things were good with Mariah right now, and I didn't want to rock the boat until I had to. Our divorce had just been finalized. It had been a fairly quick process, since neither of us contested anything.

"Mariah knows you're moving out here, but I haven't told her our plans, if that's what you mean. I will eventually, though."

Noelle cringed. "How's she going to react?"

"I don't think she's going to be happy about it, and that's why I don't want to tell her yet. It won't change my decision, and I don't want that negative energy looming over us."

Noelle nodded, seeming tense. I wondered if she was having doubts now that she was here, and it was even more real. We weren't wasting time, either, because we had our first appointment with the fertility specialist tomorrow. Noelle had taken her trigger shot yesterday, an injection to stimulate her ovaries, and both of us had already undergone pre-IUI testing. She'd worked with a doctor out in New York initially who kept in communication with the new doctor here.

"Why don't we leave your stuff for now and head out for a bit? I'll show you around the neighborhood. There are some shops and restaurants within walking distance."

She perked up. "I would love that."

The rest of the day was pretty chill. Noelle and I had lunch at a vegan restaurant I'd been wanting to try. Neither of us was vegan, but this place had some awesome veggie bowls on the menu. We also browsed some shops and stayed out until sunset. I hadn't had this much fun since the last time we were together, in New York. It didn't matter what we were doing as long as I got to listen to her infectious laugh. But I tried not to lose touch with reality, constantly reminding myself that she was involved with someone.

When we got back to the apartment, Roz still wasn't home, which seemed unusual. But I again appreciated the privacy since I knew she'd talk our ears off.

I followed Noelle into her new room and smiled as I saw her notice something I'd hung on the wall especially for her. She'd missed it the first time she saw the room.

Noelle pointed. "Oh my God. That painting. It's..."

"Indeed, it is." I smiled.

"How did you get it?"

When Noelle and I had last visited Whaite's Island, she'd admired this painting by a local art dealer on Main Street. It was a view of the beach with the clam shack at the corner, a simple but perfect depiction of one of our favorite places in the world. I'd made a note of it and called the gallery after I got back to California. I'd had it shipped here, but then life got crazy, and I'd never had an opportunity to give it to her in all these years. But I had to believe there was no better time than the present.

"I bought it soon after our last trip there. I'd been holding it for the right time to give it to you."

"What, were you waiting for my fortieth birthday or something?"

Smiling, I shrugged.

"I love it," she said. "Thank you. For this. And for everything."

She didn't have to thank me, though she'd done so multiple times.

"What time do we have to be at the doctor's tomorrow?" I asked.

"Eleven AM." She sat on the bed. "Do you think you'll have any...issue? You know..."

It took me a second to figure out what she was talking about. "I think we're beyond the point of talking in code, Noelle." I took a seat across from her. "Do you mean will I have a problem jerking myself off and coming on cue?"

"Yeah. I would imagine it's a lot of pressure."

"Unfortunately, not for me." I laughed. "I've become quite accustomed to my hand lately. And I'm abstaining for forty-eight hours so it will be...hearty."

Her eyes widened. "Is that what they recommended?"

"Yeah." I chuckled. "It's no biggie. I've survived thus far." I sighed. "You have that look, though."

"What look?" She laughed.

"Like you want to ask me something else."

"It's none of my business, but I'm curious if you've been with anyone since your separation?"

My eyes widened. "Are you asking if I've had sex?"

She nodded.

"Yes," I admitted. "With one person."

Noelle stayed silent, and I took that as my cue to elaborate.

"She's an investor in our restaurant. She lives in London. She was in town for a week once. It turned out we were both in the midst of a separation at the time. This was after Mariah got together with Andy, of course. Anyway, we bonded over our respective situations, and after a few drinks, I ended up at her hotel. It continued over the course of the week she was in town. Then she went back." I shook my head. "It was a dumb decision to get involved with a business partner. It was just sex—protected, of course. I haven't seen her since."

"What was her name?"

"Andrea."

"Sorry for being nosy. I was just curious."

"You can ask me anything you want."

"Okay…" She fell into a daze.

"Are you thinking about tomorrow?" I asked.

"Yeah."

I offered a reassuring smile. "It's gonna be good. Don't worry."

Tomorrow was showtime. Not only would I be giving my first sperm deposit, but shortly after, it would be passed into Noelle using a catheter.

"I'm so happy not to have to do this alone," she said.

I winked. "We're in this together."

• • •

It was a cool morning as we stood outside the medical building, both of us seeming to hesitate before going in. The magnitude of what we were about to do must have started to set in.

I reached my hand out for hers. "You okay?"

She took it. "A little nervous. We can't exactly come back from this, you know?"

I nodded. I couldn't understand why I wasn't more nervous. But this felt right, and that hadn't changed. I was more nervous for *her* than anything, that she might regret it. In any case, I felt like my role in all of this—besides offering up my DNA—was to make her feel comfortable.

I squeezed her hand. "This is what you want, right?"

"Yes," she answered immediately.

"There's no part of me that regrets my decision, Noelle. I want you to know that. And I also want you to know how excited I am."

"Really?"

"Yeah." I smiled.

"I think I needed to hear you say that."

"I know."

She smiled—and it reached her eyes.

I squeezed her hand again before letting go. "Let's do this," I said, leading the way through the revolving door.

There was a short wait after check-in, and then we were brought into one of the examination rooms. A nurse explained the rules surrounding my deposit duty. They'd take some time to wash the sperm sample and process it after we left, and we'd return a couple of hours later for Noelle's IUI procedure.

"So, just so you know..." the nurse said. "She's allowed to go in the room with you, but there's no contact permitted due to contamination concerns."

I looked over at Noelle and smirked. "Damn. I was counting on that."

She blushed. I might have been joking, but my imagination had been running wild with thoughts of Noelle deciding to do this the natural way or *assisting* me in that room. I'd get hard just thinking about it, though I knew it was a fantasy.

"I won't be going in. We're not together," Noelle told the nurse. "We're friends."

*Story of our lives.*

"Oh, I see." The nurse smiled. "How nice. Okay."

She handed me a cup and led me into the room where I was left alone to do the deed.

There were some magazines laid out, along with an old TV/DVD player combo—they still made those?—and some movies. It skeeved me out to think about touching the "accessories," though. There had to be some dried-up spunk residue on them. *Loads* of it. I also had my phone and could've chosen any flavor of porn I wanted.

A white towel hung off the arm of a vinyl chair. But I chose to stand, since that provided a better angle into the cup. I lowered my jeans and took a deep breath as I began to jerk myself off. Closing my eyes, I bent my head back and allowed my mind to go there—to that place it always wanted to lately. To Noelle. And I needed nothing but my imagination. I envisioned her on her knees, looking up at me with her beautiful, wide eyes, so eager as she took my cock in her mouth. This was what I remembered from years ago in the shower—except the woman in my fantasy now was present-day Noelle. Even curvier, even more beautiful than the girl I once knew.

I remembered exactly what her plump lips felt like wrapped around my shaft, the wetness of her tongue, the way she'd breathe when she took me down her throat. I remembered it all like yesterday. In under a minute, I came fast and hard, filling the cup.

After I found my bearings and closed the lid, I opened the door and went in search of the nurse.

"Speedy Gonzalez," she joked.

"That's me." I shrugged.

"You can go on out to the waiting room, or you guys can grab coffee or something and come back in about ninety minutes. It will take at least that long to process your sample. Just don't go too far."

I thanked her and went back out to the waiting room, where I found Noelle reading a magazine. She looked up and spotted me approaching. I flashed her a big, cheesy grin and two thumbs up. She started laughing. A couple of women sitting around her also cracked up. They knew the deal.

"She said we could leave and come back in an hour and a half."

We ended up getting food at a place around the corner. Neither of us had eaten much this morning with all of the anticipation, so it was good to have something in our stomachs. We probably looked like two people having an ordinary meal together. Little did the folks in that brunch joint know we were killing time in the middle of one of the most monumental days of our lives.

When we returned to the doctor's office, they took Noelle right in for her procedure. It killed me to have to stay behind, but she hadn't invited me in, and I had to respect that. It would've been a little awkward, I suppose, to admit that I'd been looking forward to seeing my cum inserted into her vagina.

I sat there, looking up blankly at the television, but I could only think about Noelle, how I should've been in there holding her hand.

It wasn't too long before the nurse came out to the waiting room. "The procedure is done, but she has to lie down for about ten minutes before she can leave. Noelle would like you to wait with her."

I hopped up from my seat and followed the nurse into the room.

Noelle was dressed and lying on the table when I walked in. When she turned to me and smiled, all felt right in the world.

"Are we in business?" I asked once the nurse left.

She chuckled. "I guess we'll see."

I sat down. "Did it hurt?"

She shook her head. "There was a little pinching and cramping, but nothing too bad."

"Pretty sure I had the easier job between the two of us."

"The nurse commented on how fast you finished." Her shoulders shook as she laughed.

"What can I say? I understood the assignment." I winked. "Been practicing for this moment for years."

Her beautiful eyes glowed with joy, the same joy I felt right now. I couldn't imagine doing this with anyone else. Sharing this experience with Noelle was the next best thing to having her as mine. Not to mention, the thought of my sperm inside her right now fucking turned me on.

# CHAPTER 23

## Noelle

**ONCE THE LYING-DOWN** period was over, Archie and I were able to leave the doctor's office.

"Do you have to take it easy for the rest of the day?" he asked as we walked through the parking lot to his car.

"No. I just can't do any rigorous exercising."

He opened the car door for me. "So bungee jumping is out of the question then?"

"Probably."

"Well, there goes my plan for us." He went around and got in on the driver's side. "When do we come back here again?"

"Two weeks."

"You think you'll do a home test before then?"

I shook my head. "They said false positives are common with those because of the hormones they gave me. I don't want false hope, so I'll wait for the actual blood test."

"Oh yeah, that would suck to get a false positive." He still didn't start the car. "Do you have plans for the rest of the afternoon?"

"No, actually. I was just going to go back to the house and organize some stuff."

"Why don't you forget about that? It's a beautiful day. I took all of today off. We should celebrate making it through round one."

Fastening my belt, I relaxed into the seat. "I'm game for whatever, sure."

Archie showed me some more of the town before taking me to see his restaurant, Fontaine's. Fontaine had been Nora's maiden name, and I loved that he'd named it after her. It was cool to meet some of the people Archie worked with, too. Based on some of the looks and nudges he got from coworkers, it seemed likely they'd drawn the wrong conclusion about me.

After, Archie insisted on taking me to some ice cream place he loved.

On the way there, his phone rang. I could tell from his side of the conversation that it was Mariah.

"Everything okay?" I asked when he hung up.

"The hospital asked Mariah if she could pick up an extra shift tonight. She knew I had the day off and asked me to take Clancy." He frowned. "I'm sorry. I have to get over there now so she can leave. We'll have to do a rain check on the ice cream."

I nodded. These types of interruptions probably happened a lot in his life. "No worries."

"Actually... I'll be making dinner tonight for Clancy now. Why don't you come over and meet her? It's just as good a time as any—unless you're not feeling up to it."

Jitters immediately set in, but no way was I going to turn down a chance to meet Archie's daughter. "I still feel great. I'd love to meet her tonight."

"Cool. I'll drop you off at your place now so you can decompress. Then I'll go to Mariah's, pick Clancy up, and come back to get you."

"That sounds perfect." Since I didn't have a car out here, I was reliant on Archie for transportation unless I called a car service.

After he dropped me at his mom's house, I opened the front door to a most unusual sight. A woman with a long, gray braid was sitting in front of a camera on a tripod in the living room. This had to be Roz. I hadn't yet had a chance to meet my roommate because she'd been sleeping in when I left for my appointment this morning.

There were multiple ring lights set up, and Roz was speaking into the camera. I listened to what she was saying...something about hot flashes. I waited until she hit pause to clear my throat and make my presence known.

She turned, raising her hand to her chest in surprise. "Oh goodness gracious! You scared the bejesus out of me." Roz smiled. "You must be the famous Noelle." She gave me a once-over. "No wonder that boy did your room up so nice."

"Nice to meet you, Roz." I looked over at the ring lights. "I didn't realize there was a production going on here."

"Oh! I was just recording a video for my YouTube channel. Menopause Roz. I have fifty-thousand subscribers! Can you believe it? Bunch of broads looking to hear me talk about the change of life."

*This woman is a trip.* "That's so cool."

"It started out as a way to vent my frustrations. I didn't even think anyone was watching, but then the followers kept coming, and I started making money. So I kept going."

"How fantastic!"

She looked me up and down again. "Archie told me you were old friends. He *didn't* tell me you were so beautiful. I can't imagine that he doesn't have an ulterior motive in giving you a place to stay, especially since he's on the market again."

"Oh..." I waved my hand. "He and I had our chance years ago, and life blew it for us."

She tilted her head. "Oh yeah? Very interesting. I'll have to hear more about that. He told me you were just friends. But now, looking at ya, I *know* he's full of shit." She rolled her eyes. "Men usually are."

"We met when we were much younger. The Remingtons were friends of my parents."

"So you met poor Nora back before things got bad, then."

I nodded. "Archie told me you were a very good friend to her and helped him out a lot."

"Well, he's obviously paying me back, letting me stay here and all. Never thought I'd have a roommate, though." She winked.

The fact that she was so pleasant brought me some relief. The last thing I needed in my hormonal state was to be living with someone difficult. Something told me Roz and I would get along just fine.

"I would love to stay and talk, but I have to freshen up," I said. "Archie's coming back with Clancy to get me. We're having dinner over at his place."

"Have you met that little sweetie pie yet?"

"Only briefly when she was a baby."

Roz grinned. "She's a delight. And he's such a good father. If your ovaries aren't already exploding, they will be once you see him with that little girl." She sighed. "Shame things didn't work out between him and her mom, but until lately, I hadn't seen a smile on his face in a very long time. He sure was happy when he came here to tell me you would be moving in."

Hearing that gave me goose bumps, and I had to stop myself from overreacting. I'd been doing that all day. I didn't know if it was the hormone medication swirling around in me or what, but from the moment Archie picked me up this morning, all I'd wanted to do was jump him. I found myself wishing we were doing this the old-fashioned way, which was completely crazy and inappropriate, given that I had a boyfriend. I shouldn't have had these feelings for Archie. But this was nothing new; I'd always struggled with my attraction to him. That would likely never change.

More than anything, knowing that a part of him was inside me right now made it so much worse. The moment they'd placed that catheter in me today, I'd felt an attachment to Archie like I never had before. This whole thing was dangerous.

I needed to work on compartmentalizing my feelings. Archie had offered to be my sperm donor. That was the end of the story. Once the insemination was successful, I would go back to New York and move on with my life.

Shortly after I changed clothes and washed my face, Archie texted to say he was outside. A rush of adrenaline shot through me. Meeting Clancy was a big deal.

As I approached the car, I could see she was sitting in the backseat. I'd barely opened the passenger-side door when she flashed her cute little teeth.

"Hi, Noelle."

The sound of her sweet voice squeezed my heart. "Hi, Clancy! It's so great to meet you. The last time I saw you, you were just a baby."

"I know. Daddy told me. I don't remember you."

"Well, I remember you, and you were the cutest back then. But you've grown into such a big, beautiful girl now."

"Thank you."

I took in her adorable face for a moment. She had many of Archie's features. Seeing his beautiful eyes duplicated and staring back at me made me so emotional. I hoped *our* baby had his eyes, too.

I hoped our baby looked exactly like him.

*Here I go again.*

Clancy also had the same light brown hair with golden highlights as her father. It even curled the same way as it fell over her eyes.

Archie smiled at me but said nothing, seeming to give me free rein to start a conversation with his kid. I was a fish out of water when it came to children. I wanted so badly to come up with something to say to her, but my mind drew a blank. *What does one talk about with a four-year-old?*

Thankfully, I didn't have to wait too long before she started talking our ears off.

"Daddy..."

"Yes, baby."

"My butt talked in school today."

"Huh?"

"I tooted."

Archie laughed. "Well, that happens."

"My friend asked me if I did, and I said no. Is that lying?"

"Well, it's lying, but it's not the worst kind of lie." He glanced over at me. "Some things aren't anyone's business. That's one of them."

"Do you toot, Noelle?"

Before I could say anything, Archie answered for me. "Yes, she does."

My mouth fell open. "And what would you know about that?"

"You used to run the water for like a half hour so I wouldn't hear you going to the bathroom at our house on Whaite's Island." He hesitated. "But one time, it didn't do the trick."

I covered my face and laughed. "Anyway, everyone toots, Clancy," I offered.

She giggled. It almost seemed silly now that I'd been nervous to meet this little ham.

"Clancy, tell Noelle who you're going to be playing at school."

"Elsa!" she shouted proudly.

"From *Frozen*?" I asked.

"Yup!"

"They're doing a play, and there are going to be two Elsas," Archie explained. "Clancy is one of them."

I turned to face her. "That's amazing, Clancy."

"Unlike me, Clancy has no problem with public speaking and performance." He winked. "I've taught her never to be afraid of such things."

"I'm impressed, Remington."

"What can I say? I learned from the best."

That evening, the three of us had a blast at dinner. Archie made spaghetti, and I took great interest in all of the various ways Clancy could twirl the pasta around her fork or slurp a noodle into her mouth. And Archie never missed a beat—catching her cup before it spilled all over the floor, wiping her face when she got too much sauce on the side of her mouth. Those were the little things. But there were so many bigger things that made him a great dad—his attentiveness to her every word, the way he always put her first. Seeing this firsthand was one of many reasons I was emotional tonight. Before I came out here, I'd had it in my head that I would raise this baby alone. Now that I'd seen what he or she would be missing by not having Archie present in their life, it made me doubt everything.

Later, I waited in the living room and surfed the net on my phone while Archie put Clancy to bed.

After he came out of her room, he walked over to join me on the couch. "Are you tired?"

I put my phone aside. "Not really."

"Then stay for a bit. I'll call you a car whenever you want to go back."

"Okay," I said, unable to stop smiling.

He noticed. "What's that all about?"

"It was really cool to see you in action tonight. You're a great dad."

"I look like I have my shit together, but some days I feel like an imposter—making up shit as I go along."

I smacked his arm. "Stop it."

"I try to make sure she never sees me down or stressed, you know? When you're a parent, you put your child first. Your own wants and needs fade into the background. But I haven't been as happy as I am now in a while. This whole thing—what we're doing, and having one of my best friends here with me—it makes me happy."

I yearned to touch him. "It makes me happy, too."

He leaned his head on the back of the couch and exhaled. "My father would've had all sorts of things to say about this situation. He would've told me I barely had enough time for one kid, that I was irresponsible having a child out of wedlock." Archie turned to me, his beautiful eyes smoldering. "But it feels right. And that's what matters to me."

I felt a little choked up. "I'm glad you still feel that way."

He smiled. "This is it for me. I don't plan on getting married again—not gonna make the same mistake twice. But becoming a dad again? That's something I wanted pretty much from the moment my daughter was born. And what better way to experience another child than to have one with you? This is a win-win situation."

"That's the first time I've heard you say you'd thought about having another child before this."

"Don't get me wrong. It wouldn't be happening *now* if it wasn't with you... But no, you're not the only one who wants this, Noelle. Not by a long shot."

His words washed over me like a warm bath. "Today was pretty amazing, the whole experience—as nerve-wracking as it was," I said.

"Sitting in that waiting area while I knew what was happening in the other room wasn't anything I'll ever forget."

"Did it freak you out a little?" I asked.

"No." He shook his head. "I was kind of in awe."

"Do you think Clancy will be okay with this?"

He thought for a moment. "She'll be very surprised, and it will take some explaining for sure. But she's alluded to wanting a sibling in the past—even after she knew Mariah and I were splitting. So that's encouraging. Honestly, though, I don't have a clue how she'll react."

I nodded. "If this first round of IUI didn't work out, what would you think about coming into the room with me next time?"

His mouth curved into a smile. "I thought you'd never ask. I would love that. I wished I was in there with you this time, but I wasn't sure how you felt."

"Now that I know what it's like, I think you should be in there. I was sorry you weren't."

"Thank you. Next time we'll do it differently—if there is a next time."

"Oh! They showed me the vial of your sperm so I could check the label to make sure it was the right name."

He snorted. "Were you like, 'Why the fuck are you showing me this?'"

"I just laughed and confirmed it was correct."

He arched a brow. "Did it look...presentable?"

"Yes." I chuckled.

"Good to know. I would hate for it to embarrass me when I couldn't be there to defend myself."

I cracked up. That felt so good after a long day. "Thank you for the laugh," I said after a moment, wiping my eyes. "Thank you for everything."

"Of course, beautiful. Thank you for letting me go on this adventure with you."

# CHAPTER 24

## Archie

**I HADN'T BEEN** that nervous the first time we came to the fertility clinic, but this visit was a different story. Noelle and I were currently waiting—anxiously—to be called in to find out whether our first IUI attempt had resulted in a pregnancy. She'd given her blood sample a couple of days ago, and the office required you to come in for the results.

Over the past two weeks, Noelle had seemed to find her groove working from home in the office space I'd set up in the corner of her room. We hadn't gotten to hang out as much as I'd hoped, though. Clancy had been sick, so I'd spent more time than usual hanging out at Mariah's. Not to mention, the restaurant had been booked solid lately. On a couple of nights, I'd dropped off food from Fontaine's for Noelle and Roz, who'd become fast friends, but I hadn't had much time to stay and chat.

I looked up when a nurse finally called us into the doctor's office. We followed her to a room down the hall. And then it was more waiting. *Why do they do that?* They make you wait in one area, then call you into another room to wait again—even longer.

I reached for Noelle's hand when I noticed her legs bouncing. Even though I was nervous, too, I was fighting not to show it.

The door suddenly opened, and we straightened in our seats.

Dr. Burns came right out with it. "Hi, Noelle." He took a seat and opened his laptop. "So, your test is negative. There's no pregnancy at this time."

*Fuck.*

*Fuck. Fuck. Fuck.*

My heart broke into a thousand pieces.

Noelle nodded, and I squeezed her hand.

"This is certainly not unusual. In fact, it's not all that common to conceive the very first time. Each cycle has anywhere from a ten to twenty-percent success rate."

Despite his assurance, I felt like a fucking failure. "You okay?" I whispered.

"Yeah." She forced a smile. "It is what it is, right?"

"The more attempts, the more likely it is to happen," the doctor said as he typed something into the chart. "So we do have you down for another cycle. We'll get your appointments squared away on the way out." He looked back up at us. "I understand that the two of you are not *together*, correct?"

"That's right," she said. "We're friends."

Dr. Burns nodded. "I tell my married clients that it never hurts to supplement with regular intercourse to maximize the opportunity the window of ovulation presents. But of course, I understand that's not an option for you at this time. If anything...changes, that's one of the things to keep in mind."

*Tell me something I don't already know, Captain Obvious.*

Noelle nodded again, her cheeks turning pink.

Just like that, the doctor excused himself, and our appointment was over. It felt almost wrong that we had to leave so fast after getting that kind of shitty news. They needed to have a room with fucking candy and alcohol or some shit where they could put people like us to decompress first.

Even worse, I had to work this afternoon and couldn't spend the day with Noelle. I would've loved to take her mind off this disappointment.

After we confirmed our next appointments at the front desk, we stood facing each other outside the building.

I pulled her into a hug and held her close. "I'm sorry."

She spoke into my chest. "It's okay. Truly. This was to be expected. That's why we have another appointment."

We'd agreed to three tries. If she had to move on to IVF—something we hadn't discussed—that would be financially tough. IUI was much more affordable.

I took a step back. "What are your plans today?"

"I have to finish writing a script that's due by the end of the week. Ironically, it's a story on quintuplets."

"Of course." I sighed. "I wish I had the night off to hang out with you, even if you were working. I could've made you dinner." Then I got a bright idea. "Would you want to do your work at the restaurant tonight? I could set you up in a corner with WiFi."

She rubbed her arms. "I'm okay being alone, Archie."

"Maybe *I'm* not." I grinned.

She smiled. "If you want me to come to the restaurant, I will." She tugged on my shirt. "But you have to make me that artichoke appetizer you told me about."

"You got it."

After stopping at the house to pick up her laptop, we drove straight to Fontaine's.

Once I got her settled at a table, I granted her wish for maple-glazed artichokes.

I set the plate before her with a smile and promised to come back with another appetizer shortly. It made me feel good to offer her a distraction tonight. She had to feel as let down as I did.

The second appetizer I brought out was calamari, followed by an entrée of eggplant parmesan. Whenever I had a free moment, I'd peek out from the kitchen to watch Noelle enjoying the food I'd prepared.

When I finally brought her a piece of chocolate cake, her eyes widened.

She wiped the corner of her mouth. "Are you trying to kill me?"

I sat across from her and leaned my arms against the table. "No, I'm just trying to make you happy, and the only way I know how to do that is with food."

She took a bite. "That's not true. There are many ways you make me happy." She smiled. "This reminds me of the last time I ate chocolate cake with you."

"That was a hot mess express, wasn't it? I still have the drawing of you from that night."

"Thank you for this," she said with her mouth full. "It did help not to be alone today, and all the special attention was very sweet."

"It's the least I could do." I leaned my head into my hands. "Can I be honest, though?"

"Sure..."

"I feel like the result was somehow my fault."

Noelle shook her head. "You heard what the doctor said. The best chance we had was twenty percent. That's not very much. Besides, if either one of us failed, it was me, Archie."

I looked up into her eyes. "Why do you say that?"

"Because your sperm was tested, and it came out perfectly viable. I'm the one with the issue."

Inwardly, I cringed. It was dumb of me to blame myself because that only prompted her to do the same.

"You know what? It doesn't matter. It's going to happen. I mean, let's face it, if it'd happened on the first shot, I would've been shocked."

"I agree." She nodded. "I was hopeful, but not optimistic."

I had to get back to the kitchen, but when my shift finally ended about an hour later, I brought over two espressos and joined her again at the table. We sat talking until they had to lock the doors.

I drove her home, and we lingered in the car once I parked in the driveway.

"You know what I wish?" I said, looking at the house.

"What?"

"That my mother were here and could understand what we're doing. I think it would make her so happy. She always loved you."

Noelle reached for my hand and offered a sympathetic smile. "That would've been really cool."

"I mean, I talk to her a lot. I've told her everything. Hopefully she can hear me, wherever she is."

"Yeah," she whispered.

"I know we agreed not to tell anyone," I said. "But have you considered telling your parents what's going on?"

She shook her head. "I'm not sure they would be receptive to any of this. I'll only tell them after the fact, if it happens."

"That surprises me. I always thought your parents were supportive no matter what."

"They are in some ways, but they have very traditional values when it comes to this kind of thing. I didn't want their take on the situation. I love them, but sometimes you have to block certain opinions out when something matters to you."

"Pretty sure they're gonna freak when they find out I'm the dad."

"Why?"

"I don't know. I just imagine them being pissed at me or something." I chuckled.

"They won't be any more pissed at you than any other person I could've chosen. I think they'll just wish I'd waited for the right man."

That felt like a punch to the gut, even if it made sense. "Well, I certainly hope they're not disappointed when they find out, because it *is* going to happen, Noelle. I promise it will."

I instantly regretted making a promise I might not be able to keep, but part of my job was to remain optimistic for her.

Noelle's phone buzzed, and she looked down.

"Is that Jason?"

"Yeah." She declined the call. "I'll call him back when I get inside."

That was a rude awakening about the reality of this situation—she belonged to someone else. I'd been conveniently putting that out of my mind.

"I'd better go," she said. "Thank you again for tonight."

"Anytime."

I wanted to hug her goodbye, but I refrained, instead keeping my hands firmly on the steering wheel. This day had been a lot. If I hugged her right now, I wouldn't want to let go.

• • •

We were one week away from our next IUI appointment, and Noelle had been taking the usual preparatory hormones. It was a Saturday, and I wanted to check on her before I had to get to work. After spending the morning with Clancy, I decided to go by Mom's old house on my way to the restaurant.

The first mistake I made was popping over unannounced. *Always call first.*

When she opened the door, there was a man standing in the living room behind her. He was talking to Roz. It had to be Jason.

*Her fucking boyfriend is here?* Adrenaline pumped through me.

Noelle looked briefly back at him. "Archie, I didn't know you were stopping by."

"What's going on?" My eyes darted to the guy as I entered the house.

Noelle let out a shaky breath. "Jason surprised me with a visit."

Before I had a chance to introduce myself, he walked over and held out his hand. "You must be Archie."

"I am."

We shook. It was as firm as a handshake could get. I had no idea what I was supposed to say to the guy. It was as if jealousy had shut down my voice box. Then when I did finally manage to speak, I got diarrhea of the mouth.

"Well, this is awkward," I blurted.

Jason's fake smile faded. "I suppose it is, a little. But it's good to finally meet you."

It was clear who the mature one in this situation was.

Roz was sitting on the couch, listening in. I needed to be careful since Noelle hadn't told her about our baby-making plans—at least I didn't think so. This must have been quite a show.

"I was just dropping by to see how the sink was working," I told Noelle. "You mentioned the other day that it was clogging."

Noelle seemed confused. Probably because she'd already told me the problem had been resolved. She squinted a little. "It's working just fine."

"Good." I exhaled. "What are you guys up to?"

"Jason just arrived about an hour ago. So we were gonna make some dinner here. I figured tomorrow I'd show him around."

"I'm only here until Monday," Jason added.

"Ah." I nodded.

Now I was down to only grunting monosyllabically.

"Why don't you join us for a drink?" he said.

"Actually, I'm on my way to work. My shift at the restaurant starts soon." If this were anyone else, I might've invited them to dinner there tonight. But no, thanks. "Anyway... Enjoy your evening," I managed to say.

"Again, it was nice meeting you," Jason said. "Long overdue."

*Bullshit.* He had to have despised me deep down. If he didn't, there was something fucking wrong with him.

"You guys have a good night." My eyes lingered on Noelle's.

Despite the somewhat apologetic look on her face, I doubted she understood the magnitude of my feelings. Especially since I don't think I'd understood them until this moment.

Once I got to work, I found myself completely discombobulated. It wasn't like I hadn't known she had a boyfriend, but seeing him in the flesh had gotten to me. And I knew exactly why.

*I need to talk to her.*

After nearly chopping off my finger while dicing garlic, I turned to my sous chef.

"I might need you to cover for me for about an hour."

He wiped his hands on a towel. "Everything okay?"

"There's a bit of a family emergency," I lied. "Nothing too terrible, but I might need to handle it."

"Whatever you need," he said, looking concerned.

I pulled out my phone and sent her a text.

**Archie: I know you're with Jason, but there's something important I need to talk to you about. I don't think it can wait. Is there a way you could make up a story and meet me for like a half hour? I can come to someplace nearby to pick you up.**

The dots moved around as she typed.

**Noelle: You're scaring me. What's wrong?**

**Archie: It's nothing bad, just something that can't wait. And I don't want to have the conversation over text.**

**Noelle: I suppose I could tell Jason I need to run to the store for something. He has a rental car, so I can take that.**

**Archie: That would be great. I'm at the restaurant right now. Just tell me where to meet you.**

She texted a few minutes later, asking to meet at Tim's Coffee, which was right in the middle of our two locations.

I'd already picked a seat in the corner when Noelle walked through the door. My blood was pumping as I readied to explain myself. I'd probably blown this completely out of proportion. But I needed to talk to her if I was going to function at work tonight.

Fear filled her eyes as she sat down. "Archie, what's wrong?"

I bounced my legs. "Where did you tell him you went?"

"To the drugstore, so I don't have all that much time. He's cooking dinner for me and Roz. What's going on?"

"I'm sorry if I scared you." I took a deep breath. "This might come across as inappropriate, but it's eating at me."

"What is it?"

"Have you slept with him?"

She moved back suddenly. "No. He just got here this afternoon."

*Here it comes.* "I don't think I can handle it if you do." I tapped my fingers against the wooden table. "I know he's your boyfriend. It's not exactly fair of me to expect that you wouldn't sleep with him, but I can't handle that as long as we're doing this. It would complicate things and maybe create doubt if you got pregnant—vasectomies aren't foolproof." I paused. "And I want you to know I won't be sleeping with anyone either, while you're out here." I looked down at the table for a moment, trying to calm myself. "I just don't want to compete with someone else in this process. I panicked when I saw him because I realized I'd never made my feelings known to you."

She blinked. "Just to be clear, so I fully understand... If I were to sleep with him, you wouldn't want to continue this."

My stomach was in knots. "That's correct."

Noelle nodded. "I hadn't had time to ponder what I would do when he came to visit. I wasn't expecting it so soon." She reached for my hand. "But, Archie, I understand where you're coming from. If something did happen between him and me, and then I became pregnant, there would always be that little bit of doubt. I know you're one-hundred percent all in, so I owe you that assurance." She exhaled. "I will not sleep with him while you and I are doing IUI. You have my word."

A boulder lifted from my chest, even as I felt like a piece-of-shit manipulator. "Thank you."

She got up from her seat. "I'd better go before he wonders what's going on. I also have to stop at the drugstore to actually buy some things so I don't go back empty-handed." Our eyes locked. "I'll call you after he leaves, okay?"

I stood. "Yeah. Talk to you then."

After she exited the café, I sat back down at the table for a bit. The relief I'd experienced just moments ago was quickly waning. My issues with Jason went far deeper than not wanting her to sleep with him. I now knew I didn't want her with him at all. I wanted her with *me*.

But I didn't quite know what was best for *her*.

# CHAPTER 25

## Noelle

**THINGS HAD BEEN** tense between Jason and me this past weekend. I'd explained to him why I thought it best that we not sleep together until I was back in New York. He wasn't thrilled, but he seemed to at least try to understand why that could complicate things. What I'd neglected to mention was that *Archie* had anything to do with my request.

On Monday morning, we had an hour to go before Jason would drive his rental car back to the airport. We were having coffee together in the kitchen. It had been tricky to have private conversations here because Roz was always around. Thankfully she'd left this morning for an appointment.

Under the table, Jason reached his legs out to lock with mine. "I've missed you more than I anticipated. I came to California because I need you to know I'm still here, even if I'm across the continent." Steam billowed from his mug as he took a sip. "It's clear from the vibe Archie gave that he's not comfortable around me. I have to wonder if there's something to that." He looked up at me. "You told me there was nothing more than friendship between you two, which, again, is the only reason I went for this. My understanding was that you'd get pregnant, come home, and our relationship would take up where it left off. I don't think you're lying to me, but I do think..." His eyes bore into mine. "If you truly believe what you said about him not having an ulterior motive, you might be blind to his feelings."

The pastry I'd eaten turned in my stomach. I agreed that Archie's reaction to Jason had been surprising, but he just wanted everything to go smoothly with our process, didn't he? If Archie wanted more with me, certainly he'd tell me...

"Archie hasn't indicated that he has feelings for me," I told him.

"Noelle, how could anyone *not* have feelings for you? You're gorgeous...kindhearted. You're crazy if you think he doesn't want you."

My cheeks burned. "Well, if you sensed something from him, that's news to me. My plans haven't changed. He and I have obviously bonded through this experience. That's unavoidable. But he's still just my good friend. And I'm still coming back."

"I hope so." He stared down into his mug. "I like to think of myself as a strong person, you know? But this situation is testing me. I feel like I'm slowly losing you, but then again, I'm not sure I even deserve you. Time will tell if we can withstand this. I *do* hope you're coming back to New York."

The hormones must have been catching up with me because I was about to cry. I wanted to tell him we wouldn't have been in this situation if he'd wanted a baby with me. I wanted to tell him that even if he was right about Archie, it wouldn't go anywhere. I couldn't trust Archie with my heart like that. I'd been burned too many times in the past. I'd watched him marry someone else, for God's sake. Quite frankly, I wasn't sure I could trust *either* of them with my heart.

But instead of unleashing all that, my feelings stayed safely tucked inside. "You coming here to surprise me meant a lot." I smiled.

"Even if my life gets hectic, you're still my priority." He reached across the table for my hand. "I want to come back again when I get home from the conference."

Jason would be at a media conference in Europe for two weeks. I nodded, but anything could happen in two weeks. My entire life could change in that time.

• • •

Archie and I had just gotten back from killing time in the middle of our second IUI appointment. We'd eaten at the same diner as last time. We'd now unofficially dubbed it "IUI and Eggs."

The stakes felt so much higher today.

When they called us into the insemination room, Archie seemed more nervous than I was, tapping his hand against his leg as he sat next to where I lay on the table.

A doctor I hadn't met before entered the room.

"Hello, I'm Dr. Sears. Dr. Burns is on vacation, so I'll be handling your procedure today."

"Nice to meet you," I said.

He looked down at a printout. "We have thirteen-point-five million motile sperm, which is a great number, even better than last time. Anything over nine million is a good result. The motility percentage is sixty, which is excellent. They're moving well."

Archie's face lit up. It was quite adorable.

"You've got some Michael Phelps swimmers in there," the doctor said with a wink. He held the tube of sperm out to Archie. "Just confirm this is you."

"That's me." He looked over at me and laughed.

Archie watched intently as the doctor transferred the sperm into the catheter. I could only imagine how strange it must be to look at his own sperm being manipulated in such a way. He reached for my hand as I slipped my legs into the stirrups. Like last time, it was pretty quick and almost painless, aside from some brief discomfort.

When the doctor took off his gloves, Archie said, "That's it?"

"That's it." The doctor smiled. "You're gonna want to have intercourse later today to get as many swimmers in there as possible."

*Um...*

This doctor didn't know our situation. He'd never met us before today. Archie and I just looked at each other. There were no words necessary.

After the appointment, we went back to his place to have coffee. Today was Archie's day off from the restaurant, and he had an hour to kill before picking Clancy up from school.

I took a sip of the hazelnut blend he'd made for me. "If this round works, it's going to be because of your super sperm. And to think at one point you were led to believe you'd be infertile."

"I got really lucky. I know that." Archie stirred his coffee. "As much as I love my daughter, I was so fucking scared before she was born." He rolled his eyes. "Well, you remember my panic attack on Whaite's Island." He sighed. "This experience is a lot different. My head is on straight. I'm excited, not scared."

"I never thought about how different this might be, compared to the first time for you."

"Yeah. I mean, I was in shock most of Mariah's pregnancy. I couldn't really appreciate it. With this, I'm appreciating and enjoying every single moment, even if the desired result hasn't happened for us yet."

I narrowed my eyes. "Speaking of all of the moments in this process... What's the room like? I never asked you."

"The spunk room, you mean?"

"Yeah." I chuckled.

"It's plain. Less is more, I guess, under those circumstances—one vinyl chair, an old-ass TV-DVD player combo, and some magazines."

"What did you choose?"

He looked away for a moment. "I don't use anything."

My eyes widened. "You didn't need anything?"

"Nope."

"Wow." I leaned back and crossed my arms. "I can't imagine that. I mean, it's one thing if you're home and relaxed in your shower or something. But when people are waiting? That would make me nervous and unable to perform." I felt my face heat. "What do you...think about?"
*What the hell? Is this the hormones talking?*

Archie's face reddened, which was odd. He was normally up for any topic of conversation.

"Not sure you want to know," he said.

"I can handle it."

"I don't know about that."

I shook my head. "You know what... It's none of my business. I—"

"I think about you."

I froze. "About me?" I swallowed.

He ran his thumb along his mug. "Does that surprise you?"

"Yeah, actually, it does."

"It shouldn't," he said, holding my eyes.

"I didn't think you thought of me like that anymore." My nipples hardened.

"You don't think I'm attracted to you?"

My face felt flushed. "I don't understand why you would choose to think about me, when you could think about...anyone."

His brow lifted. "Is that a question?"

"Yeah," I whispered. "I guess it is."

He continued to look me in the eyes. "This process—as much as it might seem procedural in some ways—is very erotic to me. I can't help thinking of you when I'm in there, knowing that what comes out of me is going to end up inside of you. That turns me on."

My mouth fell open as I struggled to formulate a response. That was just about the hottest thing I'd ever heard. I felt it between my legs. I cleared my throat. "Wow. Okay."

He took a sip of his coffee. "Now if you want to call the perv police, I'll understand."

"No." I laughed. "I get it." *Because I'm turned on by the idea of having part of you inside me, too.*

"Fantasizing about you isn't new," he added. "You've been forbidden to me for so long for one reason or another. I've thought about you a lot over the years." He exhaled. "I don't mean to be disrespectful. I know you have a boyfriend. I'm not telling you this to seduce you or anything, either. I just want you to know how beautiful you are, because sometimes I think you doubt that."

I felt ready to collapse. "I don't know what to say."

"You don't have to say anything. I just wanted to be honest." His mouth spread into a smile. "Are you sorry you asked?"

"No," I answered. "I think it's kind of sweet, in a weird way."

"Just to clarify, there's nothing particularly sweet about the thoughts I have in that moment."

Heat raced through me again. "I figured." I managed a laugh. "I feel connected to you, too, in this process."

"It's a little scary how connected I've been feeling lately," he muttered.

"Scared?" I asked. "Are you having doubts about moving forward after this one?"

He shook his head. "No. Not at all. But the lines are blurring more than I thought they would. I'm more emotionally invested. You probably figured that out based on my reaction when Jason was here—how badly I freaked out."

I nodded. "*He* picked up on it, too."

Archie's jaw tightened. "I'm not sorry if I made him uncomfortable. If he didn't want you to turn to me, he should've offered to be the one." He paused. "But I have to say, I'm damn glad he didn't." He glanced over at the clock and jumped. "Shit. I lost track of time. I have to go pick up Clancy. You want to come with me, or should I drop you back home on the way?"

I needed a break—or maybe a cold shower. "I should go home. I'm a bit behind on work." *And I desperately need to bring myself to orgasm after this conversation.*

I busied myself with finding my purse, and Archie dashed around a moment before he led me out to the car.

"Do you mind if I tell Roz what we're really doing?" I asked as Archie settled into the driver's seat.

He glanced over at me as he pulled into traffic. "If that's what you want. You'd said you didn't want anyone to know."

"It's hard lying to her about why I'm here. It'd be nice to have someone to talk to about what's happening in my life."

"It's your choice." He sighed. "I do think we can trust her. She's been like a second mother to me since Mom died."

I nodded. "Thank you."

• • •

That evening, I sat down at the kitchen table and explained everything to my roommate. She was shocked at how much I'd been keeping from her.

"That boyfriend of yours deserves a fat reward for putting up with this."

"It's a tough situation for sure," I agreed.

"Don't get me wrong, he's a catch. Jason is a good-looking man, though quite frankly, he seems closer to my age than yours. I got the impression he does very well for himself, too. But I have to ask... What are you doing with someone who can't give you everything you want?"

There wasn't a simple answer. I tried to explain. "It's not that he *can't*. It's more his choice. That's a bit of an issue I have with Jason. But, in general, I'm with him because it's always felt safe. There are some good things about being with someone who can't break your heart because..." My words trailed off.

"Because your heart belongs to someone else," Roz finished.

I said nothing. I probably didn't have to.

She slapped her hand on the table. "This is one juicy story—better than any Turkish drama I might turn on in the middle of the day with my lunch."

"Happy to be your entertainment."

She shook her head. "You're secretly in love with the man who wants to give you everything you've ever wanted. Think about that."

"Wants to give me everything *except*...himself," I corrected.

"And you won't tell him how you've felt all this time?"

"He said he doesn't want to get married again. So he's not in a place to be what I need."

"But how do you know he wouldn't make an exception for you? He's basing what he says on the fact that he thinks he can't have you." She tilted her head. "What if Jason wasn't in the way? Maybe Archie would feel differently—less likely to need to protect his *own* heart."

My body tightened in an attempt to shove away the false hope. "I know he cares about me, Roz. But there's always this fear that he's going to shatter my heart. The thing is, as much as he inadvertently hurt me by not choosing me...Archie is still the best thing in my life. I think he would tell you I'm just as special to him. That's precisely why he won't go there with me. He won't take that step. Archie has always used me as sort of a crutch. He assumes I'll be there. He values me as a friend and a sounding board, even if there's some attraction there." I looked away. "I'm the one who's been in love with him all this time."

She rolled her eyes. "You don't offer to father a baby for a woman you don't love. Maybe it happens from time to time with truly platonic people. But your history with Archie, my dear, is far from platonic. He is in no place in his life right now to be having another baby. He's got his hands full. He wouldn't be doing this *unless* he loved you—whether he knows it or not. Maybe he doesn't realize it yet." She sipped her tea. "But I do."

I willed my heart to slow down. "Well, Roz, it's nice that you feel that way, but unless that sentiment is coming from him, I have to take it with a grain of salt."

She offered a sympathetic smile. "I get that, honey. But if you do dump that old sugar daddy, Jason, can you send him my way? Menopause Roz hasn't had action in a long time." She winked. "Nobody's gotta worry about impregnating *me*."

I cracked up. Laughter was truly medicine.

# CHAPTER 26

## Archie

**I'D BEEN A** jumble of nerves since I woke up this morning. For weeks now I'd been both waiting for and dreading today.

I was supposed to pick Noelle up at 1 PM so we could go in and get the results of the pregnancy test after our second IUI attempt. But just as I was getting ready to leave, Clancy's school called.

"Hello?" I answered.

"Mr. Remington?"

"Yes."

"Clancy's not feeling well, and unfortunately, she's been throwing up this afternoon. It's happened twice. We need you to come pick her up."

"Shit," I muttered.

"Is that going to be a problem?"

I scratched my head. "Uh, no. I'm sorry. I was just leaving for an important appointment this afternoon, and I wasn't expecting this." I shook my head. "No worries, though. That's not your problem. I'll come get her."

"We appreciate that."

Mariah was in the middle of a shift at the hospital, so that left me no choice. Reluctantly, I dialed Noelle.

"Hey, what's up?"

"Hi...listen, I have some crappy news. Clancy is sick at school, and they want me to come get her right now. She's throwing up. I don't think I'm going to be able to take you to the appointment."

"Oh..." She paused. "Okay. Well, gosh, what can you do, right? No worries. I'll call an Uber and get myself over there."

I let out a long breath into the phone. "I really wish I could come with you."

"There are some things we can't control. Please don't worry about it. I'll be fine."

"Are you sure?"

"Yes, I'm positive."

"I feel like a shitty partner in this right now."

"Archie, go get your daughter and don't worry about it. And whatever you do, don't bring that stomach bug near me." She laughed.

"Yeah, that's another thing. Probably means I won't be able to see you for at least a couple of days until I can figure out what's going on with her. Hopefully, it'll be a quick virus. Sometimes they go away within twenty-four hours. Maybe we'll get lucky."

"Yeah, I hope so."

Tugging on my hair, I closed my eyes. "Listen, call me as soon as you know, okay? I'll be waiting by the phone."

"Of course. You know I will."

After we hung up, I hit the road to collect Clancy. After I'd signed her out, the nurse brought her to me. My poor girl's face was all red, and she was wearing a different outfit than she'd had on this morning when I dropped her off. The shirt looked three sizes too big.

I knelt. "Baby, are you okay?"

She shook her head no but said nothing. It was unlike Clancy not to verbalize a response. She really was feeling like crap. I had to get her home.

"Thanks again," I told the nurse before taking Clancy to the car, praying she would make it until we got back to the house.

Once we were home, I put her in the tub and started a bubble bath. Of course, right in the middle of it, she threw up again, so I had to drain the tub and start over. *What a clusterfuck.*

My heart was going a mile a minute between worrying about my daughter and wondering what was happening with Noelle at that appointment. The clock showed one thirty. Unless they were running late, she probably would've been seen by now.

I washed the vomit out of my daughter's hair and wrapped her in a towel. She looked so miserable. I drained the tub again, got Clancy dressed, and put her in bed with a bottle of Gatorade on the table next to her.

"You want me to read you a story?" I asked, smoothing her hair.

"No, Daddy. I just want to lie down and watch TV."

I nodded. "Okay, baby. Let me know if you need anything. I have some chicken broth. I can heat it up if you get hungry."

She nodded, so I left her alone for a bit, still peeking in at her through the open door. She looked so vulnerable lying there.

I realized my own stomach was a little unsettled, mainly because I still hadn't heard from Noelle. Rather than pace and stress myself out even more, I gave Mariah a quick call to update her on Clancy. Just as we were finishing, another call came through. My heart leapt when I realized it was Noelle.

I said goodbye to Mariah and switched over to answer. "Hey."

"Hi... So, it was negative."

I let out my breath in one long exhale. My heart had fallen to my stomach. I paced. "Are you okay? I mean, that's probably the dumbest question ever."

"I am okay. After the first time, I sort of braced myself to expect this. At least I know what it feels like already, you know?"

"Yeah." I sighed. "Unfortunately, I do. I was hoping for better news, but I think I was bracing for it, too."

"It is what it is."

"You say that a lot." I smiled.

"Well, there are no truer words."

"Probably."

"We can't change it, so we have to accept it."

I'd expected to feel bummed, but this was more like devastation. We'd only planned to do three IUI cycles, so only one more left before Noelle reassessed. Sure, we could move on to IVF, but given the cost and stress involved, I didn't know if she'd want to.

"How is Clancy?" she asked.

"Well, she threw up in the tub, so I started over and bathed her again. Now she seems pretty stable. She's in bed watching her favorite show."

"You're such a good dad."

"I'm only doing what I have to."

"I know, but not everyone has a dad like you."

The sadness in her voice was palpable.

"I wish you could come over," I told her. "I could cook for you or something."

"Thanks, but even if Clancy weren't sick, I have quite a bit of work to do this afternoon. I'm late on a deadline. So it's just as well."

"Will you call me later if you want to talk?"

"Yeah, but I don't want to disturb you. You're busy with a sick kid."

"I'm never too busy for you. She's probably going to be in bed most of the afternoon. I'm here if you need me."

"Is there anything you need from the store?" Noelle asked. "I could ask my driver to stop at the market and your place on my way home, since you can't leave."

"Thank you, but I think we're okay. I have saltines and some broth from the last time she got a stomach bug. When they're in school, they're always catching shit."

"I can imagine."

"You'll know what I mean someday. Believe me, you will."

"I hope so, Archie. Thank you again for, you know, giving me this opportunity. It sucks to have a negative test but..." She paused. "Gosh, I was about to say, 'it is what it is.' I *do* use that a lot, don't I?"

"Yep." I chuckled.

After we hung up, a feeling of emptiness followed me the rest of the afternoon. I kept wishing Noelle was here with me, and I worried about having only one more IUI opportunity.

One thing going for me? Clancy didn't vomit again.

• • •

The following day, my luck ran out. The first thing I did when I woke up was hurl into the toilet. And it seemed a virus wouldn't be the only thing that made me want to vomit today.

Clancy was feeling better, but still home with me, when Noelle called.

"Hey. I'm just checking in on you," she said.

"Thank you. Unfortunately, I now have what Clancy does."

"Oh no! Don't say that."

"Yep. I got it. The last couple of times she got sick like this, I somehow dodged it. But not this time."

"Maybe you're stressed or something, so your immune system was weakened."

I *was* stressed, considering all the rumination. But she didn't need to worry about that. "What's up with you today?" I asked.

"I'm calling to let you know I've decided to go to New York for the weekend."

My already-sick stomach turned.

I gulped. "For what?"

"I just need to get away to clear my head for a bit."

"Oh." I yanked at my hair. "Okay, well, I guess we all need that from time to time." I paused. "Why do you need to go to New York to do that, though?"

She sighed. "I need to touch base with Jason. He and I didn't talk much when he was here because Roz was always around. And I think I was mentally exhausted from the hormones or something. I'm feeling a little bit more clear-minded right now, so this is a good opportunity for me to address some things with him."

I kept quiet, hoping she would elaborate. But she didn't.

"Well, um, okay. Do what you need to do. You know I'm here if you need to vent."

"Thank you. I appreciate that."

"When are you leaving?"

"I booked a flight for tomorrow morning. I'll come back on Tuesday."

"Okay. I would offer you a ride to the airport, but I don't want to get you sick."

"Yeah, you need to stay away from me." She chuckled. "Actually, it works out that I'm going to New York since I can't see you anyway, right?"

"That's true," I agreed, massaging my headache.

"I'm sure by Tuesday you'll be better," she said. "Maybe we can get together then, and I'll have a report from the trip."

"Sounds like a plan." I let out a long exhale.

"Are you okay? You sound a bit down. Are you upset that I'm leaving?"

"No," I lied. "It's all good."

It wasn't her leaving that was the problem. I worried *he* was going to dissuade her from coming back.

• • •

That weekend, Clancy had bounced back, and I felt better, too. I'd just finished having breakfast with her when I dropped her at Mariah's house.

Mariah stopped me as I gathered my things to leave. "Is everything okay with Noelle?"

Her question jarred me. Mariah knew Noelle had been staying at my mother's house, but she still didn't know anything else. I got the impression she suspected Noelle and I were dating, though she had yet to ask me about it.

I cleared my throat. "Why do you ask?"

"I stopped by your mother's house the other day to pick up the grill you'd stored in her garage. When I pulled up, Noelle was sitting on the front stairs, talking to someone on the phone and crying."

*Crying?* I blinked, trying to process this. It hadn't been me she was talking to, because she hadn't been crying while we were on the phone.

"That's odd."

Mariah cocked her head. "Could *you* be the cause of her tears?"

"Why would you think that?"

"You know why. I don't need to tell you again that I've always suspected she was more to you than a friend. Now that she's in town and living at your mother's house? There has to be something going on."

*Fuck.* I had not been expecting this conversation and didn't have an appropriate response. I'd vowed not to tell Mariah anything about what Noelle and I were doing. But at the same time, I didn't want to lie. So I kept my response vague.

"Noelle is my friend. We're not dating."

Mariah shook her head. "When you finally admit she's the one you've always wanted to be with, you can let me know, and I'll say, 'I told you so.'" She sighed. "But in any case, your *friend* was upset. You might want to check on her."

My mind was racing. "Did she see you?"

"No. I decided not to bother with the grill right then. I didn't want to have to talk to her. She and I haven't spoken in years, and she wasn't in a good place. I kept on driving and figured I'd pick it up another day."

"You should've just picked it up."

"Well, that didn't seem appealing. You're the one who's made me feel uncomfortable around her because you always put her on a pedestal."

"Are we really going over this again? How many times do I need to tell you she's just a very good friend who I care about a lot? Nothing ever happened with her while you and I were together."

Her eyes bulged. "Oh... So something *did* happen when we *weren't* together?"

*Boy, I really fucked myself with that wording.* "I didn't say that."

"Yeah, you sort of did."

This wasn't any of her business anymore. "Okay, Mariah. Nice conversation, but I'm going to exit it at this point."

"Whatever." She laughed.

As I walked to my car, I wracked my brain to figure out who Noelle could have been talking to. Moreover, why the hell was she crying? She hadn't seemed that upset when she shared the news about the negative test. And she'd been in decent spirits when she told me she was going to New York. But clearly, she was hiding something.

# CHAPTER 27

## Noelle

JASON AND I stood at opposite ends of my apartment. He'd arrived looking morose, which told me he likely sensed what was coming.

I'd decided to come out to New York after a heated phone call where I admitted some of the things I resented about him. I'd been feeling hormonal and depressed after the negative test, and it all just came out. Then I'd felt guilty and realized I needed to have this conversation in person.

His head had been down, but he finally looked up at me. "You said you came home because we need to talk. I have to admit, I've been dreading it."

I walked over and put my hand on his arm. "Jason, I know you care about me. You've demonstrated that in so many ways." My breath trembled. "But I don't think we're the right long-term partners for each other. There's so much I love about you, but we're not at a place where we have the same priorities, want the same things. And that's okay. It's not your fault. You want to travel and not be tied down, and you've earned that. But once I have this baby—and I *will* have this baby—my life will change dramatically."

Jason ground his teeth. "I think you have grossly underestimated my feelings for you, Noelle. If you think trips around the world mean more to me than you..." He shook his head. "I mean, you're standing here telling me all the things you think I want. Have you even asked me, you know, how I actually feel?"

"How *do* you feel?"

"For one, I think you have some unresolved feelings for this man you're purporting is nothing more than your sperm donor. More than anything, I think *that*'s what's influencing this conversation, whether you realize it or not." He looked into my eyes. "You're not even denying it."

I owed him honesty. "No, I'm not denying it. My feelings for Archie are complicated. But they are most certainly *not* what's influencing this conversation. Aside from any feelings I might have for Archie, you and I are not compatible."

"To be clear... You're breaking up with me?" He stared at the ceiling. "You need to just say it and stop this torture."

"I'm saying I need time to be alone and not have a boyfriend, yes. I'm reluctant to tell you I want to totally end things, because I care so much about you. I always will. But it's not fair to string you along. Breaking up is the best thing for both of us right now. I need to focus a hundred percent on me and not worry about what I'm keeping someone else from doing in the process."

He scrubbed his hand over his face. "Would things be different if I had offered to father your baby?"

I had to think about that. The Archie situation would've never come into play, so I suppose things might've been different. But that was a moot point now.

I shrugged. "I couldn't help but read between the lines, Jason. Your decision to have me do this on my own spoke volumes about your commitment to me, whether you meant it to or not. But you have every right to feel the way you do. You've already raised your kids and owe me nothing."

His forehead crinkled. "Once again, you're putting words in my mouth. I *am* committed to you."

"I'm sorry, but I don't see it that way. I feel like you want to have your cake and eat it, too—have fun with me, but not be involved in all aspects of my life. I need more, a true partner. Maybe I should've thought about these things before I got involved with you. But you were very charming...captivating. Moreover, you're a good man. I want what's best for you, and part of this decision is that I don't think *I'm* what's best for you."

Jason looked away. It almost seemed like he was going to cry. That broke my heart, even if it didn't change anything for me. He held his hands up, his eyes glistening. "What am I supposed to say? Breaking up is not what I want. You're right that I've made a decision about not wanting to be a father again. If you can't get past that in terms of what it means about my feelings for you, there's probably nothing I can do to change your mind. But if there's anything I *can* do to change it, please let me know." He fell silent a moment. "Otherwise, I've never been one to beg, Noelle."

We stared at each other.

"I'm sorry it took me so long to come to this conclusion," I said. "But my experience in California has taught me a lot about what I need right now. Even though I could have this baby on my own and be perfectly fine forever, when and if I find the right man, I want him to *want* my child in his life. Because my kid deserves that."

"Okay," he muttered, staring down at the floor.

After a minute, Jason grabbed his keys and headed for the door. "I'm really sorry."

My voice shook. "Me, too, Jason." I wanted to hug him, but that would've only made things worse.

He turned around one last time. "I can't believe this," he said before storming off.

After the door closed behind him, I sat in silence for a time, feeling a mix of relief and sorrow. Something had finally clicked inside me after that last negative pregnancy test. I remembered just wanting someone to hold me; I knew Archie would've been there if he could, and that made me think. My boyfriend was *choosing* not to be a part of my journey, and he was supposed to be the one by my side, not Archie.

Sitting alone in my living room, I couldn't take it anymore. It was still fairly early on the West Coast, so I decided to call Archie and tell him what had happened. I'd spare myself from having to recap everything when I got back to California.

"Hey, Noelle," he answered.

"Hi. Are you working?"

"Actually, no, I'm off tonight. I put in for a switch in my schedule after this past crazy week."

"Do you have time to talk, or are you with Clancy?"

"I'm alone." He paused. "Something's going on with you."

"Why do you say that?"

"The other day, Mariah went by my mom's house to pick up something out of the garage, and she told me she saw you sitting on the front steps with your phone. She said you were crying. It was a couple of days before you left for New York, and I know that wasn't me you were crying to."

"I broke up with Jason," I admitted.

There was a long moment of silence.

"What?" he breathed. "Did you know you were going to do that before you left?"

"Not exactly. I knew we needed to talk, and I told myself I would base my decision on how I felt once he was in front of me, but I suspected it was going to end up this way."

I told Archie what I'd told Jason and explained my reasoning.

"Well, I definitely wasn't expecting this," he said when I finished.

"I know. I have mixed feelings. Obviously, I care about him. He's a good man who always made me feel special. We had a lot of fun together. He just isn't the best partner for me. I feel like I need a break from the stress of worrying about a relationship."

"We all know what we need. We know what we can handle. You don't need anyone or anything in your life that's causing you stress. That's the bottom line."

"I wanted to tell you now because I don't want to have to deal with anything when I get back besides staying healthy and mentally clear for number three."

"Of course." He sighed. "It feels like you've been gone a long time. I guess that's because I didn't have a chance to see you for a bit before you left, either. It seems like forever." He paused. "I was freaking out a little bit, because I thought maybe you weren't coming back, that you were having second thoughts about moving forward."

"No," I assured him.

"I'm really glad you called." He exhaled. "I know it's late there, so you can kick me off the phone, if you want."

"I don't want to get off the phone. I needed to hear your voice." I leaned back into the couch. "And I miss you." I shut my eyes tightly, regretting my choice of words, even if they were the truth.

"I fucking miss you, too, Noelle."

My eyes shot open as my heart fluttered.

"What time do you land tomorrow?" he asked. "Can I pick you up?"

"Late. I think you'll be at work. Don't worry. I'll call a car."

"We should get together on Tuesday, then."

Butterflies swarmed in my stomach, and a new kind of nervousness took hold. I no longer had a barrier keeping me from Archie. That scared the crap out of me because it opened the door to the possibility of rejection—again. I wouldn't survive that. Jason had been my safety net. Now I had none. I'd made the right choice, but tomorrow I was going back to California feeling more vulnerable than before.

• • •

Once I returned to the West Coast, I gave myself some

space from Archie. We didn't get together on Tuesday, as I told him I wasn't feeling great. Wednesday passed without seeing him, too. I needed some time to sort out what I wanted. There was one thing in particular I had to mull over before I addressed it with him.

It was Thursday before I finally made it over to his house, and I insisted on taking an Uber because he had a busy morning getting Clancy off to school. I wanted to be there as soon as he was alone, though, because now that I'd had time to think, this couldn't wait any longer.

When I arrived, his car was parked out front. My pulse sped up as I knocked on the door.

"Perfect timing," Archie said as he moved aside to let me in. "I just got back from dropping her off."

"I would've waited."

"Yeah, but it's starting to rain. Glad you didn't have to."

The tension in the air was thick as we stood across from each other.

He rubbed his hands together. "Did you have coffee yet?"

"I did. I'm good. I had breakfast already. You?"

"I already ate, too." He examined my face for a few seconds. "So...tell me if it's my imagination, but I feel like you've been avoiding me since you came back." He flashed a crooked smile, looking so handsome in a navy V-neck shirt with rolled-up sleeves. A piece of his unruly hair fell over his eyes. For some reason, today he reminded me of the Archie from Whaite's Island. His hair had grown out a bit, almost to the length it was back then.

"It's not your imagination," I admitted.

He ran a hand through his mane, his expression serious. "What's going on, Noelle?"

"It's nothing bad, Archie. I just needed time to think after everything that went down in New York."

He blew out a breath. "Look, one of the things we haven't discussed is what's going to happen after the final attempt. We agreed to three tries of IUI, but should we be talking about next steps? Is that what this is about?"

I exhaled. "Originally my next step was to go back to New York and take a breather if it didn't work out. But really, I need to return to New York for a while no matter the outcome. I have to tend to my neglected apartment. And I do occasionally have to go into the office. I can only go so long without checking in."

Concern crossed his face. "You wouldn't...consider moving out here permanently so we can keep trying?"

That wasn't so simple. "I might be able to talk to the network about a permanent switch to their West Coast bureau, but there's a lot about coming out here permanently that scares me." *You scare me.* I wondered if he could read between the lines.

"Okay..." He nodded. "Maybe we shouldn't overwhelm ourselves with decision-making right now. We don't have to commit to any kind of plan right this second. We can just take this one step at a time and see how you feel at the end of number three."

I nodded. "I think that's probably the only way I can proceed at this point."

"Understood."

Adrenaline coursed through me. This was the hardest part. "I *do* think we should give number three...our all—try everything to conceive."

Archie had been looking at the floor, but now his eyes lifted to mine. "Are you saying what I think you're saying?"

I laughed nervously. "I'm afraid to say it out loud, to be honest."

"I will, then." He moved toward me. "You want us to have sex."

"I don't want you to feel pressured into anything." I fidgeted, growing anxious.

"Are you kidding?" His eyes went wide. "This entire time I've wished we could try the natural way. The fact that it's been off the table has been very frustrating, and the only thing that stopped me from suggesting it was your boyfriend. But now that you don't have one? Fuck." He inched closer. "We *definitely* should."

A mix of relief and arousal washed over me. "The doctor said we should do it the night of the IUI treatment. So maybe we plan for that."

He cleared his throat. "Not before?"

"Well, I was reading up on it, and we're definitely not supposed to do anything for two to three days before or right after the trigger shot."

"But the rest of the time...we can?"

My body buzzed. "I suppose."

"Just tell me when..." He grinned. "Unless you're worried about taking that step?"

"I'm physically ready. Just not sure I'm mentally ready."

He lowered his voice. "You've been *physically* ready?"

I closed my eyes a moment. "This hormonal medication they have me on makes me quite horny. I can hardly sit in a damn seat without squirming half the time."

"Why the hell didn't you tell me?"

"What was I supposed to say? It wasn't like you could've done anything about it."

"I would've figured something out, believe me." He took another step closer, causing my pulse to react. "You're turning red. You were nervous about suggesting this. Is that why you've been hiding from me these past couple of days?"

"Yes," I said.

"Why?"

"I don't want to get attached to you in that way, Archie." There was no other explanation.

He looked down at his feet. "Fair enough."

Archie offered no reassurances that might cause me to take back what I'd just said. Maybe he agreed that I shouldn't fully trust him.

He looked up at me. "Going through this with you has been the most intimate thing I've ever done with anyone. Even though I haven't even touched you, I've *felt* you so strongly every step of the way, Noelle." Archie reached for my hand. "I can understand why you're hesitant, though. We've been through a lot together. You mean the world to me. And I would *never* want to hurt you." He paused and looked at me again. "Maybe you need a little more time to think about it."

*Don't forget who you're dealing with here, Noelle.* Archie had closed the door on a romantic relationship with me years ago. Yet I still loved him. Sleeping with him would undoubtedly make me love him more. That wouldn't end well. Maybe I *did* need to think about it.

"Is it *just* me who needs to think about it?" I asked.

"My body is more than ready," he admitted. "But I'd be lying if I told you I wasn't scared that sex might mess up what we have. Still, I don't think fear should stop us from doing everything we can to give number three the best shot." He paused. "Can I ask you something?"

"Sure."

"Are the hormones making you horny right now?"

I swallowed. "Yes."

"Is it possible your hormones could be making *me* horny, too?"

I let out a much-needed laugh. "I don't think so."

"Well, then it's just *you* doing this to me." His voice was low and gravelly. "You're not the only one going crazy lately. I haven't been able to stop thinking about it, Noelle. I think about fucking you all day. It's been that way for a while now. Sometimes I nearly burn food at work thinking about it."

*Oh my.* His words set my body ablaze.

Archie looked down at my chest. "Are your nipples hard right now because you're turned on?"

"Yes," I breathed.

"Let me get you off," he murmured. "Give you some relief."

My legs felt weak. "I thought you said I should sleep on it."

"Or sleep on *me*. Whatever you want." He smiled. "I'm not actually referring to intercourse right now, though. Just an orgasm."

It didn't take much to convince my needy body. I shrugged. "I mean...if you want."

"I want." His eyes sparkled. "Believe me, I want."

Archie took my hand and led me to his bedroom. He looked down at my fingers, which were trembling. "You're shaking." He lifted my hand to kiss it. "Try to relax. You've been under so much stress. I just want to make you feel good."

Vowing to try to calm down, I fell back onto Archie's bed, bouncing against the mattress.

Archie unzipped my pants and slowly lowered them, along with my panties. The air was cool between my legs as I lay there, feeling vulnerable yet tingling with arousal. It had started to rain, and I could hear the drops pelting the window.

Archie's eyes were hazy as he stared down at me. He looked up for a moment and cracked an impish grin. "Well, this is a sight I never thought I'd get to see again."

My belly shook with laughter. "Life is full of surprises."

"Sure is."

His smile faded, and the next thing I knew he'd inserted two of his fingers inside of me. He slowly pushed them in and out as he massaged my clit with his thumb, all the while looking right at me. The feeling was probably more intense than it should've been, given my long drought. I closed my eyes and became lost in the moment.

"Does that feel good?" he whispered.

Unable to form a coherent response, I bit my bottom lip and nodded.

His breathing quickened, and I could feel the heat of his breath between my legs as he continued to move his fingers in and out of me.

Archie circled his thumb around my clit. "Look at this beautiful, swollen bud. You're gorgeous."

I felt him move back, and I looked up to find him sucking his fingers. The way he closed his eyes as he did it made me throb even harder.

"Do you want my mouth on you, Noelle?"

"Yes," I murmured.

"I want to taste inside of you. Is that okay, too?"

My muscles throbbed. "Yes...yes!"

Archie lowered his face, and I felt the wetness of his mouth as he pressed his tongue into my clit. When he groaned over my flesh, it made me want to come right then and there. I'd forgotten how damn good he was at this.

Archie circled his tongue and spoke over me. "You taste even better than I remembered. Still the best thing I've ever tasted. You are so freaking perfect. God."

I bucked my hips, pressing myself against his mouth.

"That's it, baby. Grind against my face while I fuck you with my tongue."

My vision turned blurry as I reached out to rake my fingers through his gorgeous, thick hair—how I'd longed to touch it. A need like I'd never experienced grew by the second.

*What the hell am I waiting for?* I wanted him inside me so badly right now. Tomorrow wasn't guaranteed. Hadn't I learned anything from our experience in the past? I wanted him in every way—now. In this moment. I wouldn't be any less scared to sleep with him tomorrow. Archie Remington would always scare the shit out of me. But I didn't want to go another day without knowing what it was like to have him.

I pulled on his hair. "Archie..."

"Yes, baby," he mumbled over my clit.

"I don't want to wait. I want to have sex now."

His body froze. Then he slid himself up to face me. His hazy eyes widened. "Are you sure?"

"Yeah... I need you, if you're ready."

His eyes rolled back as he reached for my hand and placed it over his erection, which was straining through his jeans. "Feel how ready I am. I've been ready for twelve goddamn years." He smiled. "And I need to kiss you right now, too. So fucking badly."

"Please," I begged.

Archie took my mouth in his with unexpected force. Our tongues collided, and I immediately tasted myself. What had felt like hunger a moment ago transformed into full-on starvation. As his erection pressed into my abdomen, he swallowed my moans with each movement of his mouth.

He lifted himself to his knees, hovering over me. I swallowed as he unzipped his jeans and lowered them before pushing his boxer briefs down, freeing his swollen cock. It seemed even bigger than I remembered. The tip glistened, causing my mouth to water. Archie worked to remove his pants altogether and then repositioned himself over me. He lifted his shirt, putting his carved muscles on full display.

He stared down at me. "Can I take your shirt off?"

I nodded, hardly remembering I had it on.

He undressed me until we were both naked. Archie lowered himself again to kiss me, pressing his hard chest against my sensitive breasts.

As he lay on top of me, he looked into my eyes. "I always told myself that if you and I ever got to this place, I wouldn't make a fool of myself. I'd try to be calm and collected since it's supposed to be just baby-making, right?" He shook his head. "No. It's not just that, and it never will be." Archie moved a piece of my hair off my face. "You're so freaking beautiful, Noelle. You've always been the woman I compared all others to. I have wanted this from almost the beginning twelve years ago. I was just always scared to hurt you. I still am."

That last part might have been enough to make me hesitate or push back, if I were in any other state. But there was no going back from the level of need that had overtaken my body.

"I can't remember the last time I wanted something so badly," he rasped.

"I can," I confessed. "I was with you."

With that, he took my mouth again and thrust into me. I moaned in pleasure as he let out a guttural sound. Given his size, it probably should've hurt, but I was so wet that he'd entered me with ease.

"You want it slow and steady or hard and fast?"

"Hard." I pulled his hair before sliding my hands down and digging my nails into his muscular back.

He pumped into me with rhythmic force as our bodies rocked together.

"Shit," he groaned in my ear after a moment. "I need to slow down."

*Thrust.*

"I can't wait to fill you with my cum all by my damn self this time."

*Thrust.*

"And I'm gonna do it again and again."

*Thrust.*

"It feels so fucking amazing to be inside of you."

*Thrust.*

"I've dreamed about this. But it's so much better."

*Thrust.*

"I can't wait to get you pregnant."

*Thrust.*

"You're gonna look so beautiful with my baby inside you."

*Thrust.*

His words made it that much harder to contain my orgasm. I couldn't hold out for much longer.

Thankfully, after about a minute, we were on the same page.

"Tell me when you're close. I'm ready to explode," he groaned.

A few seconds later, I let go, allowing my muscles the release they desperately needed as I pulsated around his cock. "I'm coming, Archie."

He let out a deep groan that made my insides explode. I was just coming down from my climax as the warmth of his cum filled me.

Our bodies remained intertwined as the rain fell harder outside. It felt like we were the only two people in existence, an ecstasy I hadn't known for years. He stayed inside of me as he softly kissed my neck.

When he finally pulled out, I faced him. "That was…"

He smiled. "Fucking incredible. That's what it was."

"Yeah." I took a deep breath.

Archie pulled me close and kissed my lips. "Can you stay here with me today?"

"For a while, sure," I said casually, as if Archie Remington hadn't just ruined me for all others.

"I have to pick Clancy up from school at two thirty. But other than that, I'm canceling all other plans to give you more orgasms." He caressed my cheek. "I have to confess something."

I blinked, my heart clenching. "Okay..."

"That whole thing with me not wanting you to sleep with Jason... It wasn't just my fear of you somehow getting pregnant. I was jealous as fuck, Noelle. It hit me like a ton of bricks when I saw him here. While I'm sorry about the rash way I handled that, I'm not sorry you broke up with him. And I'm *certainly* not sorry it meant we got to have this experience today."

I rubbed my thumb over the scruff on his chin. "I'll never regret this, Archie. No matter what happens."

He and I had sex two more times that afternoon, and still I yearned for more. He'd given me everything I wanted physically. My heart, though, still wasn't satisfied because I didn't know where Archie's truly was. Now I was more terrified than ever of losing him.

Later that afternoon, after Archie and I picked up Clancy from school, he dropped me off at his mother's. Despite my fears, I was on cloud nine, still very much drunk off the sex as I entered the house. I closed my eyes, leaning against the door and letting out a long sigh.

"Oh my gosh. You've gone and done it, haven't you?"

I opened my eyes at the sound of Roz's voice.

"What are you talking about?" I asked, attempting to play dumb, though I might as well have had the word SEX stamped on my forehead.

Roz laughed. "I might be dried up at the moment, but it hasn't been that long. I remember what it was like to have that look on my face, and there's only one thing it means."

She knew I'd just broken up with Jason in New York, which made this so much worse.

"Roz, don't judge me. I know that was fast."

"Fast?" She cackled. "I would *hardly* call twelve years fast."

# CHAPTER 28

## Archie

"LIE DOWN AND relax. I'm gonna make you something special," I told Noelle, though I was probably the one who needed to relax.

We'd just arrived back at my place after our third IUI appointment. So much was now up in the air, but I was trying not to let my anxiety ruin the day. Whenever I got nervous, I cooked; that was my therapy.

"What are you making?" Noelle called from the couch.

"It's a surprise." I wriggled my brows. "Although, certainly not as good as the surprise you gave me today."

Today's appointment had been so much different than the last. For one, Noelle had decided to join me in the sperm-donation room. Even though we weren't allowed to touch, it'd been sexy as hell watching her massage her clit while I jerked myself off. Somehow the fact that we couldn't have contact made it even hotter.

"I wish I'd had a camera to snap a photo of the nurse's face when you told her you were going in with me," I said from the kitchen as I prepared her treat.

The past couple of weeks had also been a distinct shift. Noelle and I had been addicted to having sex after that first day. What had started as putting our best effort into getting her pregnant had turned into something else entirely. Noelle spent almost every night at my place, aside from the days Clancy was with me.

I finally brought out the dessert I'd prepared. Noelle had cut out dairy and refined sugar recently because she'd read it might help reduce inflammation and enhance fertility. So I'd made her a pseudo-chocolate pudding with coconut milk, avocado, and unsweetened cacao.

"This is dairy free and sweetened only with agave," I said as I handed her the parfait glass. I'd layered strawberries in the middle and placed a single one on top.

"This looks delicious."

"Try it."

She took a bite and moaned. "Wow. It's incredible."

I crossed my arms and smiled as she devoured it.

"Are you just going to watch me eat?"

"I love watching you do many things. Eating dessert is one of them."

"You're not gonna have any?" she asked with her mouth full.

"No. It's just for you."

She pointed her spoon toward me. "I can share."

I shook my head. "There's only one thing I want you to share with me today, and it's not that."

Noelle looked down at my crotch. "I can see you're ready."

"The past five days have been hard," I groaned.

We were told to abstain from sex for three days prior to the insemination today, and it just so happened I'd had

Clancy with me the two days before that, so it had been a full five days since Noelle and I'd had sex. But I'd arranged to work at the restaurant two hours later than usual tonight to allow us time together. The doctor said the most important time to do the deed was today.

After Noelle finished her pudding, she climbed over the couch and straddled me.

"What do you think you're doing?" I asked.

"Properly thanking you for my dessert."

"Are you gonna ride me right here?"

Noelle lifted her shirt before unbuttoning her pants and pulling them off. She then began grinding her pussy over my cock, which was practically busting through my pants.

Unzipping my jeans, I couldn't take my dick out fast enough. Within seconds, she bore down on me as I sank deep inside of her, unable to believe how wet she was. *Fuck*. This felt even better than the first time somehow. Gripping her ass, I guided her movements, although she didn't need any help. "That's it. Ride me, baby." I gritted my teeth. "You know how to fuck me so good."

Leaning my head against the back of the couch, I smiled up at her, so turned on by her taking control. Then I closed my eyes for a bit because the way she looked while she rode my cock had me too turned on to last very long.

Noelle began to shake as her pussy clamped down on me.

"I...I'm sorry...I'm...Oh God..." She screamed as she came.

A tidal wave of arousal tore through me as I emptied my orgasm into her.

Her hips gradually slowed as I looked up at her beautiful, flushed face. Noelle rested her head on my shoulder, and we sat together for a few minutes before she retreated to the bathroom.

When she came out, I was sitting in the same spot, wondering if it was too soon for another round. Noelle curled into me as I wrapped my arm around her, holding her close. I kissed the top of her head.

There was so much I wanted to talk about, but the last thing she needed was the stress of figuring out what would happen if number three failed. I promised myself I wouldn't broach the subject until our final appointment. She wouldn't know how she was going to feel until after she got the results anyway.

• • •

About two weeks later, on a Sunday afternoon, Noelle accompanied me to a matinee showing of the musical *Frozen* at Clancy's school. It was a welcome distraction from wondering about the outcome of Noelle's pregnancy test. She'd already had her blood drawn, and we were set to go in for the results tomorrow.

She and I were seated next to Mariah and her boyfriend, Andy. Bringing Noelle here was a big step, and Mariah likely now had zero doubt that Noelle had become more than a friend. Everyone was cordial, but we didn't say too much to each other.

Watching my little girl perform her solo in "Let It Go" gave me immense joy. Clancy kept squinting, as if trying to find us in the audience as she belted out the tune. I could never have gotten up and done that. She was braver than her dad, that's for sure. Thank God I'd managed to avoid passing on my insecurities. As her song finished, the four of us stood in a standing ovation.

After the show, we headed backstage, and I held a bouquet of flowers as Noelle and I waited for Clancy to finish talking to her mom and Andy. She'd already changed out of her costume but still had smudges of red on her cheeks from the stage makeup.

I knelt as she ran to me. "I'm so proud of you, baby!"

"Thank you for my flowers!" Clancy looked to my right. "Hi, Noelle."

"Hi, Clancy! You did so good out there."

I rubbed Clancy's back. "I heard your mom and Andy are taking you out for pizza. I wish I could come celebrate with you, but I have to get to work."

"It's okay, Daddy."

Noelle looked down at Clancy's legs. "Hey… I love your socks. I used to like wearing mismatched ones, too."

Clancy was wearing colorful socks that went to her knees—polka dots on one foot and stripes on the other.

My daughter's eyes widened. "You did?"

"Yup. It was one of my favorite things to do."

I grinned. "I can't believe I forgot that. Clancy wears mismatched socks all the time. That was one of the first things I remember noticing about you, Noelle. I guess great minds think alike."

After we hugged Clancy goodbye, I convinced Noelle to take her laptop to the restaurant so she could hang there while I spoiled her with dairy-free creations.

Everything was business as usual until I came out

to personally deliver a lemon sorbet and saw that Noelle wasn't at her table. Assuming she'd gone to the bathroom, I brought the dessert back to the kitchen so I could try again a few minutes later. When she hadn't reappeared after fifteen minutes, I started to get nervous.

Thirty minutes passed, and she still hadn't returned. I stepped away from the kitchen for a moment to text her.

**Archie: Where are you?**

The three dots moved around as she typed.

**Noelle: Out front. I just needed some air.**

*Air? What the fuck?*

**Archie: Are you okay?**

**Noelle: I'm actually not feeling great. Calling an Uber to go back to the house.**

**Archie: I'll drive you.**

**Noelle: No. You can't leave work. I've already called the car. Don't worry about me.**

Something wasn't right. Maybe she didn't feel well, but she'd seemed great all night, including just a little while ago.

I told the sous chef to cover for me and went outside, but it was too late. Noelle was already gone. With the restaurant super-packed tonight, I sucked up the feeling of discomfort growing in my chest and once again returned to work.

A few minutes later, someone I hadn't been expecting waltzed into the kitchen. Her heels clicked as she came toward me. *What the hell is she doing here?*

Andrea fluffed her long, black hair. "Long time no see," she said in her British accent.

The last time I'd seen her she was beneath me in her hotel-room bed.

I cleared my throat. "How are you?"

"Good." She beamed. "You?"

"What brings you here?"

"I've got some business meetings. Figured I'd check in on my investment. Maybe have a little Prosecco and short ribs while I was at it." Her eyes fell to my lips. "And maybe a nightcap, if you're interested. I've thought about you a lot since my last trip out here, Archie."

Those words went right through me because all I could think about was Noelle. "I appreciate that. But I'm sorry. I'm not going to be able to do that anymore."

"Because of the girl I met?"

My stomach sank.

"What?"

"I met a friend of yours in the restroom. We were chatting. I introduced myself and told her I was here to visit the handsome chef. She said she was a friend of yours."

*Fuck.* At least Noelle's change in behavior finally made sense.

· · ·

My shift couldn't have ended fast enough. After I let Andrea down easy a second time and got the hell out of the restaurant, I drove past the speed limit to Noelle's.

But when I got there, Roz answered the door.

Out of breath, I said, "I need to talk to Noelle."

"She's not here."

"What?" I entered the house and looked around. "Where is she? It's late."

"Her ex, Jason, came into town. He wanted to speak to her privately and asked if she'd take a ride with him."

My heart pounded. "Are you kidding?" *This night could not get any worse.*

"I'm sorry. I'm not even sure she would've wanted me to tell you that."

"What the hell does he want?" I spewed.

"You can't take a wild guess?" Roz quipped.

I raked a hand through my hair. "Roz... I don't know what to do."

"Come sit." She led me into the kitchen. "Talk to me, Archie boy."

Taking a seat, I put my head in my hands. "We were having a nice evening. Noelle had come to the restaurant to work on her laptop during my shift. Then a woman Noelle knew I had a sexual history with showed up. Apparently, they spoke, and Noelle must've gotten upset and decided to leave." I rubbed my temples. "This woman means absolutely nothing to me, Roz. It was just a quick fling from the past. I raced over here to talk to Noelle and..." Something dawned on me.

*Did Noelle leave because of Andrea, or because she found out Jason was in town?*

I looked up at her. "What happened when she got home?"

"She seemed tired. She didn't really have much of a chance to tell me anything before the doorbell rang. She looked shocked to see Jason. He said hello to me and asked her if they could go somewhere to talk. He didn't give her much of a choice since he'd come all this way. What was she supposed to do?"

My voice shook. "I don't want her feeling stressed right now."

"I think the biggest thing stressing her out is you, Archie. Have you given her any assurances lately? Any indication of your feelings? And I don't mean with your dick, baby daddy."

Her words hit me like a slap. *She's fucking right.*

"What's going on in that head of yours, Archie?"

It took a moment to gather my thoughts. Only one thing had ever caused me to hold my feelings back when it came to Noelle. "I'm scared, Roz. Besides you, Noelle is the only family I have."

"You're boinking the only family you have? Sounds scandalous." She chuckled. "Look, your mother would want me to give you frank advice, so I'm going to." She pointed toward the door. "That man came back for her today. I don't know what he's saying to her right now or what she's thinking, but the look in his eyes told me everything I need to know. It was determination. He's realized what he lost, and he came back for her." She crossed her arms and leaned back in her seat. "We're not given an infinite amount of time to figure things out. Sometimes we need to shit or get off the pot. And those who do it last...lose."

I'd thought I had time to figure things out. I was wrong.

Roz pointed her finger at me. "I'm not going to betray her trust and share anything she might have told me about you these past few weeks. But I'm pretty sure you can read between the lines. You don't offer to father a woman's baby, make love to her, and not expect her to be all sorts of confused, especially with the history you two have."

I pulled on my hair and muttered, "You're not telling me anything I don't already know, Roz."

"The question is… Are you going to fight for her, or are you gonna let her go back to New York with *my* future husband?"

# CHAPTER 29

## Noelle

**MY NERVES WERE** completely shot as I stood across from Jason in his hotel room, unable to imagine what he could possibly say to me that hadn't already been said.

He rubbed his hands together. "First of all, thank you for agreeing to come here with me, for trusting me. I just needed a private place to say all of this."

Keeping my distance, I nodded. "Of course, I trust you, Jason. Don't ever doubt that."

He gulped some water, seeming more on edge than I could ever remember. "I've had a lot of time to think," he said. "I've never understood the saying that you don't know what you have until it's gone, but now I do."

I sat down on the bed and licked my lips nervously.

He paced. "I've been miserable, Noelle. I was miserable the moment you left for California. From the beginning I've been jealous, sad, unable to focus at work. It's true that I wanted the freedom to travel and all of those other things you used as an excuse to end us. But nothing in life matters if you don't have someone you love to share it with." He walked over and knelt in front of me, grabbing my hands. "I love you. I never realized how much until these past few weeks. I tried to be strong, sit back while you pursued your dream of having a baby, even if it secretly killed me, but it turns out...I'm not that strong."

I pulled my hands away slowly. "I'm not sure what to say."

He stood. "I said I wasn't willing to have another child. But the thing is, I would do anything to keep you in my life, Noelle. Sure, a child at my age isn't something I saw in my future. But I've realized the only future I can accept is one with you." He paused. "And if a baby—or even two or three—will make you happy, I want to be the one to give that to you."

As endearing as this seemed, I couldn't believe it. "You don't want more kids. You're just saying this to appease me."

"I only want more kids *with you*. That's what I've figured out. There's no way I won't fall in love with our baby, even if I've been apprehensive. I was just scared—scared to start over at this stage in my life. But you know what? Starting over with *you*? I can handle that."

Did he not understand the monkey wrench he'd just thrown at me?

"This is crazy." My voice cracked. "I could be pregnant right now, Jason. I find out tomorrow."

"I know that." He sighed. "And I'm okay with that, too. As long as you come back to New York and be with me. If you're pregnant, I'll help you raise it. But if you're not pregnant, Noelle..." He paused. "I want you to come home. I want you to move in with me. *We* can start trying."

My mouth fell in disbelief. "You had a vasectomy."

"I'll schedule a reversal tomorrow."

*Jesus.* I shook my head. "I just don't understand how you could have such a dramatic change of heart."

"This didn't happen overnight. All of the things you say I like to do—going out on the town, traveling—I've done them all over these past few weeks. Nothing felt right. Nothing satisfied me or took away the pain of losing you. My mind, my heart... They've been with you this entire time, wanting to be wherever you were. These weeks have felt like years, Noelle." He moved to sit next to me on the bed. "I even opened up to Jay and Alexandra about it, something I've never done—seeking input from my kids on my personal life. They gave me some good advice. Jay told me what a great dad I was and said if I loved you, I shouldn't be afraid to become a father again. And Alexandra said she really likes you and feels like I won't ever find a better partner. Their support means the world to me. I worried whether my kids would be upset if I had a child with someone else. But it seems they want me to be happy." Jason took my hand. "It turns out, I'm only truly happy with you."

My heart hurt as I sat there, utterly confused. "Jason...I don't know what to say."

His eyes were watery. "Say you'll come back to New York, no matter the outcome tomorrow. Say you'll be with me."

I needed to buy myself some time. "I don't know."

Jason's nostrils flared. "Is it him? We should talk about your feelings for Archie if that's what's holding you back."

"Archie hasn't expressed that he wants to be with me," I said.

"Have you slept with him?"

My stomach churned. "We started sleeping together after you and I broke up. Nothing happened before then."

Jason grimaced as if my admission physically pained him. "That wasn't what I wanted to hear...but I can't fault you for it." He took my hand. "Even that doesn't change how I feel."

I looked down at our hands. "I can't even begin to process this."

"You don't need to say anything now. I just needed to let you know where things stand. Promise me you'll consider everything I had to say tonight."

Feeling more unsure than ever, I nodded.

• • •

When Jason dropped me off back at the house that night, I opened the door to find Archie sitting in the living room. He stood the moment I walked in the door.

"What are you doing here?" I asked, thrown completely off kilter yet again.

"I came to see you. I figured out why you left the restaurant."

My head spun as Roz retreated to her room.

"What happened with Jason?" he asked, a vein about to pop from his neck. "Why is he here?"

My eyes filled with tears as all of the stress came crashing down on me. "I can't rehash everything tonight, Archie. I'm spent."

His tone softened as he pulled me into an embrace. "Come here. I'm sorry." He spoke into my neck. "I don't mean to stress you out. I came to make sure you were okay. I know you ran into Andrea in the ladies' room."

I pulled back. "That did rattle me."

"I had no idea she was coming to the States, but you know there's nothing going on between me and her, right?"

"That certainly wasn't what she was hoping."

He drew in his brows. "I don't care what she was hoping. You're all I think about."

"You are who you are, Archie. You said yourself you don't have any plans to get married again. The reason I got upset tonight wasn't because I thought something was going on between you and her, but because of my reaction. It told me I'm getting too emotionally attached to you when I shouldn't be. I knew this would happen if we had sex." Crossing my arms protectively, I added, "I mean, you've given me no indication that you want a future with me. Maybe this was the wake-up call I needed."

Archie shut his eyes briefly, looking conflicted. But he remained silent, denying nothing. "I need to know what Jason said to you," he said after a moment.

I pulled myself up taller. "He says he loves me. He wants me to give him a second chance. He wants to help me raise this child." I paused, bracing for his reaction. "And if I'm not pregnant, he's decided he wants to get a vasectomy reversal and—"

"What?" Archie practically screamed, his tone jarring. "You don't believe that shit, do you?"

"You think it's so unbelievable that he could love me?"

"God, Noelle." He shook his head. "That's not what I meant at all, and you know it."

When I started to cry, a look of alarm crossed Archie's face.

My lip trembled. "Archie, I'm just really confused and tired. We have a big day tomorrow, and I need to prepare myself."

"Okay," he whispered. "I know it's late. I'm sorry." He rubbed my shoulder. "Get some sleep. I'll be here at eight in the morning to pick you up."

I tossed and turned the entire night. I loved Archie, but I knew Jason had a much smaller chance of breaking my heart. And that counted for something.

• • •

My mood when Archie came to get me the next morning was worse than it had been the night before. Neither of us had much to say, and though Archie had picked up breakfast on the way to get me, I had no appetite.

I was no closer to clarity about this situation. There was no doubt my feelings for the man next to me were stronger than my feelings for Jason, but I couldn't survive a rejection from Archie. I needed to walk away first. Offering to father my baby and actually being a life partner were two different things. He'd yet to express clear interest in the latter. There was something holding him back. And I wasn't going to stick around to get hurt.

As my thoughts raced on the way to the doctor's office, I convinced myself that if I wasn't pregnant, it would be a sign to go back to New York and reassess. That didn't mean I would never try to have a baby with Archie again, and it also didn't mean I was going to run back to Jason. It just meant I needed time to evaluate my life.

Archie and I were immediately taken to the dreaded results room. Despite the tension between us, he held my hand tightly the entire time we waited. When the doctor walked in, I noticed the somber look on his face. He took a seat across from us. Then the words came.

"I'm so sorry to tell you that your test was negative."

Archie let out a guttural sound as he lowered his head. My heart felt hollow.

"Have you discussed your next steps?" the doctor asked.

Archie turned to me, his eyes piercing as he awaited my response. He still hadn't let go of my hand. We had tried everything this time. Yet we still couldn't make it happen. Maybe it wasn't meant to be.

"No," I answered. "We had only committed to three IUI cycles. So we're going to reassess."

Dr. Burns typed something quickly on his laptop. "As I've mentioned before, many couples opt to try IVF at this point. I'm happy to go over any questions you might have about it."

I sighed. "I'm well aware of that option and will consider it for the future. But I need to pause for now and do some research. If I want to set up another appointment, I'll call you to do that."

"I understand." He smiled sympathetically. "This process can be mentally grueling, and it will certainly benefit you to take a step back and determine what you want with a clear mind."

I nodded. "Thank you for all of your help, Doctor."

He stood. "It's been my pleasure. I look forward to working with you again."

Left alone, I turned to Archie, who opened his arms to bring me into a hug. "I'm so fucking sorry," he said.

"It's okay," I whispered as I leaned against him. "We knew this could happen. The odds were still against us."

"I know, but I wanted it more than anything, Noelle. I hope you know that."

After he let me go, I said, "Archie, can we go somewhere and talk?"

His expression hardened as he nodded. "Of course."

We left the medical building, and Archie drove us to a local park. It was pretty empty, since kids were in school. We picked a spot on a bench under a beautiful tree. I looked up at the sky and tried to build up the courage to say what I needed to.

As I watched a gum wrapper blow by in the breeze, the words finally came out. "I need to go back to New York."

A long breath escaped him. "What does that mean, though?"

"I don't know yet." Staring over at some pigeons, I tried to articulate my jumbled feelings. "I feel more emotionally invested in this process than I'd hoped to. I need to protect myself. I know you care about me. That's never been in question. But I'm not sure you want the same things I do when it comes to us. It's hard for me to express what's truly in my heart when you don't reciprocate. I can't imagine a life without you in it. God, that scares the shit out of me, Archie. If I'm not able to control these feelings, I'm afraid I'm gonna lose you forever."

He reached for my hand. "I feel like we both have the same fear. I don't want to do anything to ever hurt you or to lose you. I don't trust myself, Noelle. I've screwed up every relationship I've ever had."

I stared down at our intertwined fingers. "You've been nothing but good to me, and you've gone above and beyond to make this process work. But I'm not sure continuing is the best decision for me anymore."

Archie wrapped his hands around his head and leaned into his knees. This would have been the ideal moment for him to dispel my fears, tell me he loved me, and assure me he would always be there for me.

But he didn't.

Instead, he let me go.

# CHAPTER 30

## Archie
*Two Months Later*
*Whaite's Island*

**IT LOOKED EXACTLY** the same from the outside. The house still had its wood-shingle exterior. Even the flowers out front were the same. I took a deep breath of the ocean air. I'd been here once since that fateful summer, yet I hadn't really appreciated the experience the last time. This trip felt different. I was much more relaxed and grateful for all of the experiences I'd had here, even the painful ones.

"Can I help you?" a woman asked. She'd just come out of the house and must have been wondering why a strange man was staring.

"Sorry to bother you. I lived here briefly years ago. I was just reminiscing a bit."

"Oh, that's so interesting. My family and I are renting it for the week. It's a great house."

"So, it's still a rental property then..."

"Yes."

I continued looking up at the house, lost in thought.

"Are you okay?" she asked.

*Fair question.* "Yeah, I just have a lot of memories here."

She pointed her thumb back toward the house. "Would you want to come in?"

My eyes widened. "Could I?"

"Sure."

"Wow. Thank you." I followed her to the door and wiped my feet before entering.

"Are you staying in town?" she asked.

"I flew in last night. Staying at one of the inns."

I'd started going to therapy again recently, something I hadn't done since well before Clancy was born. My therapist determined that I was still dealing with a lot of trauma pertaining to my father's death and suggested I return to Whaite's Island to face it. She thought my coming back here might rid me of some of the pent-up feelings I'd been holding on to. She'd pointed out that the last time I was here, I'd been distracted by telling Noelle that Mariah was pregnant. I'd never addressed the demons still haunting me, many of whom resided in this house.

So here I was, back at the scene of the crime. The decision to visit Whaite's Island had been last minute. My original plan was to go straight to New York to see Noelle. But I couldn't afford to botch anything up further with her, so I'd decided I should heed my therapist's advice.

The past two months, since Noelle had returned to New York, had been the hardest of my life. That was saying a lot, since I'd had some pretty rough times right after Dad died and while taking care of my mother.

It wasn't until Noelle left California that I realized it wasn't just the pregnancy I'd been hoping for. Having her there by my side was the first time in over a decade that I'd felt complete. And I'd totally fucked everything up. Once again fear had kept me from taking the next step with the person who meant so much to me. My strong feelings for her were the reason I'd always kept Noelle at bay, like a favorite piece of artwork you're afraid to touch for fear of breaking it. I was about to lose her forever—my ultimate fear—if I didn't make things right. But I couldn't fix things until I fixed myself.

The woman staying here told me her name was Jean. I chatted with her for a bit and asked whether she minded if I went upstairs. Her kids were out shopping with their father for the day, so she told me to take my time. No one else was home.

Heading up the staircase, I went straight to Noelle's old bedroom. The walls were a different color, and the old nautical motif had been changed to more modern gray-and-white bedding and décor. The one thing that remained was the beautiful view of the ocean and the lighthouse.

The last time I stayed at the house with Noelle, I hadn't gone into this room, just stood outside the door. It reminded me too much of the horrible moment when I'd picked up the phone to learn my father had died. I considered this room haunted, the scene of some of my fondest memories and also the worst day of my life. Thoughts of my dad flooded my brain as I sat on the bed where I'd been when I'd gotten that call.

As much as my father and I had disagreed on just about everything, I'd only ever wanted him to love me. While I'd gone to visit his grave over the years, I'd never felt his presence there the way I did in this moment.

Standing up to look toward the water in the distance, I spoke to him in a barely audible tone.

"I often wonder whether you're looking down at me or, no offense, up." I sighed. "Just kidding. Anyway, I wonder what you'd think of me now, Archer. I've ignored everything in your rule book and done the exact opposite of what you would've wanted. Not only did I nix the idea of law school, but I picked a profession you would've deemed too risky. You mocked me whenever I cooked anything, remember? Or when I expressed interest in anything that wasn't in line with your goals for me." I laughed angrily. "Oh...and I got my girlfriend pregnant out of wedlock. You would've loved that, too. And then I couldn't hold that marriage together for more than a few years. Quite the opposite, I singlehandedly broke it apart. I imagine you would've told me I wasn't strong enough to stick it out. You might've said I should've tried harder to maintain my family, that not only had I messed up my own life, I'd messed up my daughter's." I shook my head and scrubbed a hand over my face. "Oh! And you would've been even more outraged that I offered to father a baby for your best friend's daughter. You would've told me Noelle was too good for me, warned me to stay away so I didn't ruin her life, too. Am I right?" I walked back over to the bed and sat down. "See? All of this is what I believe, but I have to wonder whether that's really what you would say now, or whether this is my own false perception. Either way, I need to change the narrative, Dad. Right here and right now."

I spoke to the ceiling. "Wherever you are, hopefully you know I've done the best I could with what life has dealt me, even if you don't agree with my decisions. I did the best I could for Mom. That's for damn sure. Hopefully, she's with some other guy in heaven, by the way, and not your cheating ass." I sighed. "Anyway, whatever life threw at me, I went with the flow. But there has been one constant: I've been in love with the same girl. And I'm glad you got to meet her." I stood up and walked through the bathroom into my old room, continuing to talk to my father. "Maybe I'm not the best man for Noelle. Maybe there's someone else who has his shit together—someone like Jason. But I *love* her. More than he ever could. How can I expect her to trust me, though, if *I* can't trust me? A lot of my opinions of myself have come from your voice haunting me all these years. What you might have thought of me shouldn't matter anymore. But the only way that can happen is if *I* let it all go." I chuckled. "Your granddaughter performed 'Let It Go' on stage not too long ago. Even your cold heart would've loved her so much." I smiled.

Returning to the window in Noelle's room, I sighed. "Anyway... This is me letting go, Dad. What needs to matter is love. I love my daughter. And I love Noelle. I'm lucky that life brought both of them to me. I will always encourage Clancy to do what makes her happy, not what pleases people or pleases me. But I will say, I know now how hard it is to be a parent. You gave me a tough time, but you probably thought it was best for me."

I looked toward the ceiling one last time. "What matters more than anything... I forgive you for all those times you hurt me. And I forgive myself for not telling you I loved you before you died. Because after everything...I *do* love you. And I wish you were here. I wish I could've made you proud, even if I didn't travel the path you would've chosen."

I took a deep breath. I'd said everything I needed to say, and a euphoric feeling of relief came over me. Now it was time to correct the biggest mistake I'd ever made.

Downstairs, I caught up with Jean in the kitchen. "Thank you for letting me see the top floor."

She put down a lemon she'd been squeezing. "I hope you had a nice trip down memory lane."

"I definitely took a little journey up there. I appreciate the opportunity you gave me to put some things to rest."

"Of course. Enjoy the rest of your time on the island."

"You as well."

I didn't bother to explain that I was jetting out of Whaite's Island as fast as I could. Rather than wait for my flight and stay another night here, I started searching for a car service to take me to New York.

# CHAPTER 31

## Noelle

**I WAS HAVING** a lazy day at home in my pajamas, doing work and filling my teacup every hour. Needing to get myself out of this funk, I decided to call Roz. I hadn't spoken to her since coming back here.

She picked up on the second ring. "Noelle Belle! I was just thinking of you!"

She always knew how to put me in a better mood. "Hey, Roz. I wanted to check in."

"I really miss you, girl. I'm so glad you called."

"I miss you, too. I'm sorry it's taken me this long to touch base." I opened my fridge and grabbed a mozzarella stick. "How are things?"

"Menopause Roz just hit fifty-five-thousand subscribers!"

"Oh my gosh. That's amazing! It must've been your hot flash series." I chuckled. "I can't wait to binge all your videos in twenty years."

"Now stop pretending you're checking in on little old me and tell me why you're actually calling."

"I really am checking on you. I should've called you sooner."

"Well, that's sweet, but you're not the least bit interested in Archie boy?"

Archie and I had exchanged some messages over the past two months, but we hadn't addressed things between us. We were either giving each other space or growing apart. I wasn't sure which. But I missed him like crazy.

Clearing my throat, I asked, "Have you seen him lately?"

"Actually, I haven't, honey. He hasn't come around. The last time he was here to fix something, though, I saw him peek into your old room. He looked sad."

Like so many things with Archie, that confused me. I hated that he was sad, but why hadn't he reached out if he felt that way?

"What's going on over there in New York?" she asked.

"I broke up with Jason for good. I mean, we never got back together, only casually hung out, but I made a final decision."

"Really..." She sighed. "Well, I'm so sorry."

I took a bite of my cheese stick—yes, I was eating dairy again. "It's for the best. I think he had himself convinced he could want a child with me just to keep me. I couldn't let him go through with something like that when I didn't truly believe him." I shook my head. "But that's not the main reason I couldn't be with him." I paused. "I don't love him."

"You love Archie," she said matter-of-factly.

"I do." I exhaled. "And it sucks."

"If it's meant to be, it will be, darling."

"I suppose you're right," I told her. "But seriously, what's happening out there with you?"

We chatted for a while, and I promised to call more often. Then about a half hour after I got off the phone with Roz, my phone lit up with a text.

*Speak of the devil.* It was Archie.

My heart came alive at the sight of a photo, followed by a looooong message. I scrolled down before I read it. It had to be the lengthiest text I'd ever received.

My heart raced as I scrolled back up and clicked on the photo. It was a drawing of me, a sketch like the ones he used to create over a decade earlier. He'd drawn me scared before. He'd drawn me focused. He'd drawn me drunk and crazy-looking after massacring a chocolate cake. But he'd never drawn me like this. I looked sad, wearing the pink dress covered in daisies that I'd worn to his wedding. I examined the melancholy expression on my sketched face again. It was the perfect depiction of how I'd felt that day—sad, confused, and desperately in love with a man who'd just married someone else. Ironically, he'd captioned the sketch: *Love.*

I suddenly felt unsettled, scared of what he'd written. I sat down to read the message. Grabbing a pillow, I hugged it for support.

Archie: This is going to be the rawest thing I've ever written, so buckle up. I'm texting it because the next time I see you in person, I might be back to my old blubbering-idiot ways and don't trust myself to get these words out coherently.

This photo is the last drawing of you I ever created. I drew it on my wedding night. How fucked up is that? I escaped into the bathroom while Mariah was sleeping and drew you—because I had to. I never wanted to forget the look on your face. It was important to me because unfortunately, that was the night I realized you loved me. It was also the night I realized I'd made a huge mistake. If I could go back, I would've done so many things differently. I know now that you can't choose who to love based on what fits into a neat little box.

You tried to hide the fact that you'd been crying that night. But I knew. I felt it. And I'm ashamed to admit that I was in love with you, too, that day. Ashamed only because it never should have been her. It should've been you. I knew it not only when I saw the sadness in your eyes, but even when I looked out into the pews at the church and saw you in your pink dress, looking uncomfortable. My heart skipped a beat for you in a way it hadn't when my bride walked down the aisle. I'd chosen to bury those feelings deep. That was a huge mistake.

The truth is, I've loved you since our first summer together. And I can't say what might have happened if it had ended differently. But I need you to understand that back when I had to take care of my mom after Dad died, it was more important to me to make sure I didn't hold you back than to admit how I felt. I never wanted you to resent me. You had the whole universe at your fingertips, while I was stuck in California. You had career aspirations and all the freedom in the world. So I made the decision to let you go.

Then life happened. You were with Shane. And then you weren't. I was with Mariah, and we both know what happened there. Fate and timing were never on our side. And a part of me through all those years believed a false narrative that you were better off without me, which I know now isn't true. Because you loved me—that's all that should have mattered. That's all that does matter.

I also know I don't just love you because of our time together that summer. That was only the tip of the iceberg. I love you for all the moments in between, when we weren't physically together but when I knew I could count on you, when I couldn't count on anyone else.

I should also admit that, yes, while I was willing to father your baby while you were dating another man, every second you were with him killed me.

There was only ever one reason I wanted to have a baby with you. Because I love you. And I know I'd love our baby, too. I'd never regret experiencing that with you, whether we were together or not. While it disappointed me that we didn't conceive after three tries, I don't regret a second of that time—getting to know even better the strong woman you've become, getting to make love to you, and getting to experience the excitement of knowing we could be creating a life together, even if it hasn't come to fruition yet.

I am all in if you want me. Not because I'm doing you any favors, but because I can't live without you and want nothing more than to start a family with you. Even if that family is you, me, and Clancy, with no other children.

This text is already too long. But writing this down was a good way to spend the ride from Maine to New York. Now it's time for you to open your door and let me show you how much I love you.

My hands shook. I nearly dropped the phone. *He's... here?* With my heart racing, I ran to the door.

When I opened it, Archie stood there with tears in his eyes. As long as I'd known him, I'd never seen the man cry. But he was crying for me. Because he loved me.

Leaping into his arms, I wrapped myself around him and didn't waste a single breath. "I love you."

He exhaled into my neck. "I love you so much. And I'm *so* sorry for not saying it sooner."

"Eh. What's twelve years?" I joked, allowing my tears to fall.

When I could finally step back from the warmth of his arms, I took his hand and led him inside. "You said you were in Maine. Whaite's Island?"

He nodded. "I needed to go back there for closure. I hadn't intended to go see the old house, but I happened to walk by, and the person who was renting it let me inside. I sat in your old bedroom and talked to my dad. I was able to work out some unresolved issues, even if they were just in my head."

"Wow."

"I've been working on myself quite a bit since you left," he said. "But there's one thing I've never had to work on because it's always been clear to me. I've always loved you. I've just kept you tucked away, so I was never able to hurt you. But in doing so, I was hurting both of us. I understand that now."

I wiped my eyes. "I've thought about you every single day since I came back here. I've wanted nothing more than to hear you say that. Even being apart, I've fallen more in love with you since leaving California."

He took my hands in his. "I needed to take the risk that I could hurt you in order to love you. I want to have you in my life. It's not going to be perfect. There are gonna be times that I might not be there for you because of my daughter. Or there may be times when I screw up, say the wrong thing, or do the wrong thing. But I will do everything in my power not to hurt you. I will never take you for granted, and I will *always* love you."

*Should I be pinching myself?* "I've felt empty these past couple of months," I told him. "I left California because I loved you too much to stay if you didn't love me back. And I never seriously considered going back to Jason. You need to know that. No matter where I was in my life, every year, every holiday, every email... I've loved you every second, Archie Remington. So much of my heart stayed in Whaite's Island. I haven't been able to let it go. And I don't ever want to let *you* go."

"You'll never have to, Noelle." Archie caressed my cheek. "But I do need to ask you a huge favor."

I tilted my head. "Sure."

His eyes burned into mine. "I need you to move to California. I can't be apart from my daughter, and I need to be with you every day. Would you be willing to do that?"

Did he not realize that was a no-brainer? "I haven't felt normal since coming back here. I used to love New York, but I don't feel the same here anymore without you. So yes, of course, I'll come back."

Archie hugged me again. "Thank you."

"I've figured out some things myself," I told him.

He moved back to look at me. "What?"

"I think part of why I felt I needed a child so badly was that I wanted someone to love me. And while I still do very much want a child...somehow hearing you say you love me takes the immediate pressure off. Ultimately, what I've wanted in my life is a sense of family and a sense of purpose. I don't think a child is the only way to attain that. Everyone just needs their person, whether that's a child or otherwise. They need to feel like if they disappear from the Earth tomorrow, it would matter to someone."

"I get that." Archie smiled. "The best thing you could've done was leave because it made me realize I don't have forever to work out all the things that were keeping

334

me from being with you. I'm sorry it took me this long to be the man you deserve."

I rubbed my hand along the scruff on his face. "You might not have thought you were the man I deserved, but you were *always* the man I loved."

• • •

It only took me two weeks to sublet my apartment before I was on a plane to California. Thankfully, my boss had been extremely generous and agreed to let me transfer to our West Coast bureau. I'd still be doing the same job and would only need to report to the Los Angeles office on occasion.

Archie, Roz, and Clancy were waiting for me at the airport when I stepped off the plane.

Clancy held a sign that read: *Welcome Home, Noelle.*

Tears filled my eyes because it felt like I'd landed *home* for the first time in my life.

I bent to hug her first. "Thank you, beautiful girl."

"Daddy told me you're moving in with us."

I tugged at one of her braids. "I am. I hope that's okay with you."

"Yeah." She nodded. "I like you."

"That means a lot to me." I sniffled. "I like you, too."

When I stood up, Archie's arms were open and ready to receive me. His warm embrace felt so good. "Welcome home, beautiful," he said.

"I'm happy to be home."

Next I turned to hug my dear friend. "Hey, Roz."

"I couldn't wait to see you, honey. I had to tag along. I'm sad you're not gonna be my roommate anymore." She winked. "But I understand."

Taking a deep breath, I took a moment to appreciate the three people before me—my people. Ever since my parents had moved down to Florida, I'd lost the sense of family I'd felt when they were in New York. Being an only child had always been a bit lonely, but especially after Mom and Dad moved. So, Archie, Clancy, and Roz were also my family now. I'd gotten to travel the world and live out my career aspirations, but nothing felt better than being here with them.

We quickly fetched my bags from the conveyor belt, and as we walked toward the exit, Clancy turned to her dad.

"Can we go to New York sometime, Daddy?"

"If your mom says it's okay, I'd love to take you there. Better yet, we could hit Maine—maybe even see if the old house is available to rent—and drive down to New York from there. What do you think, Noelle? Maybe next summer?"

"That sounds like the perfect plan to me. All the places I love with the people I love."

Roz elbowed me. "You'd better be inviting me to this Maine house. It sounds amazing from the way Nora used to describe it."

"It was. It's magical. And you're totally invited. I said all the people I love." I wrapped my arm around her. "And that includes you."

We dropped Roz off, and then Archie, Clancy, and I headed to his house.

Archie showed me to my room—our room. He'd put up the painting of Whaite's Island that he'd hung for me in my bedroom at his mother's house. It made me happy that he'd bothered to transfer it here.

"I can't wait for later," he whispered in my ear.

*God. Me, too.*

When we reentered the living area, Archie called to his daughter. "Clancy, why don't you show Noelle what you were watching earlier?"

She ran to the television and pressed play on a show. I couldn't believe my eyes: my old pageant video from more than a decade earlier.

"I can't believe you're watching that!"

"You can still find it in the Miss America Scholastic pageant archives on their website," Archie explained. "It's playing off of my laptop. Clancy mentioned that her friend was in a pageant, and I told her you were in one once, too. So we looked it up."

Clancy giggled. "I'm Clancy Nora Remington from the great state of California!"

"That was awesome!" I clapped. "I think you'd make a perfect pageant queen."

"No." She scrunched her nose. "I want to be an actress. Right, Daddy?"

"You can be whatever you want to be, sweetheart." He looked over at her proudly before kissing the top of my head.

Archie made a special meal for us that night: penne a la vodka—what else?—for him and me and homemade pizza for Clancy.

After we finished eating, he turned to her and said, "Clancy, why don't you go finish that project in your room before you come out for some dessert, okay?"

"Okay, Daddy." Clancy got right up and did as he said.

I watched as she disappeared into her room.

"She's amazing," I whispered.

He reached for my hand. "She's happy you're here."

"Really? I worried about that. I hoped she wasn't just pretending."

"Clancy and I have talked a lot about it. She knows how important you are to me. She's getting used to the fact that her parents aren't together anymore. She's embraced Andy and now you. We're very lucky. I may not have had the best marriage to Mariah, but I know she'd never feed Clancy misinformation about me or you. She's been very respectful. Clancy looks at this like she's gaining a mother rather than losing anything."

"You know that makes me very happy, especially since I don't have a child of my own. I promise to always treat her as if she was."

"I know you will." Archie lifted my hand and kissed it. "Thank you."

We had decided to put fertility treatments on hold for a while, though a baby was still something we very much wanted. If it happened in the meantime, great. But if not, we wouldn't stress. My top priority right now was getting to know Clancy and acclimating to being back in California.

Clancy rejoined us, and Archie asked, "Did you finish your project?"

She had a sneaky smile on her face as she nodded.

"You want to show Noelle?"

Clancy reached behind her back and presented me with a large plastic Easter egg that immediately brought me back to Whaite's Island.

"Oh my." I felt like I was blushing—thankfully she had no idea why this made my cheeks heat. "I haven't seen one of those in years."

Archie winked at me.

"Open it!" Clancy said.

What had Archie put her up to?

She handed it to me, and after I twisted it open, I saw a note inside. Written on it in crayon were two simple words: *Say Yes.*

When I looked over at Archie again, he was already down on one knee as Clancy hopped in excitement.

"I know this might seem soon," he said. "But let's face it, it's really long overdue. I wasn't ready for you then, Noelle, for the magnitude of a first love. Is anyone ever really ready for their first true love? I was especially unprepared. But you...you're the bookends of my life: my first love and my last love. And I would be honored—no, scratch that, I *need* you to be my wife." He opened a ring box and held it out to me. "Please say yes."

My mouth was ajar as I looked over at a smiling Clancy. Then I finally looked down at a beautiful oval diamond, sparkling under the lights. *Holy shit!*

"Say yes!" Clancy whispered.

I smiled at her. "Well, if you say so." I jumped up and shouted, "Yes!" before leaping into Archie's arms.

He lifted me into the air. "I love you so much, baby. Thank you for making me the happiest man in the world."

"I'm *so* happy, Archie."

Clancy interrupted our embrace. "It would've been funny if she said no."

"To *you*, maybe." Archie put me down to tickle his daughter's side.

I bent to hug her.

"What would you have done if she said no, Daddy?"

"I would've cried. Because I love her that much." He winked. "But I knew she wouldn't."

Clancy tilted her head. "How?"

"Because when you love someone and they love you back, you just know. One day when you're older, I'll tell you the whole story about how Noelle and I fell in love."

"Is it beautiful?"

"Sometimes. Other times, messy. But love is like that. You'll see someday."

"Thank you for accepting me, precious girl," I said. "If you didn't, I wouldn't be able to marry your daddy."

"You're welcome, Miss New York." Clancy ran to her room and returned with a wrapped box. "I have something else for you," she squeaked.

"You do?" I took it from her. "Thank you."

After carefully ripping off the paper, I opened the box and took out a pair of socks—perfectly mismatched, one with stripes and the other with polka dots.

"You said you liked mine." She flashed her little teeth. "So I got you some."

*If my heart wasn't already bursting tonight...* "These are so cool. And it means so much that you remembered." I kicked my shoes off. The material felt buttery soft as I slipped the socks on and pulled them toward my knees.

Mismatched socks reminded me a lot of my relationship with Archie Remington. Our path certainly wasn't orderly or sensical, but somehow in the end, when the two of us finally came together, it was perfect.

# EPILOGUE

## Archie
*Three Years Later*
*Whaite's Island*

**I WIPED SOME** grass off my pants. "Where's Clancy?"

"She's popping popcorn. She'll be right out," Noelle said as she spread a blanket on the lawn.

The sun had just set, and the ocean air was cold tonight, prompting us to pull out our sweaters for the outdoor movie.

I'd just set up a screen I'd purchased in the backyard of the house on Whaite's Island. We'd managed to rent our old house for a week, but we'd had to book it a year in advance.

My eyes moved to Roz, who was sucking face with her boyfriend as she sat on his lap. "I think you two need to get a room," I teased.

Arthur ran a woodworking YouTube channel, and they'd met at an influencer's convention about a year ago. Arthur had moved into my mother's old house with Roz, and both were now paying me minimal rent. The place would likely not be sold anytime soon, but I was perfectly okay with that.

Noelle's mother brought out a tray of iced tea while her dad perused the movie selections on my laptop. Noelle's parents had flown in from Florida to be here with us. Despite my earlier doubts about whether they'd accept me for their daughter, it turned out they'd been happily surprised when Noelle and I told them we were together and getting married. Kind of ridiculous that they were apprised of both of those facts at the same time, but that's how Noelle and I rolled.

My mother-in-law came up behind me. "What are you smiling about?"

"I didn't realize I was smiling."

"Yeah. You were smiling to yourself."

"I was just thinking how awesome it is to have every single person who means something to me here."

"This week's been awesome." Noelle rubbed my back. "I wish we didn't have to leave."

"Well, we could always try to buy the house again, if it ever comes on the market," her dad said.

"Wouldn't that be something?" her mom agreed.

"Can we pick a movie now?" my eight-year-old asked as she stuffed her mouth with popcorn.

Noelle's dad brought the laptop over, and the two of them worked on picking something. Ironically, Noelle's parents had become a second set of grandparents to my daughter. Mark and Amy always treated Clancy like their own, which meant a lot to me.

I'd love to be able to tell you our efforts to have a child of our own paid off, but a pregnancy wasn't in the cards for us. Noelle and I got married six months after our engagement and about a year later, we started IVF. After several failed attempts, we decided to pursue adoption. But the wait list was long. So, we vowed to let fate do its job. It hadn't steered us wrong yet, despite the rocky road we'd taken to get here. Whatever was meant to happen would. No more IVF for now. That meant no more added stress, which was a blessing in itself.

But sometimes in those moments when you've finally let go, magic happens. And it was fitting that we were here at this special place when we got the call. When I saw the name pop up on my phone, I flagged down Noelle, put the phone in speaker mode, and walked over to a corner of the yard so we could have some privacy.

"Hello?" I answered.

"Mr. Remington? It's Nancy Cartwright from the agency."

"Yes. Hi."

"Is your wife with you?"

"I'm right here," Noelle spoke into the phone.

"I hope I didn't interrupt anything."

"No. Not at all," I said. "We're actually out of town for a week in Maine with family."

"Oh. How nice."

Glancing over at Noelle, I asked a hopeful question. "I assume if you're calling on a weekend, you might have some news for us?"

"Yes, actually. I wanted to let you know about a little boy I've just become aware of. His temporary guardians are trying to find him a new home. I know you were looking for an infant. He's a bit older—two and a half."

Noelle and I looked at each other. When she nodded, I knew we were on the same page.

"Tell me about him," I said.

"Well, his mom passed away suddenly in an accident. She was a single mother and doesn't have any family who's suitable to care for the boy. There would be no one contesting, if you chose to move forward. I thought I'd come to you two before exploring other options."

Noelle reached for my hand, and her shoulders rose and fell. I could tell she had the same hopeful feeling about this as I did.

"I've met him," Nancy added. "He's very shy but well-behaved. No major issues to speak of. He's in desperate need of a family. My heart breaks for him." She paused. "If you want, I can send you some more information, along with a photo."

"That would be wonderful, Nancy," Noelle said. "And we promise to get back to you soon. We don't want to hold anything up."

"Okay," she said. "Expect something from me in the next ten minutes."

After I hung up the phone, I turned to Noelle. "What are you thinking?"

"I don't know. It feels oddly right. He's still young enough to nurture, not to mention how badly he needs a home."

I nodded. Feeling cautiously optimistic, I took Noelle's hand as we returned to our family. I started the movie while we waited for the email. I checked my phone every minute or so until finally, a bolded message from Nancy appeared.

I jumped and whispered to Noelle, "We got it."

We excused ourselves from the rest of the pack and walked into the house where my laptop was on the kitchen counter. I opened the email and went right to the photo attached.

Noelle grabbed my arm as I clicked on it.

My chest tightened at the sight of this smiling boy. I always used to say that whenever Noelle smiled, it lit up her entire face. This kid had the same type of smile.

I finally spoke. "He's..."

"Beautiful," Noelle breathed, her eyes wide with wonder.

I scrolled up to the information Nancy sent along and couldn't believe my eyes.

I pointed to the screen. "Look at his name."

*Freddy.*

"Wow," she mouthed. "Freddy. Like Fred, your old alter ego."

"That sounds like it was meant to be, doesn't it?"

Noelle couldn't stop smiling. And it *certainly* reached her eyes. Feeling it in my bones—and in my heart—I knew this was it.

"He kind of looks like you, Archie. He's got the same wild hair."

"Actually, his smile reminds me of you," I said.

She examined the photo more closely and tilted her head. "I'm not sure who he looks like...and I'm not sure I care. He's perfect."

"Actually, I know who he looks like..."

"Who?" She looked up at me.

I smiled. "He looks like our son."

# OTHER BOOKS BY
*Penelope Ward*

Moody

RoomHate

The Aristocrat

The Assignment

The Crush

The Anti-Boyfriend

Just One Year

The Day He Came Back

When August Ends

Love Online

Gentleman Nine

Drunk Dial

Mack Daddy

Stepbrother Dearest

Neighbor Dearest

Sins of Sevin

Jake Undone (Jake #1)

My Skylar (Jake #2)

Jake Understood (Jake #3)

Gemini

The Rules of Dating (Co-written with Vi Keeland)

Well Played (Co-written with Vi Keeland)

Not Pretending Anymore (Co-written with Vi Keeland)

Park Avenue Player (Co-written with Vi Keeland)

Stuck-Up Suit (Co-written with Vi Keeland)

Cocky Bastard (Co-written with Vi Keeland)

Happily Letter After (Co-written with Vi Keeland)
My Favorite Souvenir (Co-written with Vi Keeland)
Dirty Letters (Co-written with Vi Keeland)
Hate Notes (Co-written with Vi Keeland)
Rebel Heir (Co-written with Vi Keeland)
Rebel Heart (Co-written with Vi Keeland)
Mister Moneybags (Co-written with Vi Keeland)
British Bedmate (Co-written with Vi Keeland)
Playboy Pilot (Co-written with Vi Keeland)

# ACKNOWLEDGEMENTS

**I HAVE TO** start by thanking my beloved readers all over the world who continue to support and promote my books. Thank you for sticking with me on this journey and for allowing me to have this career. To all of the book bloggers and social media influencers who work tirelessly to support me book after book, please know how much I appreciate you.

To Vi – I'm so grateful that we continue to make magic together nearly a decade later. You're the best friend and partner in crime I could ask for.

To Julie – The epitome of strength and resilience. Thank you for always inspiring me.

To Luna – Christmas wouldn't be the same without you. Thank you for your love and support, day in and day out.

To Erika – You always have a way of brightening my days. Thank you for always sharing your sunshine.

To Cheri – Thanks for always looking out and for never forgetting a Wednesday. Can't wait to hopefully see you this year!

To Darlene – A great baker and an even better friend. Thank you for being so sweet to me.

To my Facebook reader group, Penelope's Peeps – I adore you all. You are my home and favorite place to be.

To my agent Kimberly Brower –Thank you for working hard to get my books into the hands of readers around the world.

To my editor Jessica Royer Ocken – It's always a pleasure working with you. I look forward to many more experiences to come.

To Elaine of Allusion Publishing – Thank you for being the best proofreader, formatter, and friend a girl could ask for.

To Julia Griffis of The Romance Bibliophile – Your eagle eye is amazing. Thank you for being so wonderful to work with.

To my assistant Brooke – Thank you for hard work in handling all of the things Vi and I can't seem to ever get to. We appreciate you so much!

To Kylie and Jo at Give Me Books – You guys are truly the best out there! Thank you for your tireless promotional work. I would be lost without you.

To Letitia Hasser of RBA Designs – My awesome cover designer. Thank you for always working with me until the finished product exactly perfect.

To my husband – Thank you for always taking on so much more than you should have to so that I am able to write. I love you so much.

To the best parents in the world – I'm so lucky to have you! Thank you for everything you have ever done for me and for always being there.

Last but not least, to my daughter and son – Mommy loves you. You are my motivation and inspiration!

# ABOUT THE AUTHOR

**PENELOPE WARD** is a *New York Times, USA Today* and *#1 Wall Street Journal* bestselling author.

She grew up in Boston with five older brothers and spent most of her twenties as a television news anchor. Penelope resides in Rhode Island with her husband, son and beautiful daughter with autism.

With over two million books sold, she is a 21-time *New York Times* bestseller and the author of over twenty novels.

Penelope's books have been translated into over a dozen languages and can be found in bookstores around the world.

Subscribe to Penelope's newsletter here:
http://bit.ly/1X725rj

Printed in Great Britain
by Amazon